An Incident at Beauduc

Anthony Coles

To Milly and Lydia.

First paperback edition July 2020

Contents

Chapter 1   Overture to a Tragedy

A passing British or German tourist would almost certainly not have looked twice at it. Even an Italian visitor, much despised locally, would have taken one look at its crumbling, cement-patched walls and the numerous cracked tiles on the roof and searched in vain for a swimming pool or even a barbeque. They would have looked at the grey mud that passed for a garden whose only colour came from abandoned bits of children's plastic and would have driven on to better places. But, as he lay prone on the dark beach, he would have given much of the extra money he hoped to earn tonight to be back in front of his log fire with his pretty young wife. The little house, whose ownership was his enduring pride, was built to withstand that which now threatened to kill him. Like most Provencal farm houses - or mas as they are called - it was built with its broad and almost windowless back facing north for that is where his current enemy was coming from. He had burrowed slightly down into the sand while he waited in the hope of escaping the unwelcome attentions of the wind that now blew over his head, out over the Mediterranean and on towards the north of Africa with a speed that had not dropped below fifty kilometres an hour for the last two days and, at present, was almost twice that. The Mistral, the cold wind that blew down the Rhône valley, sometimes for days on end, was on only its second visit of the year so far but it had lowered the otherwise mild temperatures that they had been enjoying since the previous November to only a degree or so above zero. He was too young to believe completely in the local legends about being made anything from mildly irritable to completely mad by the icy north wind. But he also couldn't believe that he'd ever felt colder. The wind-chill took the temperature well below freezing.

His burrowing had actually made matters worse. For security he'd been told not to come during daylight to pick a suitable spot. The wind would have prevented any tourists and their overpriced and ostentatious four-wheel drives from making a nocturnal expedition down the pothole-strewn few miles of purposely un-maintained roadway that leads from the main road down to the beach at Beauduc. However someone might have seen him and his bosses couldn't risk that. So he had hidden his very heavily silenced moped in a dry ditch over a mile inland and walked the rest of the way after dark. He had picked his spot when he had arrived and it ultimately proved to be too close to the shore in the sand that was usually covered at high tide. The tide may be out now but his burrowing had exposed some very wet sand and to add to his misery the water had seeped back into his hollow. He would have sworn that the only reason it wasn't frozen was because it was salt water from the Mediterranean.

Other than the air, little else moved. The beach was almost completely barren on either side. Not much of the scrubby vegetation survived. Behind him he heard, rather than saw, the couple of decrepit shacks that passed for beach fish restaurants much lauded by the hippie gipsy arty set that came here during the summer. They creaked continuously in an agonising sort of way as the wind tried to lift them into the sea. Actually, he rather hoped it would succeed. The food was often dreadful, the prices silly and the service didn't bear thinking about. The sky was crystal clear above him and the moon was out. Normally, he thought, that would mean that the whole thing would have been cancelled but the moon was only a couple of days old and it cast very little light over the ravaged beach.

He'd prepared for the cold. The Mistral had been going for a couple of days. A pair of his wife's tights, long johns, black fleece-lined trousers and waterproofs protected his bottom half while a similar set of layers were supposed to do the same to his top. Black balaclava and corded hood pulled tight around his head and two pairs of gloves completed his kit. Windproof but not waterproof, he thought grimly. He had not been prepared for the water that now had seeped through. Rather than keeping the cold out, his carefully thought-out ensemble was now keeping the icy water in. He shivered uncontrollably. It was the only movement he was allowed. His bosses had been quite specific. Take up position and under no circumstances move until it was all over by at least half an hour. Not one iota.

He had long since lost track of time and he certainly was not going to open the small crack in the elasticated wrist of his jacket to check. They would come when they came. Winter dawn was not until eight in the morning. An eternity away. Nothing to see, nothing to hear, so he started to think hard about almost anything just to keep his brain from seizing up like the rest of him. He thought of his wife and two-year-old child sleeping in their warm beds, oblivious to the weather raging outside. The extra money would come in handy. He thought of his secret plan to finish with all this police stuff one day, to take his family into the Dordogne, find a little bar restaurant in a small village and do some cooking; his great ambition. It was an effort to find things to think about, so he did what he always did when he wanted to get away from it all and couldn't. He started to create menus. Simple food for locals, extravagant meals for the rich. It was all the same to him. There was no reason why working-class food shouldn't be just as good as food for people who had gold cards. He was proud of the fact that he came from humble Camargue family and felt little rancour towards the reality he knew for it was precisely that origin that would prevent his getting much further in his present profession.

He was beginning to warm to his mental task. Daubes for the winter, salads in summer. Some basic sauces. Nothing exotic just well-made. Local produce. He would have to choose somewhere where he could get fresh cream. Like good cheese, it was almost impossible to find in Provence and he was traditional enough to realise the great truth that much great cooking owes its greatness to the now much-maligned and unfashionable dairy product.

He was well away deep into his imagined *hostellerie* so he heard it a few seconds later than perhaps he might if he had been scanning the black horizon as he should have been. It didn't matter. It was still a distance out from the shore and he slightly delayed the inevitable. The moment he knew would come but the moment he had not been looking forward to. The noise increased. In a flurry he pulled back his hood and strapped on the pair of night vision goggles. They went over the balaclava but not the hood and his head was immediately surrounded by the icy air. Very slowly he raised his head and looked out to sea. The world was transformed into the ghostly green that he was well trained to expect.

Less than fifty yards away in front of him, a single black RIB was making its way slowly in towards the shore. Its silenced outboard motor was hardly more than idling as it nudged up into the soft sand. Four men jumped out. Two ran quickly but silently in opposite directions and out of his vision. The other two pulled the RIB a few yards up the beach and, having done so, took guns out and stood on either side, one looking inland the other out to sea. Heckler and Koch HK G36 compacts. The young man stiffened slightly. Had he been in action rather than observing, he would have been holding the same gun.

He settled deeper into his hollow. Observe. Those were his instructions. Observe and report. Nothing else. The men on the beach were all wearing full black combat gear, night vision equipment. It was almost like looking in a mirror. Lie deeper still. Less than twenty seconds later a low, dull hum came across the sand. A black dune buggy but electrically powered. It stopped at the RIB, the driver dismounted and collected a man who had been sheltering under a canvas in the rear of the boat. He then took a backpack from the buggy and passed it over to the boat. The two got back into the buggy and equally silently turned it around and vanished out of sight along the beach towards the south east. The whole operation had taken no more than thirty seconds. He settled back to watch the re-embarkation of the RIB and its small crew.

He knew that there was no point in doing anything. Not turning around nor trying to get to the Sauer SIG Pro official issue 9mm. buried somewhere in the folds of his clothing. It was all too late. Hopeless. So he just went back to thinking of his pretty wife and child sleeping only a few miles away while the .45 soft nose slug from his killer's silenced Glock 30 entered the back of his head, exploded against the inside of the front of his skull and blew the resulting mush of the young policeman's brain deep into the black Provencal sand.

Chapter 2   First Debrief

'Three? All three?'

The voice that surfaced briefly above the general hubbub was incredulous and worried

'All of them?'

The shouting match between three of the five people around the table had ebbed and flowed across the table for a few minutes. The local Provençale bosses of the Police, the Gendarmerie Nationale, and the man from the Direction de la Surveillance du Territoire (DST), had been joined by two more who had remained silent so far throughout the meeting. The first dressed in a grey business suit represented the oddly named anti-terrorist unit Recherche, Assistance, Intervention et Dissuasion (RAID). The second and chair of the meeting was a slight, elegant woman dressed in a grey silk suit and ivory blouse. She sat at the head of the oval table quietly watching. Unlike the others who sat surrounded by sweaty palm prints and untidy piles of papers, the polished table in front of her was completely bare save for a small mobile phone. She sat relaxed but erect, her hands folded lightly in her lap, moving her head slightly from time to time to watch each member as he spoke or rather ranted.

She let the recriminations continue but in reality she had stopped listening. Actually, she knew what she was going to say before the meeting started. This was just going through the motions and now she was bored with it all. She raised her hand slightly from her lap and waited. The noises gradually subsided and all four men turned their gazes towards her. Each had similar thoughts. Who was this fast tracked, precious bitch from Paris, sitting self-importantly at the head of their conference table? This was nothing to do with her. She would soon find out that it was a man's world down here in Provence and women generally weren't welcome.

'Gentlemen. I don't think this is getting us very far. This meeting was not convened to discuss in any detail what happened two days ago. The responsibility for that particular fiasco will be investigated by others and questions of blame or responsibility will be settled then. I have been asked to accept your individual reports and then to see how we go forward in this operation.'

'Asked, Madame? By whom, may I ask?'

The question came from the Colonel of Gendarmerie who had command of the regional force. The career soldier had difficulty keeping the contempt for this well-dressed civilian woman from his voice.

'By the office of the President, Monsieur.' she replied, with an exaggerated courtesy.

The RAID man smiled slightly at the intentional omission of man's rank while the gendarme went the colour of his scarlet shoulder flashes.

'And what makes the Office of the President think that they can interfere in this matter. My force is answerable to the Minster of Defence through the Ministry of the Interior.'

The man was becoming positively truculent. The others looked on with interest.

'In fact, Monsieur,' the emphasis was greater now and the elegant woman allowed a touch of steel to enter her voice, 'the chain of command is the other way about. Even the gendarmerie has it civilian masters. However, that hardly matters at this point. I will now tell you what is to happen. There will be no discussion.'

The three policemen looked in varying degrees outraged. Even the man from the anti-terrorist squad shifted uncomfortably in his seat. None, however, spoke as the woman went on.

'In the early morning two days ago a simple observation and surveillance operation on the beach at Beauduc in the Camargue, an operation that was planned jointly by you four, went terribly wrong, resulting in the death - the execution rather - of three young policemen and a complete absence of any information about what happened. Person or persons unknown, I believe is the expression. A valuable piece of intelligence from our colleagues in Tunisia has been wasted to say nothing the lives of three officers, each of whom had families and admirable career prospects in their respective services. Your plans for following whoever landed came to nothing. To say you lost them would be inaccurate. You cannot lose something you never had.'

She continued to survey the hostile group in front of her as she continued contemptuously.

'The responsibility for this fiasco is yours and yours alone. As of now you are all suspended from your posts. This meeting will close now and reconvene in two days in my house in Arles. At that time, you may present proposals as to how we move forward in this matter and only incidentally try to persuade me why you should continue to be employed at all by the Republic.'

'And what, Madame, is wrong with the offices of the Gendarmerie in Arles for our - your- next meeting?' The Colonel made no attempt to conceal his contempt.

The woman gazed at him with as patronising an expression as she could muster.

'Almost everything, Colonel. I would remind you that your recent track record in organising anything with any efficiency or confidentiality at all is less than impressive.'

She turned her attention back to the meeting as a whole.

'If I am satisfied with your proposals, I will give some thought to your individual reinstatement. If I'm not, your suspension will be converted into dismissal from your service with full loss of rank, privileges and all pension rights. The decision will be mine, mine alone, and there will be no appeal. Have I made myself understood?'

She glanced around the table. Inevitably the silence was broken by the Gendarme who by now had become completely claret coloured.

'And by what authority, Madame, do you think you can do this?'

She didn't reply, just stretched an elegantly manicured hand to her mobile phone and touched a single button. The machine's speaker was switched on and everyone fell silent as it rang out. It was answered, and a look of complete horror crossed each man's face as a very familiar voice emerged from the machine.

'Good afternoon, Madame Blanchard. I take it that I was right, and a confirmation of your authority is needed?'

'Good morning, Monsieur Le President. I am afraid it is.'

The group around the table stiffened as if a single man. The voice continued:

'Gentlemen. Let me make it perfectly clear to you. Madame Blanchard is acting under my direct orders and carries my complete confidence and my full authority in whatever she wishes to do. Do I have the pleasure of your understanding?'

All four recovered well enough to confirm that they had indeed each understood.

The RAID man found himself idly remembering that Dumas's infamous Cardinal Richelieu gave Milady de Winter a similar carte blanche, which had proved to be a somewhat unreliable authority. The voice from Paris intervened again.

'Goodbye, Madame and good luck. I look forward to hearing from you.'

'Goodbye and thank you, Monsieur le President.'

The line went dead. Madame Blanchard stood up, slipped the now silent phone into her handbag and walked briskly out of the room leaving four astonished faces looking after her.

Chapter 3   The Old Man

The old man was off his game. Way off. Normally Gentry would have had to work very hard to stop the wily old bird swamping him. However, today, he played as he appeared, wistfully and somewhat preoccupied. Over the three years they had been getting together for weekly games of draughts and a chat at the back of the rather scruffy Café de Paris, just below the Place Voltaire, he had come to respect his opponent's skilful use of the variants of the Polish game that they both enjoyed. Marcel Carbot may have been well into his late eighties - not a great age for residents of Arles who are notoriously long-lived - but he could be utterly ruthless in his game as Gentry had frequently found to his cost. His opponent insisted that they played for money. That was a matter of honour, although none actually ever passed between them. Just as well, Gentry thought with a slight inward smile, because the balance of the account would definitely not be in his favour.

This time there was little conversation either and that was certainly unusual. The old man enjoyed talking about his youth in Arles before and just after the Second World War as much as Gentry enjoyed listening. But today he was uncharacteristically quiet and Gentry found he had to overlook a couple of his opponent's mistakes to make the game last.

'Marcel, old friend, it is probably none of my business, but you seem out of sorts today. What's wrong?'

The old man sat back in his chair and slumped slightly.

'I am sorry, David. You're right, of course. I'm not good company today nor have I given you a good game.'

'Tell me, if you wish.' The old man sighed.

'My grandson, Jean-Claude, I believe I have told you about him?'

'Yes, of course. Is he not serving with the gendarmerie?'

9

'Well, yes. He has recently been seconded into the DST.' Gentry immediately felt a slight frisson of anxiety. He knew more than his friend might imagine about the Direction de la Surveillance du Territoire, the French counter-terrorism unit and very little of it was good. However, he knew better than to press. In time, the old man continued, and Gentry was distressed to see a tear in the corner of his eye.

'He was apparently killed in a training accident four days ago.'

Gentry remembered that his friend had spoken with great pride of the boy and his career. The family tradition was one of military service. His son had served with great distinction in the Algerian war being awarded a Croix de Guerre posthumously. They had never found his body. Many years ago, Marcel himself had been the recipient of that most rare of decorations for valour in France, the Médaille Militaire. Both had had the personal entitlement to wear the Fourragère. The loss of his grandson would have been felt keenly, especially after the death of the son.

'I am truly sorry to hear that, Marcel. I know how proud of him you were. If you need it, I would be honoured to take you to the funeral.'

Gentry knew that the boy's own family now lived in the north of France although he had recently come back to his roots in Provence to marry a local girl and raise his young family. It had been a decision that particularly pleased his grandfather.

'Thank you, my friend. The funeral will be in Paris, I'm told and I will travel by train. I would be grateful for some company. If it not too much trouble. Someone is sending a car for me and Jean's wife and child.'

'Of course, I'll come with you, if that is what you wish.'

His companion lifted his head and smiled his thanks through eyes that were now full of tears.

'He has already been cremated. The service will be a

memorial only.'

Gentry hoped that the alarm that was set off in his head when he heard this didn't show on his face. Indecently fast cremations were, in his experience, always suspicious. Gentry waited for the old man to compose himself. He had been on the receiving end of numerous debriefings over the years in the Service and he knew the value of letting distressed people let the knowledge out in their own time. After a while Gentry signalled for a marc for them both. And they each downed the larger than usual measure in one. The bartender obviously knew that something was wrong with the old man.

His companion took a spotlessly clean handkerchief from his pocket, wiped the tears without embarrassment and straightened in his seat.

'I'm told it wasn't an accident.'

Gentry knew there was no point is asking how the old man knew. He did. That was enough. He had been born in the Camargue and that is where his sons and grandson had settled. They were all part of its community and it was a very closed community. People took care of their own. Even residents of the town of Arles only a few miles away were separate. Someone had told him that the army was lying and he, like Gentry, was more inclined to believe them than the authorities.

'Where do the army say the accident happened?' 'In the Alps.'

'And where did it actually happen?'

'Beauduc.'

Gentry focused. Although the Camargue is actually the Rhone delta where the great river finally spills into the Mediterranean, there are surprisingly few sand beaches; at least beaches that are accessible to the general public. The whole area is a national park and there are very few public roads. Even fewer go down to the sea. There are beaches at Saintes-Maries-de-la-Mer and

11

Isle des Sables but Beauduc is a particularly inaccessible spot served only by about three miles of track that is in such bad condition that it takes an hour to drive over it in an ordinary car. Gentry had never felt the slightest inclination to go there. Like his friend Smith, he didn't understand sand and disliked beaches. He did, however, know enough about the place to be certain that no-one went there in January for pleasure. It did, however, explain how the old man knew that it wasn't a training accident. Nothing could happen at Beauduc without the locals knowing about it or, he thought grimly, usually being involved.

Gentry knew in an instant what was really troubling the old man. It was not just the loss of his grandson. It was not knowing what happened and not having any way to find out. He looked across the forgotten game set on the small table between them and felt a momentary regret.

'Would you like me to see if I could find out a little about what went on, Emile.'

There was immediately almost a childish like hope in the man's eyes.

'Can you?'

Gentry nodded, laying a gentle hand on the man's arm. 'Yes, I think so.'

In truth, Gentry's answer should have been 'no, but I know a man who can', but this seemed both a good deal too flippant and it would have been a reply that would have added to his friend's discomfort.

'Thank you. I would be grateful. The funeral will be a great deal easier if I knew that someday I would know the truth.'

'Possibly, Marcel. Only possibly. You must understand that.'

'Yes, yes. I know. Possibly I know…' Standing up abruptly, he held out his hand.

'Time to go home, I think, David. I am afraid I have not been very good company today. Perhaps next week. I will telephone you when I hear about the arrangements for travelling to the service. Thank you again.'

With that he gave Gentry a firm handshake, squared his shoulders and walked slowly erect out of the café door. Gentry retrieved the day's local newspaper, Le Provence, from the bar, collected another Marc, refraining from taking a large measure from his friend Smith's very special personal bottle held behind the bar, and settled back into his corner seat. He wanted some time to think but sitting staring vacantly into space would have caused some raised eyebrows in the bar where he was well-known. Someone would have come over to talk to him about the old man and his recent tragedy and Gentry didn't want the distraction. Burying himself in a seeming detailed perusal of the newspaper he hoped would be a signal that he didn't want to be disturbed.

He could see perfectly well that something was going on. Official explanations of unorthodox happenings were once his stock in trade and this sad little story smelled familiar if unpleasant. However, he felt that he had to do something. After a while he got up, settled the bill and walked slowly the hundred or two yards through the narrow medieval streets back to his house. It was, he felt, time to pull in a few favours.

His study was tiny. It was a rectangular glass-walled loggia tucked in right under the roof, five stories above the ground, on top of the rambling old house that was his home. It was accessed by a spiral stair from the inside of a cupboard in his bedroom on the floor below. Once a roof terrace and therefore flag-stone floored, it had a complete view over a three-hundred-and-sixty-degree panorama over the city, the great curve of the Rhone to the north, the main town and beyond it to the west and the Alpilles mountains and back up to the Amphitheatre and St Trophime to the south. Unlike the rest of his deceptively large house that was habitually shuttered and very dimly lit, it was completely glazed on all four sides. Also, unlike the rest of the house, it was not furnished in a comfortable gentleman's club combination of mahogany, dark leather, wood panelling and oriental rugs as befitted a retired British civil servant of independent means and little desire to conduct an extensive social life – or any social life at all for that matter. The loggia was minimalist in the extreme. A large glass-topped stainless-steel table bearing a single low voltage brushed steel desk light and a matching upright office armchair. A similar but smaller side table containing a MacBook Air that seemed to float above the glass. The table also held, more prosaically, a single file that always contained papers to be worked on, a pad of paper and a draughtsman's pencil. Only one problem at a time ever came up to the loggia and it stayed there until it was dealt with. A small satellite phone and the Mac. The rest of the furnishing consisted of a bottle of Banff single malt, a Georgian panel-cut tumbler, and an original Charles Eames recliner and foot stool. Apart from the desk light, the room was lit by whatever God provided from outside although the glare of the full Provençale sun in summer was controlled by photosensitive glass.

To say that it wasn't overlooked would be small exaggeration, but no buildings of any proximity were even at the same level let alone higher. It was one of the reasons he had chosen the house years ago. Those with a mind to could possibly have observed from a considerable distance but would find that the glass remained annoyingly difficult to see through even at night even when lit from the inside. Bullets would have had an equally difficult passage. The loggia was set back from the edge of the roof on all sides just far enough to prevent it being visible from the street below. He was the only person who ever entered the room and precious few knew it was there. The men who constructed it came from the Service in London as did all the materials. They had done the job privately still bound by the Official Secrets Act but had departed Arles considerably richer.

Gentry sat at the desk, started the laptop and made a few calls.

They got together most weeks for a drink and a game of chess or sporadically for a drink and a chat at one of the many bars around the town. Neither was a regular meeting. Smith had come to Arles slightly later than Gentry and it was a great surprise to them both. In spite of working together for many years they had never discussed what turned out to be a mutual love of the beautiful old town at the north end of the Camargue. Smith had been coming off and on since his childhood. His father had been stationed in Marseille after the Second World War, Nazi hunting in the south of France for allied intelligence. Arles had proved to be fertile ground in spite of a history written subsequently that was all resistance and no collaboration. Gentry had fallen separately for the old Roman town. When it came time to retire and escape the ghosts of England, both real and imaginary, Arles was the natural place to go. Gentry had discovered the town later in life but it drew him as powerfully as it did Smith. So, when Gentry was looking for somewhere to set up his antique book business, a large rambling *hôtel particulière* buried in the centre of the old city that was sufficiently remote and unfashionable a location to prevent all but the most serious collectors finding him. It suited him well.

Very occasionally, one or the other broke the pattern of meetings. There was usually a particular reason. On this occasion Gentry's telephone call confirmed that this was indeed one of those times. His original instinct that his old friend Smith would be the man to help was proved right.

So it was later in the afternoon when he made the call. The phone had rung a few times. Smith was obviously not at his desk and before long the answering machine would click in. Smith never checked his answering machine. Gentry was not entirely sure that Smith ever bothered to learn how it worked. However the phone was finally answered.

'Yes?'

'Smith? Gentry.'

The public school tradition of referring to close friends by their surnames came naturally to them both. Neither asked how the other 'was'. They knew.

'Do you have a moment? I want to ask your advice.'

'You mean my help.'

Gentry laughed. 'Yes, I suppose I do.'

'Fine. Come on round.' 'Ten minutes.'

Gentry sat back to collect his thoughts. It was one of those extraordinarily clear sunny days that you get regularly in Provence in the winter and the view from his loggia was breath-taking. He ordered the facts he had learned quickly and easily and there were precious few to order. Five minutes later he had walked around the Amphitheatre and up into the Place de la Major and was knocking at Smith door.

There was the customary enthusiastic greeting from Arthur, a large rescue greyhound from the darker recesses of East London who had joined Smith in his retirement. His host had already prepared drinks, a Banff malt for Gentry and a supermarket cooking scotch with Perrier water for himself, and they sat on a slightly worn pair of sofas arranged at right angles, Smith on one with Gentry and a delighted Arthur on the other. Gentry started.

'I need a favour.'

It was a rare admission. Very rare. And because of that Smith took it seriously.

'The grandson of a friend of mine was killed recently in a special forces training accident, or so his grandfather has been told.'

'And you don't think that's true?' Smith could read the signs.

'I don't know, but I do know that there are some very high-flying people, military and otherwise, looking into it.'

'You better tell me about it,' said Smith, topping up their glasses.

The story did not take much telling. As ever, Gentry was precise and economical. It was a briefing just like the old days and Smith listened in silence until Gentry finished. There were some obvious gaps in the narrative, but Smith knew that was leaving them was Gentry's way of getting him involved.

16

The cremation was the good indication that something was up. There was no reason for it and there was an obvious conclusion to be drawn, but Smith was not entirely certain what he could offer that Gentry couldn't. More than most, Gentry was the silent investigator. His local contacts were extensive, and he was perfectly capable of ferreting about in the problem without Smith's somewhat more pragmatic and occasionally muscular approach. The answer obviously lay in something that he hadn't mentioned, and Smith knew he was expected to ask.

'OK, why do you need me?'

No point in beating about the bush. Other than sympathy for his friend, Smith could not conjure up much enthusiasm for the story. The reason wasn't long coming.

'I'm told by a friend in the Elysée Palace that there is a very high-level investigation going on and this is not into some common or garden training accident.'

Smith wasn't remotely surprised that Gentry had a contact in the French President's official residence. Gentry's value throughout his career in what might inaccurately but conveniently be termed the British intelligence service owed much to his ability to network quietly and efficiently throughout the world.

'The committee charged with the investigation consists of four very senior policemen and a high-ranking spook. The chair is a personal appointee of the President himself.'

Smith was happy to continue playing Gentry's game. 'And?'

There was obviously an 'and.'

'It is your old friend, Suzanne Blanchard'. There was short silence.

'Ah,' said Smith softly, 'I see.'

There was another moment's silence – actually rather a long one while Smith took stock.

'And what precisely, do you wish me to do.' Gentry looked across at his old friend.

'Well, to be frank, given that you still hold enough evidence if not to convict her, then at least put her in the frame for the murder and ritual castration of her late husband , I thought you might be in a position to ask her what actually happened on the beach at Beauduc.'

'Hum,' said Smith, as he reached for the bottle once more.

Chapter 4   Lunch with Madame Blanchard

Arles seemed dead. Actually, to all intents and purposes, it was. The temporary excitement of Christmas and the New Year, modest enough, had faded and January was slipping imperceptibly into February. You don't really get a proper winter in this bit of Provence. Occasional days of sometimes heavy rain and cloudy skies and, of course, the odd Mistral. Temperatures can drop to freezing at night from time to time and the consternation caused by early morning ice-filmed puddles tends to occupy the street conversation around the town well past the time when the ice actually disappears in the morning sun. Very, very infrequently it snows. The value of a ten-minute light snowfall is fifty-fold that of a morning frost. Days are spent in the local boulangerie discussing the vagaries of the weather. The topic even has the ability to supplant the usual obsession with matters medical that occupy so many conversations in southern French. It is a mistake to think that the customary greeting 'comment allez-vous?' will remain phatic. Ask it and you risk having the question answered in encyclopaedic detail and at length, supported with written records of blood pressure, cholesterol and other details of all measurable bodily functions that can be carried around in notebooks in handbags (both male and female). Doctors and pharmacies are outnumbered only by bakers in France and there is a good reason for that.

This particular morning was cold and the early risers that Smith usually met on his regular 7:00am walks with Arthur were to be seen prodding suspiciously but balletically at the frozen puddles with tentative feet and rolled umbrellas. The wind was already up as well. Not a true Mistral yet but getting that way. There would be compensations for those that would stop to look. If people managed for a second to transcend their own idea of discomfort and look around them they would see. The air often cleared and the view north east over to the Alpilles and beyond even to the Mont Ventoux could be breath-taking. A truly clear view tends to be a winter luxury in Provence.

Gentry's request had been unsettling in an amicable sort of way. Smith had already crossed paths with Suzanne Blanchard and that was why Gentry had called. A year or so before Smith had unearthed evidence that she had killed her paedophile husband. At least, that it what Madame Blanchard thought. His evidence, if that was what it was, was relatively flimsy circumstantial but the elegant Madame Blanchard didn't know that. Guilt can make fools of most people and she was no exception. Gentry was right. It certainly gave him an entry even though she was now promoted from her job as a senior Brussels Eurocop to something seemingly much more exotic. Smith was uncomfortable. He valued his solitude. He had no desire to be any more visible or involved than necessary. His retirement had already become too eventful although a certain Madame Aubanet, the main reason for the more recent and somewhat unwelcome visibility, was significant compensation for that. But locking horns with an ambitious woman whom he disliked, and he was pretty sure didn't like him, who was acting directly out of the French President's office investigating a matter of national security, was not exactly something he relished. By now, she almost certainly had powerful friends and such pond life was, in Smith's experience, to be avoided. But Gentry had asked for help and that was good enough. He owed Gentry a lot; his life to say the least. The two went back a long way as did their mutual debt. Smith sighed, thought for a moment, mentally squared his shoulders and dived into the problem.

The first thing to do would be a fishing trip. He had an advantage. Given Madame Blanchard's fears, she would be surprised at his contact, especially as she seemed to have risen even higher in whatever she thought of as a career path. After the events of the previous year she had tried to contact him a couple of times possibly to find out how deep was the shit she assumed Smith knew she was in, but he had never returned the calls. He didn't like this slim, tensioned woman, who suffered terminally in his opinion by comparison with her cousin Martine at whose behest he had performed what they both considered a service. Martine and he had become close, if occasionally tangential, friends ever since. Suzanne Blanchard was an altogether different paire de manches. He did not trust her further than he could throw her elegant arse and although that might have been further than she would imagine, but was it still not far enough.

Having made himself his customary mug of espresso and

made sure that Arthur had a good supply of biscuits and fresh water, he went up to his study at the top of his little house next to the Arles Arena. The dog had a dislike of the slippery stone stairs and it took a lot to make him climb them. He preferred to lie just outside the kitchen door and wait for cats to kill. He was an expert at this particular form of pest control, as, actually, was Smith in a slightly different way. It was still dark outside and Smith's study room was cold. He fired up his PC and waited until the lengthy and completely unnecessary start-up procedure that all who are the unwilling recipients of that nice Mr Gates's operating systems around the world have to suffer, ground its grudging way into life. He looked at his Outlook contacts. He still had a mobile telephone number for her.

By now it was eight in the morning; a good time for catching someone off-balance but in this particular case he had the feeling that whatever time he called, she would be up, perfectly coiffured and at her desk.

'Madame Blanchard. Good morning. This is Peter Smith.'

To give her credit she recovered quite quickly. But not quickly enough. The gap was palpable. However, that said, the recovery would have done credit to a grand prix driver finding himself sideways at two hundred kilometres an hour.

'Monsieur Smith. How nice to hear from you. How are you?'
'I'm well, Madame. And you?'

'Also, well. To what do I owe the pleasure of this call?'

Smith was pleased to see that her tolerance of pleasantries was even less than his own.

'Well. Madame. I was wondering if it might be possible to meet sometime soon and have a chat?'

Her reply took him completely by surprise but nevertheless delighted him. He was not unpractised at interrogation and he had just felt his original advantage extended to thirty - love. However, it was his serve after all.

'How did you know I am in Arles? I only arrived an hour or two ago.'

He didn't, of course, It was the sort of mistaken assumption that people often made when they forget they are using a mobile phone. Smith took the greatest possible pleasure in drizzling a gentle 'Ahhh' down the phone. No more. Again, the recovery couldn't be faulted.

'I wonder if I might have a word sometime soon, Madame?' He heard the hesitation clearly.'

'Whenever you wish, of course. I am at home.'

Smith remembered the elegant little house on Avenue Haussmann that she had shared with her late husband until, of course, she had killed him by cutting off his testicles, stuffing them in his mouth and holding it closed until he bled out - or so he suspected. She continued:

'Perhaps you would like to come to lunch today?'

Smith sensed that she was aching for him to decline the invitation and suggest a more neutral location and a later date to give herself a little time to prepare.

'How very kind, Madame. I would be delighted.'

This time the gap was infinitesimal, and few would have detected her disappointment. People never understand that eighty percent of all communication is non-verbal and, properly versed and practiced, much more can be learned over a telephone conversation than just from what is actually said.

'At one o'clock then, Peter.'

'I shall look forward to it, Suzanne.'

He could sense clearly the stiffening that went with this exchange of Christian names. Hers was sarcastic. His had been mischievous.

'Well,' he thought, as he put the phone to one side, 'that was a bit of luck, I think.'

He hadn't expected it to be so easy. He had no idea that she had been in Arles and as a result of having his bluff called somewhat he had also left himself rather too short a time to plan the meeting. It would be playing it on the fly, as they said, in the Land of Hope and Glory. He felt momentarily comforted by the use of the foreign metaphor.

Gentry had given him very little information. That in itself was unusual. Gentry was normally the one who had all the details and who had to put up with Smith's improvisation. This time it seemed that it might be the other way around and Smith would have to prepare to lead. For once Gentry was acting on impulse and things might get a bit bumpy because of it. Gentry was never someone who could make it up as he went along. That ability, or perhaps it was a gift of some sort, was one of the few areas where Smith maintained an advantage. The more outrageous he became in their periodic chess games; the more Gentry was likely to be taken unawares. He had always been regarded by Gentry as somewhat reckless, whereas, in fact Smith's success both in their chess and in their somewhat less orthodox ventures together was actually based on more learning then Gentry would have given his friend credit for. Scholarship was the domain that Gentry had chosen for himself and Smith never had the heart to tell him that being still and knowing everything was not the only way. You could mix the Apollonian and the Dionysian perfectly successfully if you knew when to change the proportions, a bit like seasoning soup. Smith did, Gentry didn't. It was as simple as that and explained the basic truth of their long relationship; Gentry was important to Smith but Smith was essential to Gentry.

He had to find a way of getting Gentry back in his usual place, focused into the picture. He knew his old friend well enough to know that if this problem, whatever it was, ever became operational, then Gentry would need to be where he had always been, in the background - knowing rather than doing.

He decided against calling his friend to tell him of the meeting with Suzanne. Gentry would feel honour bound to offer a briefing and given that lunch was less than three hours away, it would be a waste of time. Gentry would know he was doing a bad job of it and that would make him morose. No, the whole thing would have to be impromptu. He took stock of what little he had.

The boy had apparently been killed on a training exercise. It was perfectly possible, of course. Military and police accidents do happen regularly and in France where the borders between the two services are more than a little blurred, the chances of a relatively unqualified young man being in a situation for which he was less than fully trained, were correspondingly high. The fast cremation was also not, in itself, suggestive of anything other than exactly that – a fast cremation. What was, of course, odd was that a high flyer like Madame Blanchard seemed to be heading up some sort of investigation. The military usually took care of its own. The last time he'd had contact with Madame, she had been a very high-ranking police official working in the anti-fraud department Europol, the European police force based in Brussels. Now she seemed to be working for the French government and her involvement in any sort of enquiry would in itself suggest that all was not strictly kosher. Certainly, a routine training accident would not concern her. That was, of course, his way in.

However, it was important not to push her too far at this early stage. Whatever was going on, she would not want to tell him about it; at least not in detail. However mighty she might imagine was his possible hold over her, it would not do to have it tested too far. She was operating with some high-level backing and if she became sufficiently exasperated or threatened, she was in a position to make life unpleasant for him. Better not push his luck, at least not to start with.

She was as he remembered; slim, medium height and immaculately turned out. Her dark brown hair cut straight and neatly into the nape of her neck. Small pearl stud earrings and a single rope of twisted gold threads around her neck. Elegant tailored linen slacks in a colour that used to be called Eau-de-Nile in Smith's childhood and seemed no longer to exist. Slightly heeled Gucci's. Smith thought grimly: she had inherited her late husband's taste for the Italian's leather tassels. A ravishingly baroque silk Lacroix shirt tucked into a wide belt pulled a notch tighter that it might have been had it not been intended to emphasize a waist that Smith felt he could have encircled with his joined hands. Not that he wanted to try. One fewer button than might be strictly tasteful was fastened showing the beginnings of a cleavage that owed more to the corset-maker's art than to God. He had to admit she looked stunning in that way than many French women have, slim and slightly jagged. He had the feeling that unclothed, she might disappoint.

She pulled the door wide to let him in and extended her hand.

Her smile was as thin as she.

'Peter, what an unexpected surprise.'

The grip was firm but correct. At least, he thought, she hasn't tried to pretend that he was welcome. Somehow it put it him at his ease. He decided to follow her lead and not pretend.

'It was good of you to see me so quickly. I do hope this isn't too inconvenient.'

She smiled at his use of the word: too. There was no question that it was, of course, inconvenient as well as unwelcome. However, with the skill of a practiced politician she had obviously decided to make the best of it.

'I am afraid for lunch you'll have to have what comes. Having only just arrived, there is not much in the fridge apart from a few essentials that my housekeeper got in for me when she knew I was coming. You will have to make do with an omelette and salad and cheese. That is, in any case, about the limit of my culinary talent.'

Smith decided to be gallant, a mode which, like many British men, he found quite easy to slip into.

'Madame, that sounds perfect. Why don't I do the salad while you cook the omelettes? Perhaps we can talk while we cook.'

It was a calculated gamble. He needed information, information that she might be very reluctant to give him. The only way he was going to get it was to leave past difficulties well in the background. She was already unhappy enough about his appearing without the voicing of actual threats to make matters worse. There were few people who would readily describe him as charming. There were very, very few that knew him well enough. However, like most Englishmen, he could turn it on when necessary as long he wasn't required to keep it up for too long.

It worked. This time her smile was genuine, and her manner changed from suspicion to gentle mockery in a flash.

'I am beginning to see what my cousin Martine sees in her Englishman, Monsieur Smith. Yes, I would enjoy that' Smith followed her into the kitchen where, like the rest of the house, the furnishing was modern, excellently equipped and in immaculate taste.

'There is a bottle of Krug in the fridge, Monsieur, and some glasses in the cupboard above the dish washer.'

Smith worked quite hard to keep up with this new domestic bliss. In a few minutes she had gone from being defensive and rigidly contained to smiling, relaxed and, dare he admit it, rather sexy in an informal sort of way. This was a side of her that he hadn't seen before. It crossed his mind that he was being flirted with. Then he remembered the testicles. On balance, however, he was happy if a little disconcerted. There was actually a perfectly good chance that what had happened to the old man's grandson was indeed a training accident. They happened all the time. Although if it was, he couldn't immediately see why she was involved. He didn't want to waste his advantage. As he passed the first test of his new coolness – getting the cork out of the Krug without making a hole in the suspended ceiling or breaking one of its elegant recessed low voltage spotlights – he thought he should try it on a little more.

'Peter, Madame, please'

'Very well.' And, anticipating his next quandary, she continued: 'The makings of your salad dressing are in the cupboard next to the glasses.

Smith poured the drinks. They both set to work producing lunch and before too long they were seated either side of the kitchen table. She had found some smoked trout to enliven the omelette and he was flabbergasted to find some British Coleman's mustard powder which, in his opinion, was the only thing that could make that greatly overestimed bastion of French cooking, French Dressing, remotely interesting. A pair of baguettes lay on the table between them. The food, simple enough, was excellent. He felt slightly surprised without actually knowing why.

Time for business. Actually, he had no idea how to start. He was on the point of suggesting that they just finished lunch, chatted amicably for a bit, finish the Krug and then agreed to meet later somewhere where they could start to dislike each other again. Then, halfway a mouthful of an admittedly delicious omelette, surprisingly it came to him. Honesty. Or rather partial honesty which was as good as he ever seemed to manage these days.

'Suzanne, I've come to ask for your help.'

She looked across the increasingly untidy space between them with a look that was by some distance warmer than that which had greeted him three quarters of an hour before, and just expressed anticipation. He plunged in.

'A few days ago, a young special forces policeman called Jean-Claude Carbot was apparently killed on a night training exercise - officially in the Alps but actually on Beauduc beach here in the Camargue. The man's grandfather had asked me to find out whether or not it was an accident. The matter is being investigated at a very high level and you have been brought in to head up the enquiry. That, by itself, means that it wasn't a simple accident.'

She looked across at him very sharply. There was quite obviously no point in being ignorant. She knew enough about Smith to understand that he would not have made contact had he not known. She also realised that he was the only reason that she held her present exalted position and had not taken up permanent residence in some European women's prison. However, there were some motions to be gone through.

27

'What would you say, Peter, if I said that I have absolutely no idea what you are talking about?'

By way of reply Smith refilled their glasses and said nothing. She smiled grimly.

'I thought so.'

There was a long pause while she came to terms with the fact that for a second time in a couple of years, she had crossed paths with this infuriating Englishman. He was very much more than a casual bystander. She also knew that he could ruin her. At the same time, she knew that he could help her as well. He had some unorthodox skills and she might need them at some stage. As if reading her mind, he said:

'Be straight with me, Suzanne. You know that I can help in ways that your official friends might not either be able or willing to. I can't imagine that you are going to get much co-operation from them. You may not want my involvement but I am afraid I am in, like it or not.'

'Why, Peter. What business is it of yours?'

'I agreed to try to find out what happened for the boy's grandfather.'

'Is he a friend of yours?'

'No, but I owe someone a favour.' 'Just a favour?'

'Yes. Just a favour.'

'As before, you are a good man to have as a friend, Monsieur Smith. I know that. And a bad enemy. And I know that too.'

Her smile was brief.

'Again, I can see what my cousin sees in you.'

'Madame, perhaps not quite as obviously, I am your friend as well.'

She looked levelly at him. They both were remembering some horrors of the recent past.

'Yes, perhaps I could understand that in time.'

Her voice was uncertain as she accepted the inevitable, drew a deep breath and started to tell the story.

'A little time ago, we received information from contacts in Algeria that Hassan Agreti, a senior strategist for Al Qaeda, was coming to France to oversee the planning of a series of terrorist actions in France, Spain and Italy. He was coming by fishing boat, transfer to a RIB and a landing at Beauduc. We planned to observe his arrival and then follow him wherever he might lead us. We planted more than thirty men along the coast five kilometres either side of the Beauduc beach. None of them saw anything but the three men covering what turned out to be the actual landing site were shot dead. The young man you're interested in was one of them.'

'Shot?'

She nodded slowly.

'One shot each to the back of the head with a .45 hollow point.'

'They didn't hear their killers then.'

'Presumably not.'

'So now you have been given the job of finding out who grassed.'

'Basically, yes.'

'And you are surrounded by department chiefs all trying to cover their backsides.'

'Again, yes.'

'Who are you reporting to?'

'The President.'

'Directly?'

'Yes.'

He didn't have to make a long, low whistle for them both to hear it.

'Madame Blanchard, I'm impressed.'

There was pride in the slightly inclined head gesture. 'Thank you, Monsieur.'

'Who are you dealing with?'

'Police, Gendarmerie, DST and RAID.'

Smith was appalled and for the first time felt slightly sympathetic.

'Christ. With that lot busy peeing around the edges of their patches you were lucky that you only lost three.'

Smith sat back to think quickly. The President. That was pressure for him as well as her. He remembered all too well how these sorts of things could go wrong. He still bore the scars of a similar infiltration that, in spite of everything that Gentry could do to prevent it, ended with a couple of nights in a Somalian interrogation cell. He shuddered as the suppressed memory returned for an instant. Trying to coordinate a number of mightily bureaucratic French military and police services, each obsessed with their own status was a recipe for instant disaster.

She nodded slowly.

'Yes, had I been involved from the start, it would not have happened. With that many different agencies, I'm surprised that the press and television didn't get to hear of it, let alone Al Qaeda. It was a complete fuck-up and heads will roll in time. I would have organised it very differently.'

It stuck Smith with a certain irony that, had not France at last abolished the death penalty a very few years before, Madame's head might well have been literally rolling, struck from her shoulders by Madame Guillotine. Her late husband may have been a disgusting paedophile, but even French law does not allow you to execute him yourself. More's the pity he thought.

'You've made rapid progress from Europol, Madame.' A thought struck him.

'Or perhaps you have been in counter-terrorism all along.'

'I am pleased to hear that at least a small part of my life is not an open book to you, Peter. However, I have a meeting here later this afternoon with the local departmental heads. They are required to give me some sort of explanation.'

'You have come back here, Suzanne. Is there a local connection?'

She nodded.

'My personal contacts say there is. The leak, we believe, came from one of the local agencies.'

Smith sighed.

'Then you have absolutely no chance of making progress and you must know it. You know what they think of police, military and outsiders here. They hate them. The local plod are morons who wouldn't know a terrorist if he wore a lapel badge. In any case, they won't tell you anything even if they knew something, which they probably don't. There are people here who will know exactly what happened, but they won't talk to you. You are going to need some help.'

She looked across at him with a sly smile on her lips. 'Why do you think I agreed to see you so quickly, Peter?'

He reflected that there were actually a number of possible answers to that, some of which she would not have liked. There was obviously some sort of attempt at regaining lost ground, but Smith was prepared to let it go at that. She continued:

'Does this old man actually have grounds for suspecting anything?'

Smith found himself getting quickly very angry and decided it would do no harm to show it.

'Madame, this 'old man' as you rather dismissively describe him, served France with great honour during the Second World War and later in the Algerian War. His son died in his country's service. They both received your highest award for bravery. He is an old-school patriot who is completely devastated by the death of his grandson. I would thank you to treat him with the respect he deserves while you run around covering your undeniably elegant arse. Because of what is involved here, he may well have to be told lies but I will not allow you to dismiss him as if he were some sort of inconvenience.'

She was very surprised by the anger in his voice and was immediately and genuinely contrite. She stretched her hand out across the narrow table and touched his arm lightly before withdrawing it slowly.

'Peter, I am sorry. I spend too much time being a politician these days. Of course, you are right. I have forgotten how to be civilised. He is obviously a good friend of yours'.

Smith looked across the table at her. 'Actually, Madame, I have never met him.'

She looked across the table with astonishment. This Englishman never ceased to surprise her.

Smith went on quickly. 'Apology accepted, Suzanne.'

He shared out the last of the champagne as they helped themselves to cheese. Champagne, even good stuff, was not his favourite tipple, having developed a taste for cheaper crémant . His usual budget only ran to a champagne that hurt when it went down his throat. He preferred a crémant that was often infinitely better value and didn't taste like paint stripper. However great champagnes managed to taste dry with most food but very slightly sweeter with cheese and this was one of those occasions. Time to make a pitch, he thought.

'Whatever lengths your predecessor may have gone to keep the Beauduc operation secret, he had no chance of succeeding. With that many agencies involved it was absolutely bound to get out. Your three men were targets the moment they were assigned to the job.'

She sighed, 'Yes, I'm afraid you're right.'

'Whatever actually happened on the beach, it's sure that it is now common knowledge in the Camargue. That sort of thing doesn't happen without at least some of the locals knowing. I would guess that is why the old man started wondering about the boy's death. He presumably heard something. Indeed, if your Arabs had planned their operation correctly, which they appear to have done, they would have known that too, which means there is someone very local who probably helped. Is that why you are here in Arles?'

'Yes, it is, although I have very little hope of making much progress. I am not particularly well thought of in the Camargue as I think you know.'

They sat in silence. Smith knew enough about the reasons. Her immediate family had been branded collaborators during the Second World War. They were one half of one of the oldest Camargue families. The other half had been with the resistance. The split and hatred had not stopped when one brother had executed the other very soon after the liberation of 1944. For her uncle, Martine's father, Emile Aubanet, it still hadn't. Hardly surprising as he had been the one to pull the trigger all those years ago.

She looked at him directly.

'Who are you working for, Peter?'

33

'What on earth do you mean?' His surprise was genuine.

'Well, as you might imagine I am in a good position to find out most things about people if I want to. Although it has been very unofficial, I have been trying to find out about you since we last met. And in spite of having some very highly placed friends both in France and England and in spite of calling in all sorts of favours, I find that the man I know as Peter Smith, while he certainly exists, seems to have no history to speak of.'

Smith contented himself with trying to raise a single eyebrow is an insouciant sort of way. It was a skill he had never actually mastered, and he was conscious of looking only as if he had a slight twinge of facial cramp. Inwardly he was pleased that much of his past remained buried, irrevocably filed in a place that even the Service wouldn't give anyone access to. That had been the price of his retirement. If she couldn't find it, then probably no-one could. He had a lot to thank Gentry for.

'I can assure you, Madame, I am not working for anyone. I am retired after a completely undistinguished career in both academia and business. I have two daughters and two ex-wives, a greyhound, a little house near the Arena and a very mediocre bank account.'

'Bollocks.'

It sounded odd coming from a smart lady dressed like a fashion plate.

'How could you cook omelettes without getting a single mark on your elegant trousers?' he wondered. He also didn't reply, so she continued.

'I heard about the episode last year coming back from the Marseille opera with Martine. Yours were not the actions of a retired school teacher.'

Four shots, two kills he remembered with a grim satisfaction. Double taps. Silence was still the best policy although a trace of the frown that he thought he had kept inside must have made it to his face as she quickly added:

'I assure you that I got this from contacts in Marseille not from Martine.'

He just looked steadily across her and said nothing. This was getting entirely too personal and he could not continue to say nothing although he had been able to do so under infinitely greater pressure in the past. Time to move things along. He found he had begun to like this odd woman. Actually, if he'd thought about it, he might have from the beginning. His own rather unorthodox morality actually allowed him to approve of what she did to her husband. He would have done it himself had he had the chance although it would have probably been done with less Provençale theatricality. Martine also liked her in spite of the family feud and that counted for a lot - increasingly so, he found. He decided to try her direct approach.

'Do you want my help?'

She looked at him steadily. She was risking a stellar career by confiding in this secretive Englishman. She had no control over him, no authority. She was almost certainly breaking a large number of national secrecy laws. However, the fact that he was responsible for her remaining at liberty or even alive, for that matter, must count for something. She took a deep breath.

'Yes, Peter. I believe I do.'

'My question was whether you want it, not whether you need it.

There's a difference.'

It was a subtle point but she got it. A slight uncertainty shuddered through her and she attempted to row back a little.

'There are conditions, Peter.' 'No there aren't Suzanne.'

She sighed: 'No. I suppose there aren't.'

'What exactly are you trying to do? Is your job to find out

what went wrong last Saturday night, who was responsible for leaking the information, catch up with your terrorist, find out what they are up to and put a stop to it? What is it?'

'My brief is to find out what went wrong and if there was a leak, where it came from.'

'Nothing more?'

'No. The rest is up to others.'

'Thank God for that. I am too old to rush around after terrorists. But I'll help you if you wish.'

'Why?'

In spite of knowing the answer, Smith found that it was a more difficult question to answer than he first imagined, and he took his time replying.

'Soldiers of all sorts get killed in battle. That's normal. Not pleasant, perhaps, especially in some of the more unorthodox battles that people have to fight these days, but normal, possibly even right. That is, after all, what they are paid for. Soldiers expect the possibility. To be killed because someone betrays you, someone who you have a right to depend on, is different - very different. That is not right. That boy was murdered serving his country, not killed or even executed. Murdered. For me there's a difference. But I think you know that already.'

'If I didn't before, I do now. You seem to speak from experience, Peter'.

He made up mind. What is life without trust? Perhaps it was time he found out. He looked directly into her eyes and held her gaze.

'Yes. I do. And that's an end to it.'

It was both a question and a statement. Her glance never wavered.

'Very well.'

She glanced at him very sharply.

'You're assuming that they were betrayed, Peter. Do you know something I don't?'

'Not specifically, Suzanne, but I know enough about this sort of thing to smell a betrayal when I get downwind of one. The lies to the grandfather and the hasty cremation of the body, your own appointment. For all their youth these men were highly trained, and you don't just walk up to people like this and casually out a bullet in their head without being equally well trained. Perhaps it's just my instinct. But for me this is certainly a betrayal and jour job, I would suggest, is to find out by whom and that means someone very high up knows something. You're to discover who are the traitors or to provide information that will enable your boss to cover it all up'

She grimaced at the memory of the number on her speed dial.

Suddenly it was time for him to go. He saw nothing more to be gained by staying on and he found himself enjoying her company more than he felt he should. She was playing a little game with him as well as addressing the serious stuff and he was uncomfortable. He got up.

'Thank you for lunch, Suzanne. I enjoyed myself.' She reached out and laid a light hand on his arm. 'I am glad to have you on my side this time.'

'I think that if you remember correctly, Suzanne, I was the last time. It just may not have felt like it at the time. Good luck with your meeting this afternoon. I doubt whether you will learn much. By now even this motley collection of policemen will have got their stories straight. Let me know what happens.'

He leant towards her in that slightly diffident way that Englishmen adopt when preparing to offer the traditional Provençale farewell three kisses on alternating cheeks. He never knew which side to start. Given how little the kisses actually usually meant, he regarded the whole performance as unnecessary. However, as he lowered his head towards hers, he felt her hand settle on what in polite company might be described as his lower back. He wasn't sure, but he could have sworn that another blouse button had come undone. At the last second, she turned her head and planted a light but firm kiss on his lips. Slightly startled, he moved quickly away towards the street but was forced to turn back as she called after him. She was standing in the doorway in an exaggerated contrapposto, hand on hip, smiling broadly.

'Do you really think my bottom is nice, Monsieur?' 'Yes, Madame, I do.'

'Nicer than Martine's?'

He quickly turned away with her delighted giggle pursuing him down the street. It was only after he got home and closed his front door behind him that he felt into his pocket as he was supposed to and took out a small screw of paper. Inside was a small high security door key and a note that read 'the meeting is at 4:30pm. Be careful. You will not be alone.' The note prevented him from asking further questions. He looked at his watch. It was half past two. She would expect him to arrive just after four.

The atmosphere was hostile as the meeting assembled in Suzanne Blanchard's elegant but very minimalist dining room. Table and chairs by Matteo Thun. Paintings courtesy of her late husband's excellent modern art collection. The four men were dressed as before, two in uniform, two in suits. Madame again was formal in a dark grey pinstripe suit, tight skirt cut to the knee. White blouse and very high stilettos. Again, the table in front of her was bare save for the telephone whose presence was as symbolic as it was practical.

'Gentlemen. Thank you for coming. Before we start, I would like to say that there will be no records of this meeting so please do not take notes and whatever recording devices you might have in your briefcases or pockets should be switched off. I am also not interested in hearing you read from files or prepared statements so please put all that away too.'

There was a general shuffling around and discomfiture while note pads, piles of files and other general bits and pieces were removed from the table and returned to brief cases. Madame waited patiently for the hubbub to conclude while Roger Gallion, Commandant of RAID, looked on with a slightly amused smile, secretly pleased with himself that he had anticipated this and had brought nothing.

Again, it was the gendarme, Claude Messailles, who objected. 'And how do we know, Madame, that you are not recording this meeting without telling us.'

'You don't, colonel. Right let's start. I see no reason for this meeting to be very long. I don't want extended attempts at explanation or excuses for what happened at Beauduc. Nor do I want to hear attempts to point fingers at other departments. I am not interested in attributing blame between you at the moment. I want to know the answer to three questions only. The first is do you know who leaked the intelligence, secondly, do you know who or what group did the killing, and thirdly do you know where the terrorist who was landed at Beauduc has got to?'

She looked around the table.

'Let's start with a simple yes or no to those three questions, shall we?'

She turned to the RAID chief.

'The men who died were yours, Gallion so we will start with you.'

Gallion's face was utterly devoid of any expression as he stared

down at the glass table top. His reply was almost a whisper. 'No, no and no, Madam.'

'Granais?'

'The same, Madame,' intoned the Commissaire of the Police

National e.

'You other two? '

Lefaivre from the DST and the gendarme Messailles also just shook their heads. Madam Blanchard became briskly dismissive.

'Right, thank you. Colonel Messailles and Commissaire Granais. You may go. Please see yourselves out.'

The two uniformed men looked at her completely shocked.

Messailles spoke first:

'Madame I must protest. We must be part of this enquiry. You cannot just exclude us just like that. In any case, if, as you threatened when we last met, that you intend to remove us from our posts, you must give us the chance to defend ourselves.'

The man was clearly rattled.

'Colonel Messailles. Your personal future in the service is not at the top of my list of priorities. However, I will get around to you in time. You could spend the intervening time hoping that I give you a greater chance to defend yourself, as you say, than the three young men on Beauduc beach were allowed. Good day to you.'

She looked on as the two policemen rose uncertainly from the table and left the room. As the door clicked shut, she immediately became more business-like and addressed the remaining two.

'Right. To business. Drinks gentlemen? Gallion was the first to recover.

'Er, yes. Scotch please.'

His companion nodded his agreement. Suzanne Blanchard got up from her place at the head of the table and went over to a side table against the wall, returning with a small tray containing a whisky decanter, matching tumblers and a jug of water.

'Please help yourselves. Mine's half and half.'

To say that it became clear to the two men why this woman was doing the job she was, would be overstating things a little, but they began to get some idea. Once the small group had re-assembled around the table, Madame raised her glass.

'Gentlemen, I give you the security of France and the memory of three brave young men.' The two nodded and drank silently.

'Lefaivre, your DST planned this operation. Gallion, your men were on the beach. Talk me through what happened. The condensed version, please. Please forgive me if I ask questions as we go along'.

The DST man nodded and took another pull from his whisky.

'As you know, three months ago we received information from our network in Algeria that the terrorist planner Hassan Agreti was to be landed in France. There is a small Al-Qaeda cell in Marseille and they were to organise the sea crossing and hide him when he got here. He was to come from Algeria by fishing boat and transfer to an RIB, landing on Beauduc beach.'

She shot a question across. 'Why Beauduc?'

Lefaivre shrugged.

'I don't know exactly but I would guess because it is remote, access is difficult and there would be a minimal chance of a casual passer-by to see what was going on.'

Madame frowned.

'This whole thing seems much too well-organised for important details like that to be left to chance, Monsieur le Directeur.'

He shrugged slightly and continued.

'We had a man placed in the Marseille cell so we were relatively sure that the information was accurate - although given that the man has now completely vanished, I have a feeling that our penetration of this cell is either not as complete as we thought, or there is another cell in Marseille we know nothing about which is, of course, also worrying in itself. The decision was taken not to arrest the terrorist but to let him run and see where he went.'

Gallion joined the conversation.

'We were informed of the Beauduc location a day before the landing and set up a standard observation operation with three men actually on the beach with others either side to pick up the surveillance.'

'Protection for the beach party?'

'Yes, standard cover three hundred metres back with mobile units to cover the two escape directions.'

'Out to sea?'

'None. We assumed that as the trip from North Africa could have be planned to end anywhere, there was little likelihood that the man would re-embark and land somewhere else.'

Madame frowned. There was a lot wrong with that particular assumption, but she decided to let it go for the moment.

'How many men were involved?'

'Two assault groups, twenty men'.

'Satellite surveillance?'

'No.'

For the first time Lefaivre looked uncomfortable as he saw her sharp glance across the table.

'We requested it but we were told that it all the satellite time was assigned and there was no time to change it.'

'Told? By whom?'

'I don't know. I am afraid I was too busy trying to organise the operation to ask. I shall find out, however.'

'Do that. Did anyone try to buy satellite time off the Americans, they always have it to spare.'

'It was generally agreed that we didn't particularly want to share this operation with them. Their security leaks like the proverbial sieve. We also had no reason to suppose that the operation would need this level of backup. We had twenty very well-trained men in the field. There was no reason to suppose that everything was not under control.'

Inevitably Madame Blanchard jumped on this with something approximating a snort.

'Perhaps had you not been so confident, you might still have ended up knowing where your target has gone, to say nothing of a full complement of twenty men instead of seventeen plus three well-trained corpses.'

The DST planner nodded quietly.

'Yes, Madame, you are right, of course.'

It was an unexpectedly handsome admission. Lefaivre clearly felt the loss of the men keenly. She felt that it should be acknowledged but the knowledge of what she might have to do to these two men prevented her from doing so. She waited for the briefing to continue. It was Gallion.

'Our men were in place by ten o'clock.' 'Who was command on the ground?'

'Sergeant Lucien Girossi. He is the best men I have. Visibility was good; a two-day-old moon. It was very windy and cold but a perfectly good night for observation.'

'So what happened?'

'At twelve minutes past three, seventeen of the twenty men on the operation received a radio message that the operation was cancelled and, as specified in the standing orders, that they should withdraw for extraction by helicopter.'

'Leaving the three on the beach completely unprotected?'
'Yes. Perhaps I should explain.'

Madame Blanchard interrupted:

'Just carry on with the narrative. It's important we get the chronology right.'

Gallion raised his hand slightly in acknowledgement.

'Two times are usually set for a group to arrive at the extraction point depending on whether the withdrawal is covert or overt. This was a fast overt extraction and they had a window of ten minutes to reach the helicopters. When they arrived they found that they weren't expected by the crews and they were three short. Five went back to check and found them dead on the beach. They brought the bodies out, cleaned the beach and the whole unit took off at three forty-five.'

Suzanne Blanchard was pleased that both these men knew when to stop talking. The ensuing silence was only slightly broken by the sound of her topping up their glasses.

'Gentlemen, please forgive me for asking what are to you some obvious question. However, as I will undoubtedly be asked, I need some answers. Have you any idea who gave the order to withdraw?'

'None. All radio communication is usually recorded on our computers and there is no such message.'

'Is there a backup?'

'Yes, at different locations at the local HQ and in Paris.

Transmissions are re-encoded and sent via satellite.'

'Re-encoded?'

Yes, the original transmissions are always encoded. The system for data transmission to the recording uses a different encryption algorithm. We use AES 256-bit encryption keys for both.'

'Perhaps. All members of the team have to have the same key to share the communication. However, it should be understood that no member of the team would have been expecting any radio communication. They are trained to operate independently under radio silence using their own initiative. Radios are only used in emergencies. In fact, no official communication took place until the first attempt at extraction and Girossi informed HQ what was going on.'

'How could you limit reception to seventeen out of twenty?' 'Unfortunately, that's not too difficult. You just have to change

The encryption key in the three you want to exclude.' 'Can that be done remotely?'

'Yes, you can target the transmission to an individual radio and they are all individually identifiable. However, you need a lot of insider information even to begin to plan doing this.'

For the first time in the briefing, Gallion stirred.

'I think, Madame, we can assume that whoever did this, had the required level of both expertise and access. It was unfortunately planned properly. Estimating five minutes for the support troops to get out of vision of the beach and another five minutes for the beach to be back in vision when your men came back to investigate, they would have had not much more than ten minutes to kill the three men, land their terrorist and make off.'

She looked at the two men at her table.

'Right. Thank you for your report. I have four questions and would like your opinion, but I want you to go away and think about it. Firstly, why kill the three? They could just as easily cleared the whole team off the beach with a radio order and no-one would have been the wiser. However, to find out why, you usually have to ask who. Thus secondly, who exactly are 'they'. This is too big, too well organised, resourced and executed, to be some small isolated terrorist cell from the suburbs of Marseille. Then I want your opinion as to where this newest addition to the French terrorist population might be. I want you to find him. Finally, and I do mean finally, I want to know where the leak is. Let me make myself absolutely clear, gentlemen, if you find some answers, any answers you will take no action without consulting me first. At the moment you are both on my 'to be trusted' list - very precariously. Abuse my trust, and that means acting without consulting me, and I promise that you will be manning a tide observatory in Saint Barthélemy within twenty-four hours. I expect a report from each of you every day - verbal not written - more frequently if necessary. Do you have any questions?'

Neither man did.

'Finally, you might like to wonder why, with all your planning, resources, high tech gadgets, and God knows what else, neither of you seems to realise that in all likelihood everything you did at Beauduc was observed.'

'You mean by American or Russian satellite?' 'No.'

'By the terrorists'

'No. By a bunch of farmers with nothing more sophisticated than a horse, a ten foot wooden pole with a spike on top and two thousand years of familiarity with the Camargue. If you don't understand that you have no hope of solving this problem. You really don't know much about this part of the world.'

The two men left. Madame Blanchard sat for a moment at the table. She got up, collected another glass from the side table and sat down again.

'You can come in, please, Roland.'

46

A section of the book case that formed half of the end wall of the dining room opened and a thin, casually-dressed, handsome man in his mid-thirties entered the room. Roland DuPlessis was an old friend. They had begun their police careers together in the École spécial Militaire de Saint-Cyr and also worked together when Suzanne Blanchard had been at Europol. He was currently colonel in charge of GIGN or the Groupe d'Intervention de la Gendarmerie Nationale.

Layers of bureaucracy proliferate in France faster and thicker than fleas on a dog. So it was with the various police forces. The Police Nationale have their subdivisions including a highly trained anti-terrorist, RAID, so does the Gendarmerie Nationale and the GIGN was it. They hadn't been involved with the Beauduc operation and she had called him in as an old and trusted friend to assist her investigation.

'Well?'

He poured himself a scotch and sat down.

'It could have been some sort of warning as well as an insertion.'

'A warning to whom?'

'Crack that, and you will, as they say, crack the case. I have to admit I am not sure if my group would have done much better.'

'So one question is why were you not involved.'

'Suzanne, there are many departmental rivalries and the intelligence and anti-terrorist communities are not one great happy band of chums. This is particularly true with the planners and policy makers. At a military level there is more cooperation that you might imagine. Something to do with shared dangers, I suppose.'

'Roland, I want you to do some digging. A lot of digging if necessary. If you get any flack let me know. I can clear the way although unless I come up with something pretty soon, I am not sure how long my support will last.'

The man took a last swig of his scotch and rose to leave. 'OK, I'll see what I can do.'

When she got back from escorting DuPlessis to her front door she found Smith sitting at the table, not, she noticed with amusement, in her seat but helping himself to a drink. The front door key was on the table.

'I'm really getting too old for this hiding in cupboards business, Suzanne.'

As she passed behind his chair she planted a kiss on the back of his neck.

'Oh, I wouldn't say so. Older men can be sexy too.'

'I wasn't talking about sex. Suzanne.'

She pulled her chair back from the table so he could get a good view and sat, hitching her skirt up entirely too high for it to be just for comfort and crossed her legs. She wore stockings not tights. Smith couldn't remember if he had even met someone who could flirt and talk about terrorist murders at the same time. She wiggled her stiletto at him.

'Well?'

'You have great legs, Suzanne, but possibly a lousy taste in friends. I think a question you need to ask is why your friend DuPlessis and his incontrovertibly effective anti-terrorist group were excluded from the planning of this operation. I understand that he may be an independent set of eyes and ears to help you but you do need to ask yourself why he was officially left out of this whole debacle; rather luckily I would suggest.'

'He told me that they were assigned somewhere else. They are a very small group, you know. They simply weren't available, I gather.'

'I'll get that checked. It's not something you should take on face value, Suzanne. '

Her expression became sad and tired at the same time. She sighed.

'Ah, it would be disappointing if there was anything suspicious there. I have known him for a long time. By the way, how did you avoid bumping into him when you arrived?'

'I arrived before he did.'

'But I thought...'

'Yes, I know what you thought, but I tend not to not to be entirely predictable. I have found it to be useful habit.'

She nodded.

'And one that I suspect has saved your life from time to time. Does this mean that you were in the house while I was changing?'

'Madame, I am not a voyeur.'

'How very disappointing. If I'd known I would have put on more of a show.'

The borders were getting a bit too blurred for Smith's taste. 'Suzanne, I agreed to help but...'

His host tossed her head back and laughed shortly.

'All right, Peter. I'm sorry. Of course, this is a serious matter for both of us and I value your help. It would seem that you might be the only one I can trust in this ghastly business. You must forgive me if occasionally I, shall we say, relax a little too much. For me, it's necessary from time to time. Not for the first time, I find myself coming second to my cousin. However, back to business. What did you think of the meeting?'

'I thought you were good. It was right to get rid of Granais and Messailles. I presume they are both good at their jobs but they don't seem to know anything about all this, although I have a feeling that there is more to Messailles than meets the ear. I was less

49

impressed than I should have been with Gallion and Lefaivre. They were entirely too chummy for my liking. Given that you currently have the power of life and death over them, they were too relaxed. They should have been fucking angry and they weren't. That would worry me. The only time that you caught them on the hop was with your comment about their being watched. They didn't like that. I think your farming friends might be having some unwelcome visitors over the next few days. I must warn Martine.'

'I already have.'

On seeing his slight surprise, she continued:

'You aren't the only person to talk to my cousin, you know.'

'Finally, as I said, I'm definitely not sure about your friend DuPlessis. Need to check up on him.'

'All right, what next?' She was all business although Smith noted that the skirt was no lower; a touch higher if anything.

'We need to know exactly what went on. I need to talk to Martine and I need to get some satellite info.'

'I thought there wasn't any.'

Smith shook his head.

'Bollocks. You can't tell me that facilities to photograph an Al Qaeda terrorist landing on the shores of France were refused because the damn satellite was booked out to something else. They must think you are an idiot to try that one. The Americans might have some as well. In the very unlikely event that they really didn't know about this operation, they have enough cameras up there to make it probable that they have caught something while they were doing something else. Hell, wait long enough and it'll probably appear on YouTube or Facebook.'

Suzanne became business-like.

'What can I do?'

'Keep the pressure on your people. Ask for reports more often than they want to give them to you. Ask them questions to which you know the answers. All the usual sort of thing.'

'And you?'

'Oh, I'll just get on my merry way and ferret around a bit. I will let you know when I stumble into something useful. In the meantime, Suzanne, I suggest you take care. These are some powerful people with egos to match, to say nothing of the fact that you are the one woman I have come across in this entire sorry story and this is, after all, the land of Nicolas Chauvin. One or more of them, probably with close links to the Élysée Palace, could easily be responsible for the murders of three men. If there is a culprit to be found, they are playing a very high stakes game and are well resourced. If I had to guess at this stage - and it would be a complete guess - I would look closer at your friend DuPlessis. I don't like the smell of him.'

'We have been friends for a long time, Peter.'

'Well? So what? Just be very careful - especially of him.'

Her face mirrored the sorrow that she was obviously feeling.

'Thank you Peter. I think I know that but I appreciate your concern.'

'If I were you, I would have a chat with that rather important employer of yours and organise some close protection. A couple of men out of the GSPR would be good. In fact I would insist on it if I were you.'

'I am not sure if the President's security detail would be very interested in me, Peter.'

'They would be if he told them to. He is the one putting you in harm's way.'

'I will have a word, if you wish.'

'I do. Please let me know what is arranged. I don't want any embarrassing meetings.'

'Does that mean you will be looking after me too.'

'Whether I do or don't, you won't know.'

She smiled at him with a mock insouciance.

'Peter, you care. I'm touched.'

'Surprisingly, perhaps, I do. However, I also don't want to have to spend too much my time worrying about you. However, I'll take my leave of you now. I have a date with a chess board.'

She escorted him to the door and stood on tip toe to kiss him full on the lips.

'Thank you again, Peter. I do appreciate your help. In fact I have the feeling that without it, I will really get nowhere with this investigation.'

He looked down at her.

'Perhaps you shouldn't have taken it on in the first place. Suzanne.'

Chapter 5 Chess with Gentry

The two friends concentrated on the beginning of game in silence. They were seated either side of the masterful small Renaissance chess table, each at their customary ends, glasses of whisky at their elbows, a neat Banff single malt for Gentry, a Monoprix cooking, well-watered with Perrier and ice for Smith. A huge log fire in the grate with Arthur spark out asleep in front of it, they were surrounded by Gentry's books that were, in theory at least, his stock in trade. It was a stock, as Smith had noted many times before, seldom changed, in spite of theoretically being for sale. The last thing that Gentry actually wanted to do was sell any of his books and he went to considerable lengths to avoid doing so. The entrance to his shop was as invisible and as inaccessible as was possible, giving onto a narrow courtyard that was surrounded by the rest of the fine old house, buried deep in the maze of little streets and tall medieval buildings that lie to the immediate north west of the Amphitheatre. Few people who passed knew of the great collection of books and pictures that lay within and a single, undersized doorway was the only entrance, above ground that is. The small amount of light that entered the two small mullioned windows into the courtyard had long since faded and the room was lit only by occasional, hooded library lamps over dark book shelves and brass-banded mahogany display cases. It was a perfect room of great tranquillity.

This time Gentry played white and opened with Giuoco Piano and, on seeing Smith's relatively conservative early reply, quickly slid into the Evans Gambit. Normally he would have started with Ruy Lopez when he played white at their weekly evening meetings and Smith wondered, for a moment, whether his old opponent was trying to disturb the status quo this time. The two had been playing together for years off and on and in an impossible variety of places and, considering that they were completely different in their general approach to the game, were very well matched. Gentry was methodical, with an encyclopaedic knowledge of the game. His positions were well constructed and secure. While Smith knew more about the tactical canon of the game than he ever admitted, or Gentry ever knew, he was much more unorthodox preferring to drive the game along rather and wait for mistakes. Not for the first time he thought how well the great game reflected their relationship as well as their personalities. Smith was unorthodox, at his happiest and best when having to improvise with less than an ideal amount of information. He played his chess in the same way. As a result he often won from unlikely positions whereas he lost usually because he had missed something. It was to Gentry's continual frustration that Smith was slightly ahead on win count, not that either actually really bothered to keep score.

This time Smith wondered whether Gentry was hoping that the more methodical approach engendered by the Giuoco Piano might frustrate him and consciously set himself to be more patient than usual.

As the game progressed, Smith briefed Gentry on his conversation with Suzanne Blanchard. Their games were never conducted in silence with the sort of concentration that usually characterises serious chess. Each knew that the other was working harder at the game than he pretended but the regular evening rendezvous was always a time to talk as much as anything else.

After Smith had finished his account, Gentry took a long draw from his malt.

'Well, my old friend obviously can't be told the truth. Madame B was more than usually candid with you and she is at considerable risk if anyone finds out. The old man is an honest man, but he really cannot be expected to take this particular secret to his grave – unless, of course, someone puts him in it prematurely.'

'Yes. I agree. However, I think he could be trusted with the knowledge that his grandson died on some sort of secret mission for his country. The old soldier might be content with that. He might even be proud.'

'I should fucking well hope he would be.'

Smith looked up sharply. Gentry's obscenity was all the more shocking for its complete rarity. He continued, angrily:

'A bunch of incompetent, over-promoted security people who couldn't organise a piss-up in a brewery make a complete Horlicks of a simple intercept and surveillance operation that I could have organised in my sleep. This charming old soldier has lost his son and now his grandson for France. He has no one left. And for what, I ask? It makes me bloody pissed off.'

Smith remembered grimly times in the past when he had been at the sharp end of such operations controlled by Gentry and they had not always passed completely without incident. He also remembered, however, that he had not, as yet at least, had the inside of his head atomised by a .45 bullet. He leant across the table and laid a hand gently on his old friend's arm. Looking into his face he saw a look that he had only seen a very few times before. Normally it was Smith that got angry.

'Life is shit and then you die, my old friend. How many times have you said that to me when I have come back from a job in a mess?'

Gentry slumped back into his seat. Smith continued, searching for a way to get Gentry back on track.

'The old man needs your certainty not your anger. Yes, you must probably lie to him but only in a way that will at least give him a proud memory for that's the only thing he will have left. You've done this before; may I remind you. However, I need your certainty, too.'

Gentry looked up sharply. 'Why, may I ask?'

'I've told Madame Blanchard that I will help her to find out what went wrong.'

Gentry slumped back in his chair, rolled his eyes heavenward, let out a long sigh and let in a large swig of whisky. A not unskilled feat of coordination, Smith thought as he waited for his friend to recover.

'Oh Christ, Peter. Why?'

'Not entirely sure, old chum, maybe I'm a bit bored.'

'You had better be careful or you'll get your bored ass shot off.' 'Not with you watching it, I won't'.

'And what makes you think I would want to do that, yet again?' 'Because, David Gentry, you may think that you are completely content in your bachelor retirement but in reality you're as bored as I am.'

There was a pause while Gentry came to terms with the fact that his friend was right. A long sigh indicated acceptance.

'All right,' Gentry's voice was resigned, 'What's first.' Smith rounded on him with an abruptness that surprised him.

'Nothing for you unless you get on board quickly. Not your old friend, the draughts player, Suzanne Blanchard nor I have any use for you if you continue to sulk. Unless I have your complete attention, I'll do it without you.'

The two had never really fallen out in all the years they had worked together. Both knew how much they depended on each other and that knowledge had prevented previous disagreements from ever becoming real problems. They both had different jobs and they had both been very good at them. Together they were close to an ideal partnership. Gentry usually had control. He planned, organised, supplied, advised, very occasionally, instructed. Smith just went out and did the job and with the priceless ability to make things up when the plans went wrong, as they often did. Their missions were usually successful – surveillance, infiltration, transportation, kidnapping, occasionally elimination – whatever Her Majesty's Government had required at the time. Only the last one in Somalia scarred them enough for them both to want to draw a line under it all. Her Majesties Government had reluctantly agreed. Gentry looked across at Smith.

'I'm sorry, Peter. You're quite right. Of course I'll help. I got you into this. I won't let you down.'

Smith smiled. 'Never thought you would. You're incapable

of it.'

Gentry suddenly switched in to business mode. 'All right, what do you want to do first.'

Smith was relieved that the crisis had passed, for the moment at least. He also became business-like.

'Right. My first point of call will be Martine.' He saw a broad smile cross Gentry's face and immediately went slightly defensive. Over the last year he had become entirely too fond of Martine Aubanet, something that he had attempted to keep from both himself, the lady and Gentry without any success at all. He continued to a slightly mocking companion.

'She or her father will know what went on at Beauduc if anyone does. I need her help in talking to the right people.'

'I thought that Suzanne Blanchard was persona non grata in that part of the family.'

'Only with the old man, I think, and for perfectly legitimate reasons. Martine is prepared to let dead collaborators lie, as it were.'

'I often wonder,' mused Gentry, 'whether our modern desire to forgive, forget and move on, as they say, is entirely right. Nothing wrong with a bit of well-placed enmity, even revenge, I've always felt.' Ignoring the aside with which he had complete sympathy, Smith continued forcefully, not giving his companion a chance to reminisce:

'I want you to find out about the official end of all this. Who exactly organised it; what the hell was actually supposed to be going on. I cannot believe that this was a simple surveillance operation. No one in their right mind lets a major terrorist loose in their country in the hope of following him somewhere interesting. If they really wanted to get some information they would have picked him up the second he landed on the beach, killed everyone else and electrified his gonads. I want to know where the information came from and how good it was. Who was the North African connection? What was the provenance of the information? Who prepared the operation?

Who was involved? Who was local liaison? Who picked the observation teams? Who planned strategy? I also want to know why there was no protection for the guys on the beach. No second layer backup. Or if there was any, why was it useless? Why no air observation? Was there any satellite surveillance? I want to know about the GIGN man, Roland DuPlessis and why his group was excluded from the operation. He is significant because he seems to be the one who Suzanne trusts in all this and that makes her vulnerable to him if he isn't straight. I personally think he's suspect at the very least.'

Gentry looked interested.

'And why have you taken against this man, Peter. Apart from your usual suspicion of absolutely everyone, you seem to have focussed on this DuPlessis very early?'

Smith thought for a moment.

'Firstly Suzanne' trusts him. That makes him dubious in my book. Secondly the GIGN was left out of things. Thirdly I noted that while we were both observing Suzanne's cosy but pretty inconsequential meeting, DuPlessis was hiding in the space behind the library door and was using a nifty little directional microphone and a mobile phone to send the whole conversation God knows where. I could see he wasn't just recording it. That could have been done much more simply.'

That really got Gentry's interest.

'Ah if only we knew where that signal was going we would be a lot closer to solving this little mystery, Peter.'

Smith nodded and continued.

'OK now another question.'

Gentry looked passively at his companion and wondered in which direction he was heading now. Sometimes it was hard to keep up.

'Why Suzanne?'

Gentry knew this was a rhetorical question. Smith was thinking our load.

'I'm perfectly aware that she is a capable investigator, or at least used to be presumably before she started flying a desk. She also has Provençale connections. However, she is simply one of many who could do the job. She is certainly French but not from any of the mainstream French agencies and the French are particularly chauvinistic about this sort of thing. She is senior but not senior to enjoy direct authority from the President. It's all a bit of a conundrum.'

Gentry finally made a modest sortie into the monologue.

'If you ask me, which incidentally your haven't to date, it is more to do with Suzanne herself than with any qualifications she might have for the job. Put briefly, the President of France wants her specifically for the job. Why is the question you should answer.'

'Exactly. So I want to know what the official word is on Madame Blanchard. Last time I saw her she was a senior Eurocop with a dead paedophile husband, probably murdered by her . It seems to me to be a long way from there to swaggering around the halls of the Elysée. Why is she involved? Maybe she is screwing the President.'

He paused.

'What the hell am I telling you this for? You know already.'

He glanced at the handsome Georgian carriage clock on the mantelpiece over the now moribund fire, his retirement present to Gentry. It was close to one am.

'I want all this as well as all the other stuff I have forgotten within eight hours. After that, the rest of your retirement is your own.'

'Will it be?' Gentry smiled quietly.

'Almost certainly not. Now fuck off and start working.'

As if to emphasise the urgency of the issue, Smith lent forward and poured another large measure of Banff into his friend's glass.

Chapter 6   Martine

It had taken most of the morning and a decent lunch - a baguette, pâté and camembert - shared with an expectant Arthur for the slight feeling that he had indulged a little too much the previous night to abate. But as usual, she answered him within a ring or two. Also as usual her tone expressed her delight at hearing from him. Equally as usual he felt a pang of guilt and regret at not being in touch with her sooner. Ever since their first meeting last year and the adventure that had ensued, he had thought that he might have found what he imagined, at least, was what he wanted. A *compañera*; someone who would be part of his quiet retirement but not be too much part of his life. He had had two wives, both of whom had departed in the particularly British civilised manner that left both sides dissatisfied. A proper bloodbath is the right way to end a long-term relationship not a polite handshake. The only thing the modern world achieved, it seemed to him, was obfuscation rather than clarity. What should count should be winning not continuance. When he came to the south of France he had a vague thought of finding someone, near his own age, attractive, cultured, intelligent. Someone with whom he could share the few passions left in his life other than Mozart and Arthur, and that was sitting across a dinner table with someone to look at and talk to. Sex remained down the list of priorities due primarily to lack of confidence itself born on unfamiliarity and a failing medium-term memory. Martine had remained annoyingly attractive – or was it gratifyingly? Maybe he was not as emotionally moribund as he'd hoped.

'Peter, how nice to hear from you.'

It had indeed been a week or two since he last called.

'Martine, I wonder if you would like to come here for supper? I feel like cooking.'

'Only if it's tonight.' 'Oh, why?'

'Because I want to see you again.'

He had a sudden picture of her, sitting in the great Mas buried in deep in the Camargue, where she lived with her father. She was strikingly beautiful, rich, intelligent, beautifully dressed and mannered and fulfilled all the criteria of his ideal *compañera* except for the fact that he also fancied her something rotten. That, of course, was not part of the picture and his inability to come to terms with it was a major impediment, for him at least, in taking any relationship further.

He was both pleased and worried by the obvious fact that she was prepared to wait for him to make the correct decision.

'Yes, tonight.'

'Excellent. What shall I wear?'

He was somewhat flummoxed, not for an answer but at the question. She had never asked it before. Needless to say, he fell into the trap.

'Er, I was thinking of just us.'

Her voice sank an emotional decibel lower. 'Ah. Business or sex?'

Perhaps she had got bored waiting. At last some latent chivalry came to the rescue.

'No, Martine not entirely business. Yes, I have a problem that I want your help to solve, but I also want to see you again.'

Without actually intending to, he had been completely honest. 'In that case,' she replied triumphantly, 'I shall be business-like and sexy. I will also bring dessert. See you seven.'

Without anything further she rang off.

Smith looked at his watch. He had five hours to clean the house, go shopping, shower and change and cook something. Martine Aubanet and her family owned, amongst other things, a number of restaurants in the town some of which served food of a quality that would have put to shame many of the local over-hyped, Michelin- rated establishments frequented by the Arles glitterati. The restaurants were tucked away in inaccessible places, looked unprepossessing but served exquisite food to locals at prices that the locals could afford. Well-heeled, self-important tourists were invariably turned away with mumblings about reservations. You can't have a reservation in a restaurant that doesn't accept them. They were also definitely plastic free zones. He thus felt a little diffident about cooking for her. A quick glance in the freezer located a few paupiettes that had been surplus to requirements when his daughters had last come to stay. He took them out and stood them on a plate on his garden table to defrost in the pale light of the winter sun. The rest relied on a quick trip to Monoprix, the Asda Walmart of France.

He walked down to the supermarket, though the deserted Place Voltaire, and across the Place Lamartine at the north gate to the city. It had been the site of most of the fighting when the town was liberated from German occupation in 1944, only after an aerial bombardment from the American air force that not only took out the road and river bridges across the Rhone, but, for reasons best known to themselves, also destroyed a wide swath through the medieval town to the immediate north east of the Amphitheatre and on down towards the Rhone. Amongst the many victims of this pointless bombardment were most of the houses on the Place de la Major and Van Gogh's famous Yellow House on the Place Lamartine. Smith always took particular pleasure in informing hopeful American tourists who now asked for directions to the little building that famously housed Van Gogh for eighteen months and Gauguin for three that it was their own air force that had reduced it to shingle. By fortunate misadventure they managed to avoid the complete destruction of the Roman amphitheatre and the patron church of the Guardians of the Camargue that stood outside his little house, Notre Dame de la Major.

Once home from grocery shopping, he found that the paupiettes had, of course not defrosted. Bugger. So he browned them off anyway, quickly in hot mixture of seasoned olive oil and butter and put them in a large casserole. Hopefully an hour or two of very slow cooking would make them taste of something more than just salmonella. Next was a very primitive but potent tomato, shallot, garlic and herb sauce thrown together with more than the usual amount of alcohol. He poured it over the meat and set it to stew very slowly. The butcher made good paupiettes, veal not turkey, with a stuffing that was handmade rather than re-constituted, and Smith knew that there would be enough proper meat juice to give some balls to the sauce. He half boiled some potatoes as a preliminary to slicing and frying them. A tomato salad with some chopped, almost dead, chives from his winter garden would complete the main course. Monoprix had offered no cheese of any note so he had to rely on a couple of bits of sheep cheese he had bought expensively off the market at the weekend. The starter was a simple salad with some slices of pear fried in butter and a dash of Pernod on some green salad with a light vinaigrette sweetened slightly with honey. His guest would provide the conclusion to the meal.

Wine gave him pause for thought. Martine's father owned some of the few really great vineyards in the area. His wines were exquisite and never made it into the market. They were also utterly untypical of the region. The general Côtes du Rhone wines that surrounded Arles were, in general, good without being exceptional. The vins du pays were invariably good and wholesome in the genuine sense rather than that patronisingly pejorative sense in which the word is usually used. The really good ones were also cheap. Some, especially those that had jumped on the 'bio' bandwagon, were dreadful value for their inflated price. Emile Aubanet produced small quantities of a red to rival the Grand Crus from Bordeaux; a sweet white that equally that would bear comparison with the very best. Even a crémant that was better than most so-called champagnes by a country mile. There was no way that he could rival that. His local wine seller offered some excellent table wine from a vineyard on almost the last cultivatable bank of the Rhone before it dissipates into the Camargue near Mas Thibert, the little village that was offered as a home to the refugee harkis who had fought with the French during the Algerian Wars. The St Pierre was excellently and conscientiously made and was supplied from a petrol station-style hand pump into whatever container you felt like bringing at a princely sum of one and a half euros a litre. It tended not to last for more than a month or so, but, for some reason, that never seemed to be a problem for Smith.

Once the meat was on, he set about cleaning up. His house was a dusty one. Apart from the fact that those in charge of the immediate post-war rebuilding looked no further than concrete for their main method of construction, passage of cars and lorries into the Place past his front door inevitably made for dust, especially as he tended to keep his windows open in all but the most severe northerly winds. He liked the air and if he had to keep his big tiled wood stove burning fiercely to compensate, then that was no great hardship. The result was that the house was dusty. He also hated housework. The obvious solution was a femme de ménage of whom there were many available. However at ten euros an hour, they were simply too expensive. He had been toying with Quentin Crisp's solution of ignoring the dust completely and then paying someone to come in once one could no longer open the door. However the problem had not yet got to that point. Cleaning over in an incompetent sort of way, he put a match to the fire and it was soon time to shower and dress. He poured himself a large, well iced cooking whisky and Perrier and went upstairs.

Yes, it could be described as business and sexy. Martine Aubanet came into the house looking completely devastating and she knew it. She wore a mid-grey, pinstriped business suit complete with immaculately creased trousers; a white lightly frilled blouse beneath. Pearl stud earrings and a double row pearl choker around her neck. The only other jewellery was, as usual, a silver Saintes Maries Camargue cross at her lapel. Her dark brown hair was caught up to the top of her head in that distinctive style of Arlesian women. The outfit was rounded out by dark grey stocking or tights, Smith would not allow himself to guess which, and a pair of outrageously high black Christian Lacroix stilettos that were all thin straps and tapered heel. She stood taller than he did. How the hell she drove her Range Rover in them he could only guess. Smith was stunned. She was delighted. Ignoring the customary triple touching of cheeks that denoted a greeting in this part of the world irrespective of the sex of the participants, she planted a long and passionate kiss directly on his lips.

'Right,' she said with glee, 'that does for the business, when do we get to the sex?'

Martine Aubanet – she had reverted to her maiden name after the murder of her husband, Robert DuGresson – was obviously in a thoroughly good mood. Not for the first time, Smith found himself wondering why she was obviously so fond of him. It was true that he had sorted out the problem of the murder of her late and thoroughly un-lamented husband and the relationship that developed afterwards still refused to die, due in no small part to her refusal to let it. There were almost fifteen years between them and somehow he couldn't bring himself to believe it.

Arthur in the meantime had lost all his habitual sense of dignity and gone completely hysterical. Martine was one of his very favourite people and he was quite uninhibited in telling her so. He was a very large greyhound indeed and perfectly capable of standing up and putting his forepaws on her shoulders, stilettos and all. In fact that was what he was doing now. Smith started to admonish the dog but he knew full well that she encouraged him. She sat at one end of Arthur's sofa, oblivious to the dog hair. He jumped up beside her and immediately lay with his head in her lap, utterly content.

'Martine, you look wonderful.' She nodded.

'I know. Have you any idea how uncomfortable these bloody shoes are?'

'Er, no.' Smith was rapidly losing touch with reality.

'Christian told me that they are actually only meant to be worn in bed.'

'Er, oh yes.' The thought was simply too much for Smith who busied himself in preparing another whisky, identical to his. It was no surprise at all that she knew Christian Lacroix. The great designer was a famous son of Arles and Martine was one it's richest and certainly most stylish inhabitants.

The next hour or so passed entirely too quickly. They talked about the Aubanet businesses, about the farm and her father's bulls.

Apart from being part of a family that lived and worked in the Camargue, her father was one of the most successful breeders of bulls on the great marsh. The rest of the extensive and varied family business was in the hands of Martine and was involved in a very wide variety of activities ranging from farming to property, wine making, and general trading. Everything, however, was based locally and many of the businesses, especially the small hotels and smaller firms were not necessarily run for profit. The Aubanet family had been living in the area for many generations and they took their social responsibilities seriously. It was just as well, Smith often thought, for the French government certainly didn't.

To his surprise and intense relief, the paupiettes turned out to be excellent. As he hoped, the otherwise potentially banal tomato sauce had been transformed by the meat juices. The starter was done to perfection. It is entirely possible to over-fry pears - which was possibly a slightly odd thing to do in the first place. This starter was Smith's only personal contribution to international cuisine. The conversation was, as it always was between them, wide-ranging and easy. As usual he felt utterly content in her company. Arthur had taken up permanent residence, prone on the floor at Martine's feet and was happy to accept a regular supply of titbits from her plate. He knew the family as well as Smith and her father was similarly inclined to spoil the dog on their not infrequent visits to the mas. Before long they were sitting again on the sofas, drinks at their elbows.

'All right,' she said, 'now the business.'

Smith tore his gaze away from those extraordinary shoes and looked across at his guest. It was a real effort of will to bring up the whole matter, the evening was going so well.

'I presume by now you have heard about the events at Beauduc the other night.'

All trace of coquetry vanished, and she immediately became very serious.

'Yes, I have. It was a dreadful business.'

'And you have heard that your cousin is in charge of the investigation?'

Martine looked rather sharply at him.

'No I haven't. Although, I'm slightly surprised. I wouldn't have imagined that Europol would have got involved in what seems to be to a domestic French issue.'

'I think that she is now working for the Elysée, at least on this particular problem.'

There was never any question in her mind as to how he knew this. He just did. She had learned at an early stage when he got involved in the aftermath of her husband's murder that Smith had ways of doing things and knowing things that possibly didn't bear too close an investigation. All she knew was that she had been the fortunate recipient of his varied talents. She also owed her life to him. There was much she was prepared to take completely on trust from him. In the year since then she had gradually fallen in love with him, something that was completely obvious to everyone who knew her with the possible exception of Smith himself. She was prepared to live with that fact – for the present, at least. However, she could take a good guess at why he wanted to talk about the Beauduc business. She knew the family of the murdered policeman, especially the grandfather. They were Camargue people. She also knew exactly what had happened on the beach and how it differed from the official story given to the families. The official surveillance of the landing may well have been a dreadful failure, but it had not gone unobserved by the locals. She waited for him to explain his interest and to ask for her help. She had, of course, already decided to give it in spite of some misgivings about his getting involved again with something that, on the face of it, wasn't really any of his business.

'I have agreed to help Suzanne find out where the leak was.' She looked at him levelly.

'Now why on earth would you want to do that, Peter? I thought you didn't like her very much.'

'Well, actually a friend wants me to find out what happened.

It is a family thing.'

She took some time to respond. She had an inkling what friendship meant to Smith and was always slightly humbled when she came across it. She knew he had very few friends. Equally she knew that there was absolutely nothing he would not do for them. Unlike others she knew from many walks of life, his preoccupations were different. While most people networked as hard as they could in some sort of effort to make an ever-larger bed to lie in, Smith did the opposite. He had pruned until there was no more foliage. Unlike everyone she knew, those few that finally remained in Smith's life were more important to him than he was to himself. That is what made her love him. She knew that she was one of those.

'How can I help?' Her voice was as level as her question was honest. Whatever it was that made Smith want to investigate Beauduc, the fact that he did was good enough for her. He told her as much of the story as he knew while she listened intently.

'I need to know exactly what happened on that night. Who was there and why. I need to know what happened in reality. Why it all went wrong and who was responsible.'

He turned more directly towards her, took her hand and continued:

'Martine, what I need from you is only, and I repeat only, the names of some people to talk to. Under no circumstances must you do more than this. This is not some local or even regional problem; it is very much more than that. You and your father may have two thousand year's Camargue loyalty and tradition that will protect you from most things. It may well be that this is different, and that safety might not be quite enough now. There is no mercy in the world of terrorism and I need your promise that you will do no more what I ask.'

Her usual tendency to make light of things whenever she felt he was getting solemn vanished for she knew he was deadly serious.

'Of course, Peter. I promise. But what about you? Surely there is the same danger in all this for you as well.'

Smith knew only too well. But unlike Martine, he knew what it was and could quantify it. He knew that the secret of survival is to remain more valuable alive than dead and, with Gentry's help, that is precisely what he had been doing off and on for the last forty years working in various far-flung parts of the world. Suzanne Blanchard was his first line of defence for as long as she herself had the protection of the Élysée, at least. Gentry would have to monitor the extent to which her position of influence might change as her investigation progressed. She had probably already made some powerful enemies and she would only survive for as long as she kept winning.

'My dear, I have managed to survive into my retirement. I fully intend to enjoy it now it has arrived.'

She wrinkled her nose and gave a small harrumph.

'Not for the first time, Peter, I note that you have a funny idea of retirement. Usually that is not the time one embarks on a one man hunt for a gang of international terrorists.'

'I'm doing no such thing. All I want to do is to find out enough to be able to lie honestly to an old man.'

'Lie?'

'It is unlikely that he can ever be told the truth.' 'Ah,' she said quietly, 'I see.'

He looked down and was surprised to see that he was still holding her hand. Tenderly he raised her palm to his cheek and cradled it there for a moment. It was an unexpectedly gentle moment that slightly surprised them both.

It was late, well past midnight. Her coda to the evening was to issue an invitation.

'It is my father's birthday on Saturday. He's having a big party in the evening to which, of course, you are invited.'

Smith at once squirmed inwardly. He knew full well that

since their adventure during the previous year, he had become something of a notoriety amongst the friends and acquaintances of the Aubanet family. Although he was honoured to be invited he had no desire to present an alternative focus of attention when the object of the party was to celebrate the old man's birthday. It was because she knew of his difficulty that she continued quickly.

'However, he also knows that you would like to decline while being polite enough to accept if asked. So he intends to ask if Arthur would join us on Sunday to inspect the new season's calves on the farm and then for a small family lunch . You are, of course, welcome to come as well.'

Her father had also taken a great liking to the dog. They both took genuine pleasure in each other's company. Emile Aubanet's bulls were his greatest passion and the invitation to look over the new arrivals meant much more than one to champagne, tapas and chatter.

'Please tell him that we should both be delighted.'

'Excellent. Shall we say ten o'clock? And perhaps by tomorrow morning, I might have some news. Now I must go.'

He rose with her.

'You're not driving yourself home, Martine.'

It was both a statement and a question.

'No, Peter. Jean–Marie is driving me,'

Memories of some excessively exciting car journeys with her and Jean-Marie as driver were still relatively fresh in his mind. Much to his relief but no little surprise she had accepted his request that she was not to drive on her own. He had also personally spent considerable time with Jean-Marie teaching him some of the aspects of defensive driving and use of a handgun that do not naturally occur in driving schools' syllabi.

They went to the door together and, sure enough, the black

Range Rover was parked in the street outside his house. Jean Marie jumped down from the driver's door.

She turned to Smith with a look of concern on her face.

'Take care, Peter. I don't like this business very much. I do not like the fact that you are choosing again to put yourself in danger. I will not even try to dissuade you but you must allow me to be worried. You are important to me.'

'As you are to me, Martine. I hope you know that by now.'

She placed a gentle prolonged kiss on his lips and turned away down the steps and into the waiting car. The last thing he saw as the Range Rover slid down the hill and past the side of the great Roman amphitheatre that was Smith's main reason for buying his little house there in the first place was a mischievous grin and a wink from the young driver.

It didn't occur to him that half past midnight was an anti-social time to telephone anyone. Nor was he surprised that the mobile phone was answered half way through its first ring by a man who was clearly neither asleep nor unhappy at the interruption.

'Peter. How nice to hear from you.'

Smith had no idea how Girondou possessed a technology to circumvent the device on his phone that prevented his caller-id being sent but he was talking with the head of one of the major crime families in Marseille and was not particularly surprised. Maybe it was just as simple a thing as Smith being the only person on earth to dare to call him at this time of night.

'Alexei, I am sorry to call you at this hour.' A deep chuckle wafted over the ether.

'No, you're not, Peter. You are the only person who would dare to. Others have tried but they have usually finished sleeping in bridge foundations.'

Girondou had an unnerving and very un-French ability to make fun of himself although there was a slight chill of authenticity about this particular jest. He continued.

'Actually, I was half-expecting a call from you. I had hoped that you were going to take me up on my offer of a job. I still feel more comfortable with someone of your abilities on my side rather than anywhere else but as your assurance of moral neutrality has proved to be accurate, I am resigning myself to the fact that you do not wish to associate yourself with my particular version of the dark side of life. I presume this is about Beauduc. If my memory serves it is my turn to offer you lunch. Tomorrow – or rather later today - at noon?'

'Yes, that'll be fine.'

Girondou's information network was second to none so the presumption came as no surprise. However, it was late, well past his usual bedtime. So, having let Arthur out to visit the garden one last time, he shut up the house and went to bed.

Other than the fact that it was high, about four metres, Smith estimated, flanked by an equally high, creeper-covered wall that ran either side until it went out of sight at far bends in the road, there was little to help the casual passer by identify the big and rather beautiful wrought iron gate as the entrance to the home of the most powerful criminal in the South of France. Alexei Girondou was the head of the crime syndicate that controlled most major felonies along the coast between Italy and Spain and inland until you get within spitting distance of Lyon some two hundred kilometres north. Not that you would be able to tell when you met him. He was medium in height, weight and appearance. Always immaculately dressed with a deep tan and exquisite manners he was every inch the successful, sophisticated businessman. Which, in a way, he was.

The house was built on the cliff just above Sausset-les-Pins, on the strip of land that encircles the south shore of the Étang de Berre to the west of Marseille. The location was predictably scenic; an unbroken view to the south over the Mediterranean and to the east across the Bay to Marseille so memorably captured by Cézanne at almost the same time that Van Gogh was working in Arles. Behind, the house was sheltered from the wind and unwelcome observation by the L'Estaque mountains. It was an archetypal spot. The sort of house that everyone imagines rich residents of the Côte d'Azur to inhabit. The location was also thoroughly practical for a man of Girondou's calling. The A55 AutoRoute was within five minutes fast drive along one of three different routes, all maintained in a surprisingly good state of repair. The sea was two or three minutes down the hill. The airport of Marignane was a five-minute helicopter hop to the north east. Fast – very fast – transportation was available in both places. The mountains also disguised the fact that the house and idyllic rural location were surrounded by the most powerful protection of all – the vast expanses of industrial development that extend from the oil refineries and chemical works at Fos, Martgues and Istres to the west to the newer commercial developments between L'Estaque and Marseille in the east. This had been Girondou's power base while he rose to the top in a typically bloody set of wars with his rivals. It was his kingdom. The criminal world of Marseille is not based in the Vieux Port where everyone just looks like a criminal and tourists hunt for Popeye Doyle doubles. It is here where the power really lies. Girondou lived amongst his friends. No one drove onto the D5 from Martique or from Marignane down to the coast without being noted and checked. Equally, no one came within a couple of kilometres of the gate without specific approval of the men sitting in front of banks of TV screens in the pretty little gatehouse just inside the great iron gates.

When Smith arrived at the gate it was open, and he drove straight through, receiving a wave from the deceptively cheery old gatekeeper. Fortunately, he had remembered that the windscreen of his battered old Peugeot 307 was very dirty and he had leaned forward in his seat as he passed though les Ventrons a kilometre or five back so that the camera could get a good view. Face and number plate recognition software had done the rest. It all looked rather peaceful as he felt the slight bump of the pneumatic bollards set down in the roadway; bollards that could be raised to the height of a metre in a tenth of a second and that would stop a truck. He tried not to think of the firepower that followed his slow progress down the winding leafy drive lined with olive trees and oleander bushes.

His host was waiting for him at the bottom in the wide sweep of the courtyard entrance. It was one of those clear sunny winter Provençale days where because of the light, it felt less cold than it was. Girondou greeted his guest with genuine pleasure and offered a firm handshake. He was dressed in that style that the very rich affect in Provence that gives proper meaning to the overused and widely misunderstood expression of 'smart casual'. Plain cream cotton shirt and slacks, polished Gucci loafers and a cashmere sweater knotted loosely around his shoulders. No rings, just a vintage gold Cartier tank watch at his wrist.

'Peter. It is good to see you again.' He meant it, as did Smith. 'You also, Alexei. Thank you for asking me here.'

His host suddenly became serious.

'Peter, there is a slight change of plan. When Angèle heard that you were coming she cancelled a hair appointment and the girls dumped a shopping trip to the Canebière. They both have new boyfriends, and this seems to necessitate a complete change of wardrobe. However they all want to have lunch with you. Do you have the time to stay and eat with the family and perhaps we can talk afterwards?'

'Alexei of course I have the time to talk later and the chance of having lunch with three of the most beautiful women I know is not to be missed for an old man like me.'

His host grimaced.

'Only the English can flatter like that. How you can say things that would sound like a tired chat up line coming from a Frenchman is beyond me, but it certainly seems to work. Come.'

They went through the house and sat out on the terrace with its spectacular view over the sea. Not for the first time Smith wondered at the way his friendship with this man had developed in the six months or so since they first met. Here he was sipping a chilled Grand Cru Chablis to beat a fizz of any quality and exchanging small talk with a man who controlled or had committed virtually every crime imaginable. He was managing director of a business that carried out murder, extortion, fraud, kidnapping, prostitution and, in all probability drug dealing, arms trafficking and almost every other form of illicit money-making activity. Smith had worked for the British Government in a surreptitious way for much of his life and there were very few of those crimes that he too had not committed in one form or another. The fact he did it on orders from a part of Her Majesty's Government that doesn't change with general elections made little difference to him. They were similar in many ways. The rest of the world would almost certainly think differently but he had long since stopped bothering what the world thought.

He and Girondou had bumped into each other last summer when he had been looking into the death of Martine's husband and, in the process, had found out considerably more about the gangster than might possibly have been good for him. Girondou had taken a chance and trusted the Englishman when he said that he wasn't interested in passing on anything to the police, his only concern being the investigation of the murder of what turned out to be a thoroughly unlamented paedophile. Smith had, of course, kept his word and the two had gradually become friends in spite of Girondou's regular but unsuccessful efforts to recruit Smith into the family business.

After about a few minutes their conversation was interrupted by the arrival of the ladies. At first glance all three looked like sisters. The twins were seventeen and as nearly identical as makes no difference. Their mother might have been twenty-five years their senior but looked only five at most. They were three staggeringly beautiful women, tall, slim, raven haired and all obviously delighted to see him. The girls rushed up to him and the three were enveloped into a communal hug. Madame Angèle followed at a somewhat more sedate pace and, holding his hands tightly, placed three kisses on alternating cheeks. Alexei had no secrets from these three and they all knew what they owed to Smith's silence. He stepped back and looked at them. There was obviously a Bardot retro thing going on amongst the young for the girls were almost identically dressed in turned up baggy jeans belted suicidally tightly to emphasise their tiny waists, plain white tee shirts and flat espadrilles. Their mother was in a haut couture version of the same theme - blouse, slacks and again canvas shoes. Smith was reminded of his own, somewhat older daughters. He whispered something to one of the girls and they ran off only to return with the box of chocolates he had bought for them from Madame Legrand, the fabled choclatière of Arles and a small posy of flowers. Buying a present for a family that either had or who could afford everything was difficult, especially on Smith's budget but it amused him to buy something extremely fattening for these three beautifully shaped women. They would consume the chocolates voraciously and it would, of course, make absolutely no difference to their shape. Madame Girondou accepted the flowers with pleasure and rushed off to find a vase.

Lunch was taken on the sheltered terrace and passed in a general chatter of domesticity. For some reason they had adopted Smith as a sort of honorary uncle and he took pleasure in being brought up to date with the girls' progress in school – a report accompanied by much wrinkling of noses – and their new boyfriends, who seemed to hold their interest rather more. He could not help feeling slightly sorry for the boys. Dating these two would be an intimidating prospect for many reasons. Both their parents looked on with pride as their daughters monopolised the conversation. They excused themselves before pudding, but not before inviting themselves to stay with him during the Easter Feria in Arles. They then left to take up their dates and Smith was amused to hear that the two boys in question had been waiting in another room throughout lunch. Family meals were a priority in this household and Smith found himself admiring the fact.

Having caught up with Angèle's news during cheese and pudding, the meal finally came to an end. She knew that there was some business to be discussed. Rising from the table she said:

'I'll leave you two to it. I am going to get my hair done and run a few errands. Peter, come again soon. Please tell me if having the girls for Feria would be too much.'

'Not at all. It'll be nice to have a houseful once in a while. They may have to bunk up together if my two come as well but they haven't let me know yet. In the meantime, thanks for lunch. As usual it was lovely to see you all again.'

She planted a single kiss on his cheek and left. Smith turned to his host with a smile as avuncular as his honourary position demanded.

'You are a lucky man, Alexei.'

'Yes, I know. Do you want to sit and talk or walk?' 'I rather think I'd like to walk.'

The temperature had dropped a little but the afternoon was still bright. Having put on coats they started out to walk through the maze of paths that ran around the hillside. It was an entrancing walk and one regularly came upon spectacular views interspersed with clumps of oleander bushes and a variety of pine trees. Had Smith not been trained he would have missed the fact that they were observed and guarded every foot of the way. They were good, he thought. Not visible but definitely there.

'OK, Peter. How can I help?'

Smith had wondered how to explain something that he really didn't understand himself, so he settled on telling his host everything and again retold the story in its entirety. When he had finished, they walked a little in silence. Girondou turned.

'I understood from the beginning why you involved yourself in the killing of DuGresson last year. You're a sucker for a beautiful woman and your slightly, shall we say, unusual sense of morality enabled you to abhor the paedophiles while remaining indifferent to the sort of things I do. That is why neither the Aubanet family nor I have ever been bothered by the flics and why Madame Blanchard is now a senior investigator basking in the undiluted authority of the President of France rather than serving a life sentence for the murder of her husband. You are an honourable man, Peter, at least in the sense that I understand it, but why this, my friend? You must know that these are much more dangerous waters than the last time.'

Smith took some time to collect his thoughts. He knew that he did not owe this man any sort of explanation, but he felt that he wanted to offer him one. Friendship, for him, was an all-or-nothing business.

'Much of what you do, Alexei, I too have done in the past. The only difference between us is that I did it on the orders of Her Majesties Government; people who actually are responsible to no-one other than their own sense of self preservation and a belief that they are doing it for England or some other preposterous idea. I could always have said no – I think – but I didn't. But now I don't accept there is a distinction that makes you a criminal and made me an honourable soldier taking orders in an unwaged and almost certainly illegal war. I have long since given up any wish to understand the morality of all this, even if there is one; which I doubt.'

'I do, however, tend to make my morality up as I go along and even if you get through all the agonising and the conscience pricking and the self-analysis, I have always found decisions about right and wrong surprisingly easy to make. What I see in this story is simple. I see a young man who only ever really wanted a family, and career having his brain atomised because people in high places were either incompetent, or betrayers of trust. I see a young widow and a child who had a future before last week and now only have a dreadful past. I see an honest and proud old man who will now die in sorrow. All this because some men with authority and no conscience were either incompetent or duplicitous or probably both. All my life I worked for people like this and I have come to hate them.'

He continued with a shake of his head.

'I am not stupid enough to think that I can fight terrorism. Much as it disturbs me, I have no appetite for that sort of thing, nor, I suspect, would I be able to do anything if I had. But I can do something for the old man. I can find the people who caused that young man to be killed.'

'And punish them?' Girondou knew it wasn't really a question.

There was a long pause. Smith's voice was almost a whisper.

'Yes, if no one else will.'

Girondou slipped his arm through Smith's and the two men continued their slow walk in silence. After a while arguably the most powerful man in the south of France looked across at the Englishman.

'Christ, Peter. I hope you never come after me.'

Smith felt he was almost talking to a child.

'I won't, never fear. You and your family are my friends.'
'You don't forgive betrayal, do you Peter?'

'Oh no, never. I know what it's like.'

Their walk had finally brought them back to the house and they arrived at Smith's car. He took off his coat and threw it onto the back seat. His host asked him to wait for a moment and disappeared into the house. When he appeared a couple of minutes later he handed Smith a plain brown cardboard box.

His host explained.

'It is a secure satellite phone, my friend. Given who you are dealing with, I wouldn't trust any of your phones or even your emails. Do you actually have an email, by the way? '

Smith ignored the question.

'And this phone is secure? 'Oh yes.'

Seeing the slightly questioning look, he continued:

'Encrypted. I am on speed dial 1. Your number is in the memory under 'me'. I though you would like that. The GPS chip is activated but can only be read by me. '

'If you find yourself in, shall we say, difficulty, dial 9 twice. You need not stay on the line, nor will the phone make a noise. As long as you don't go much further north than Lyon I can have men to you in ten minutes. While I think of it, you might advise Madame Blanchard to take a similar precaution. Given who she is investigating, I can't think that her calls go unaudited.' He added with a grin: 'She does not get the Girondou get-you-home service, however. She can look after herself.'

'Thank you, Alexei. I appreciate your help. I owe you.'

'No, you don't. Its what friends do. In any case, the girls would kill me if I didn't help.' His tone became serious.

'Of course, I'll help you as far as I can, Peter. However, you must understand that I can't jeopardise things here. I need the goodwill of people in many places both here and in Paris and while I can lose one or two if necessary, the whole thing depends on a certain level of confidence and trust. I will go further for you than for anyone else but even for you I may have to have limits.'

'I understand.'

Girondou nodded in the direction of the hidden cardboard box. 'I will call you later tonight with a quick report on what comes

to light first.'

'Could you get me a few more of these? Four perhaps?' 'Of course. I will have them to you later this evening.'

With that the two men shook hands and Smith drove back up the drive and set course back for Arles.

He got home sometime in the early evening and still feeling the benefit of an excellent lunch decided to forego supper, take Arthur for his evening walk along the river a little early and settle in with a glass of whisky and a book. However, before he left he put in a quick call to Suzanne Blanchard. As soon as she answered he spoke over her in order to stop her identifying him.

'Hi there. I am just going to take Arthur for a walk. Meet you outside the Hospitallers in a few minutes.' With that he put the phone down without allowing her to speak further.

He had no doubt that she would get the message so a few minutes later he and Arthur were walking along the river wall west in the direction of the Tranquetaille Bridge. Although it was only seven, it was dark and overcast and the river was flecked with angry white marks as the wind crossed the surface . He arrived at the Musée Réattu, the fifteenth century Grand Priory of the Knights of Malta - the Hospitallers of the Knights of St John of Jerusalem. He saw leaning into a strong northwest wind, a slim figure in jeans and a heavy blouson jacket, walking towards him under the dim lamps that light the riverside in a half-hearted dimness. The face she turned up towards him to be kissed in greeting was concerned. She put her arm though his, having made the usual fuss of Arthur who, on this occasion, was less interested in greeting than on scanning the areas for cats to kill. For him also, old habits die hard. They walked together along the river, hunched against the wind.

'This is all rather unorthodox, Peter, to say nothing of chilly.

82

Has something happened?'

'I just wanted to have a quick word as soon as I could. Firstly, your telephones are in all probability being bugged, as, most likely, is your house and your emails.'

She looked around her.

'No,' continued Smith, 'no-one following.' 'Does this mean you are making some progress?'

Very conscious of the fact that the right answer to that particular question was no, he replied with some caution.

'A little.'

'Any idea who might be interested in what I say'.

'An idea, no more. However, I should know more tomorrow.

How are your enquiries going?'

'Well, the great and the good of the police and security services are all running around in small circles and unlike you, my progress is being somewhat hampered by having to go through official channels, as they say.'

'You're getting nowhere, in other words.'

'Quite.'

They walked on together for a while. The wind was getting stronger .

For no reason he could actually put his finger on, he walked back up through the deserted town with her until they stood in front of her front door. She opened the door and stood to one side.

'Would you like a nightcap?'

'I would but I have work to do.' 'Ah. A pity.'

She looked up at him.

'All this is going well beyond what we agreed, and I am grateful to you, Peter. But why?'

Smith found himself momentarily embarrassed. The question hadn't really occurred to him and as often happened when he was confronted by something personal and unexpected, he told the truth.

'A family thing, I suppose.' She laughed without passion.

'I am not sure if Emile would see me as part of his family.'
'Perhaps not, but Martine would. You should allow old men

their opinions without necessarily being bound by them. I wouldn't like to saddle my daughters with my sins.'

The small white face that looked up at him was not that of the self-confident, presidential investigator, but of someone much more alone than that. Smith felt a twinge of sympathy, or perhaps it was the cold getting into his shoulder where a fragment of a Russian bullet remained after the surgeon said he would have to take his entire shoulder off to get it out.

'Lock the door, Suzanne, and call me at any time if you need to.'

He kissed the still upturned face and waited until the door closed behind her and he heard the locks turn over.

By the time he got home it was slightly past eight thirty. Thoughts of a good book had faded slightly but the whisky still sounded good. Fortunately, there was a rerun of an Australia - South Africa rugby international on his satellite channel.

In spite of a long and on-going campaign to rid his life of the myriad and increasing number of ring tones, bleeps, electronic alarms, miscellaneous bits of pseudo-music that came associated with every gadget from mobile phones to toasters, he had still not entirely succeeded. He never bothered to learn which was which. Rather like the registration numbers of his many cars, he never felt the need to commit them to memory. However, inevitably some were familiar. This one wasn't. Momentarily he was flummoxed. Then he realized that it was his new phone. After a moment' delay caused by a slight uncertainty as to how the thing actually worked, he answered it.

'Peter.' As only one person was likely to be at the end of this particular electronic round trip into space and back it was a statement rather than a question.

'Alexei.' Again, the possibilities were limited.

'We have managed to dredge up some preliminary bits of information for you. A hard copy will be delivered to you by one of my people in about five minutes, so don't bother with notes. I'll give you the essentials. We started with the members of Madame Blanchard's investigation. Of the four under scrutiny, you can pretty well discount Paul Granais, the local commandant, of the Police. You can also discount the departmental chief of the Gendarmerie Nationale, Claude Messailles.'

'Oh? May I ask why?'

The answer was as simple as it was obviously true. 'They are both mine.'

'Ah, and that means they are..?' Smith voice trailed away. He found it difficult to use the word honest.

A rich chuckle winged its way from space after an annoying second or so delay.

'I think that reliable is the best word. Granais is a time-serving bureaucrat with very little ambition other than to retire early in comfort with enough money to support his wife, three children and two mistresses. God knows how he is going to organise his life when he no longer has an excuse to get out of the house. Messailles is a more considerable man. On the surface he seems to be a blustering, arrogant pig. Actually, below the surface he actually is a blustering, arrogant pig but he's also sharp as a knife and very, very good at his job. He could well make Director General of the Gendarmerie Nationale one day, which would be handy for us. They both have personal idiosyncrasies that have enabled me to come to expensive understandings with both of them – a passion for money and a predilection for coke respectively. However, while I understand why these two were at the meeting, they are the men responsible at a local level for all activities of the Police and the Gendarmerie, the chances of their knowing anything specific are remote. One of the two groups that actually planned the operation, the DST, very roughly equivalent to your MI5 in the UK was there, with a medium rank man from the planning department called Lefaivre. Don't know too much about him. However, the GIGN Intervention Group, the gendarmerie special anti-terrorist group within the gendarmerie seems not to have been represented. '

'I thought the DST only operated outside France'.

'Well, originally they did, but I think these niceties have long since vanished.'

'And the last man?'

'Now there, there seems to be some more fertile ground. The RAID man at the meeting was not any local official but the Commandant, Roger Gallion himself. He is the most interesting of the lot. Although RAID is nominally under the police command, they have a considerable independence. I also know little about them other than to express the pious hope that they were not involved directly. They are a very small, highly specialized outfit, numbering fewer than one hundred all told, and can claim to be the best-trained and best equipped anti-terrorist unit in the country if not the world. I would guess that they formed the beach party. It would be hard to find any problem there, I would have thought, there are so few of them. But I can always be wrong. However, I would say that if this particular unit has been turned into traitors, then France is in deep shit. What is interesting is that the GIGN wasn't there. They would have been involved in planning if not in execution. So combine three anti- terrorist groups, all bitter rivals with the well-known French ability to make mountains out of molehills, and you have a recipe for disaster in spite of the undeniable talents of the parties involved.

This whole thing could just be a monumental cock-up.'

'Alexei, I think that a cock-up theory would make matters worse rather than better. In any case, whatever crossing of wires might, I repeat might, have led to this, somebody talked.'

An image of a sharply-suited young man in a Washington bar came quickly to mind and then was put to one side almost as quickly. Smith knew that it was a long way from being a cock-up but chose not to start the discussion. He broke off to answer a knock on the door. A quietly dressed man stood outside and handed across a bulky manila folder and another cardboard box. Behind him in the street below, Smith could see the inevitable Range Rover. Two men stood front and rear looking out across the square. Having made his delivery, he shook hands, and turned back down to the car. The sombre trio vanished into the night.

'The cavalry has arrived, Alexei. Many thanks.'

'One day you may have cause to be thankful for that cavalry, Peter. In the meantime, I will see what I can dredge up about events at Beauduc. Take care, my friend.'

'Good night, Alexei and thank you. Kiss the ladies for me. I am in your debt.'

'No you're not. You should come more often and kiss them yourself. You're old enough.'

It suddenly occurred to him that Girondou and his family might not have too many personal friends.

'I will, Alexei, I will.'

Chapter 8 An Interlude for Exercise and Paperwork

Whatever other priorities might come and go from time to time, the morning ritual was prescribed. Arthur was a creature of habit. Up at six, an hour around Arles irrespective of the weather, a shower and strong espresso and then whatever life-administration had forced its way to the front. It is a relatively easy routine in the summer when temperatures regularly rise above thirty degrees by 11:00 am and often don't sink below that until 8:00pm. If you want to get anything done, realistically it has to be done either side of those times. By mid- morning all trace of any overnight cool has gone and most Arlesian shutters are all but closed, mosquito screens are lowered, and the population prepares to do little or nothing for the next few hours except, of course, eating and sleeping. Smith had always found it difficult to sleep in the middle of the day and had never quite got the hang of the siesta. During winter, however, the 6:00 am start had other compensations. He was one of a very small number of people who were up and about. The town was usually deserted and the trip around the windswept streets was a continuing pleasure. The early morning walk was an additional enjoyment because the town's population of dogs, as disrespectful of the local regulations about wearing leads as their masters were about parking, tended to keep the same hours as their households. Thus, the winter morning walk was also more relaxing for Arthur whose adaptation to a French retirement from the dog tracks of East London had not succeeded in diminishing his desire to kill any moving quadruped smaller than a horse.

Today he realised that, other than Girondou's files that were waiting on his desk, he had little immediate on his plate. He therefore decided to make his morning walk somewhat longer than usual. So it was still dark when he struck off northwards away from his house, down the hill from the Amphitheatre and headed out of the town through the old Roman city gate, at the Cavalière, across the Place Lamartine and continued north out of the town along the Avenue de Stalingrad. Not for the first time he found himself musing about the conventions of naming streets. In Arles the same street had appeared in many different guises over the years. The oldest street names were often religious. The revolution put a stop to that and there followed the wholesale re-naming of streets after individuals, usually of the best revolutionary credentials. During the German occupation in 1942 many had been changed again to reflect a more right-wing bias, the Place de la République changed to Place Pétain, for instance, only to be renamed in haste after the Germans left back to their previous socialist names. Before the second World War the main road north from the town had been the Route d'Avignon which was precisely where it led. Now is was the Avenue de Stalingrad although he did wonder if that cities socialist credentials would remain strong enough to withstand the political correction that revisions of history tend to demand on occasions.

He passed under the pair of railway bridges that carried the main line from Marseille into the station and the smaller branch line that had led to Lunel across the river bridge. This bridge had been the target of numerous American bombing raids in the summer of 1944 to prepare the way fro the Operation Dragoon when the Allies landed in the south of France. The bridge had resisted the traditionally haphazard American bombing before it was finally dropped into the river to hinder any German withdrawal. In the process much of the Cavalière Quarter have been levelled. Causalities or collateral damage as it is these days called included much of the elegant suburb of Tranquetaille on the north bank of the river, Van Gogh's famous Yellow House and indeed Smith's somewhat less famous house on the Place de la Major. He lived in the version that was reconstructed after the war.

The road was one of the less attractive ones that led out of the town. Very quickly after the bridges it changed into one of those unlovely ribbon development strips of mixed shops and small warehouses, car dealerships and fast food restaurants. The whole thing reminded him of some American towns where commercial interests had overridden either good taste or good planning - or more likely, both. However, he stuck to his route north until he passed the prison and then turned eastwards, crossed the narrow ribbon of the suburb of Le Trébon onto a series of byroads that crossed the numerous water-filled dykes and small canals that irrigated the old Crau marsh that separates Arles from the rich farming country to the east. The route would take him on an extended loop that gradually turned south past the Mas Lacroix where the last small German garrison had been based before their withdrawal in August 1944, past one of the new cemeteries that had been built outside the town and then back south and into Pont de Crau and thence back into Arles. It was a long walk and one that he only took in winter. In summer there were too many mosquitoes living in the marsh and in the water channels to make it enjoyable. Arthur had realised that this wasn't the sort of countryside that suited a longdog. There was little to chase and even less space to do it in. So, he contented himself to walking slowing at Smith's side with the lead drooping in a gentle curve between them.

As usual he tried to use the time wandering through the countryside mentally to run through the story so far, as it were. He usually thought that this was the right thing to do; long periods of thought, analysis and introspection all leading to a plan of action for the future. Gentry's way. Actually, for him it was a waste of time trying. He just wasn't that sort of person. Deciding what to do next had never been a problem for him and most of the time he was right. Even when he wasn't and making things up at the last minute failed him, he unusually got himself out of trouble, often by extreme violence.

He was, however, intrigued, as much by Suzanne and her investigation as anything else. Certainly, there was more than met the eye about the recent happenings at Beauduc. Suzanne was a police heavyweight but to send her with seemingly unlimited powers to head an investigation, seeming sanctioned by the President himself beggared belief. The propels at the recent meeting represented most of the main forces of anti-terrorism in France let alone just law enforcement and to think that somehow, they were involved in some sort of combined training exercise at unfortunately resulted in the deaths of three young soldiers was unlikely in the extreme. These groups hardly talked with each other under normal circumstances. There was obviously a bigger agenda here and the fact that the Élysée was so directly involved leant a thoroughly sinister hue to the whole thing.

Having threaded his way roughly south east across and around numerous water filled dykes and ditches he found that he had slightly missed his way. There were precious few actually foot bridges. He had reached a large expanse of water and realised that he had reached the Étang de Gravière considerably to the east of his immediate destination. It was a big enough marsh to remain full of water even during the summer. Now it was teeming with birds of all sorts from ducks, coots, herons and even the odd flamingo. He finally found a dyke that ran across the water and before long was standing on the road that runs between Pont de Crau and Barbigal. This was familiar country. If crossed his mind to make a rally long walk out of it and strike north and head for the village of Barbigal and the famous roman grain mill that had been built nearly two thousand years before on a spot where two aqueducts converge before they continue towards Arles bringing a constant supply of water from the Alpille. The canal falls some hundred feet down a sheer escarpment and the Romans had constructed two parallel rows of eight water wheels to power a flour mill. The mill, of course, had disappeared but the site is one of Arles's more memorable if less publicised attractions.

However, his trip had taken longer that he intended, and he felt like something to eat and drink rather than proceeding further north he turned south down the road and made it to the village of Pont de Crau after twenty minutes further stiff walking. He wasn't particularly bothered about not visiting the mill site and the only other thing in that direction was the Chateau of Barbigal, a rather lumpen sort of a castle with a renaissance-style façade with a round tower at one end and a square one at the other. The castle is now given over to the profitable business of weddings for people with a lot on money. It was also struggling to shake off a wartime history as it was adopted as the out of town headquarters of the occupying German infantry regiment when they were forces out from the Hotel Jules Cesar in the centre of town by the American bombing of the Rhone bridges. This piece of history tends not to be mentioned in the wedding publicity.

Before too long he was seated at a corner table in the small cafe in Pont de Crau that he and Gentry used occasionally when they wanted to talk. It was a small very traditional place on the main road just opposite the water powered electricity company that once produced power for Arles. That had long since ceased working but the cafe usually had a good simple plat du jour and Smith liked that simplicity as much as he valued the privacy of being out of the town of Arles. It was also one of the few cafe's that has a car park at the back away from prying eyes. He final reason he went from time to time was their liking for Arthur who was always sure of some tit bit or other. Todays menu was a lamb stew followed by apple tart.

So, both Smith and the dog happily ate a light meal while he tried to force himself to be analytical. It took about two minutes to realise that it was a complete waste of time. Something was going on, but no-one was going to tell him. Certainly not Suzanne who, for all her newly discovered familiarity, wasn't going to tell him anything; willingly at least. He smiled slightly at the thought of using some of his extensive repertoire of more roust interrogation techniques on her but quickly dismissed the idea. He could ferret about with some of the people at Suzanne's recent meeting, but he suspected that Girondou's files would tell him most of what he needed to know. He could set Gentry loose on the problem if not. So, with a mental shrug of the shoulders he changed tack and concentrated on his lunch which was more than usually good. Arthur clearly thought so too as he had disappeared in the general direction of the kitchen. If history was anything to go by he would emerge reluctantly later walking a good deal more slowly than when he went in.

So rather than planning anything, he fell to musing on the one thing that had been troubling him from the start. Why on earth were the three soldiers killed in the first place? On the face of it a clandestine landing of a terrorist on a Provençale shore should have been just that; clandestine. The murders would only have drawn attention. Perhaps that was the point. A message of some sort. But what message and to whom from whom were all unknowns. Whatever the reason it certainly brought down a high-level investigation but again perhaps that was the intention. If so it then comes down to it the question was who could possibly benefit. Of course without know who the "who" were it was an impossible question. He assumed that the terrorists had little to gain from it, especially as the landed man seemed to have disappeared into the safety of the dark side of the South of France. Perhaps Girondou could help although he was pretty confident that he would have been told. The police themselves were another possibility although he could couldn't image why. Perhaps Girondou's files would yield something but he didn't think so. Personal vendetta was another reason but that was entirely too convoluted. there were easier and less complicated ways of killing someone. That really only left one possibility; red herring., or at least a diversion of some sort. But at that point he ran out of ideas.

It was still a bit of a walk home so he settles his bill and extracted a thoroughly well-fed greyhound fro the kitchen and set off down the main road and followed the line of the remains of the Roman aqueduct into the town from the east. He took the little bridge over the railway line and headed back up the step into the place de la Major, acknowledging the wave of his local wine merchant as he passed the little shop. By the time he got home the temperature risen enough for him to settle down in the garden with an early whisky with Girondou's files in a stack in front of him. Arthur was flat out on the terrace beside him intent only on sleeping off what had obviously been a thoroughly good lunch. As he reached for the first file a thought struck him. He lifted his mobile and called Gentry.

'You free for a word later on?'

'Of course,' came the reply immediately. 'How long?'

'How about eight?'

'OK.'

Smith continued:

'Can to do a little digging on a few people first?'

A hollow laugh came over the airwaves.'

'Why am I not surprised, Peter?'

Smith allowed the sarcasm to pass and read from the titles of the files in front of him.

They contained what looked like a set of standard personnel files on senior employees covering all the major figures that Smith had come across so far and some that he hadn't. They could have been management files for any major corporation. Apart from detailed CVs and psychological profiles, the files also contained information that was slightly less usual: lists of assets, properties, boats - Gallion owned a small plane - details of immediate family and mistresses and boyfriends with addresses for all of them. What seemed to Smith to be complete financial breakdowns including credit history and bank statements current to the last thirty days. Each file concluded with a single page analysis of the individual's strengths, weaknesses and pressure points. Not for the first time Smith saw the secret of Girondou's success.

As Girondou had mentioned, Granais and Messailles were both directly on the payroll although each did not know about the other. This made sense. As regional commanders of the Police Nationale and the Gendarmerie Nationale they were each able to be of most assistance. Both had Swiss bank accounts containing very considerable sums. Smith was interested to note that his gut feeling about DuPlessis, the GIGN man, was born out by his dossier. The Lieutenant in charge of this elite unit had been earmarked as a possible target should Girondou feel the need of an influential contact in French counter-terrorism. The man was married but also had an Iranian mistress who also seemed to have a lot more money in the bank than one would expect. Gallion and Lefaivre seemed to be solid and were not on Girondou's list of potential allies despite Lefaivre's homosexuality and Gallion's passion for recreational flying. Neither hobby seemed to demand excessive amounts of money.

What was more interesting were a couple of dossiers on people he had not heard of, both in the DST. Given that it was this department that first obtained the information from North Africa and planned the subsequent operation, these two names he would pass on to Gentry for further investigation. Both were senior and that was the general tenor of all the dossiers. They were all senior people able to influence events in a general sort of way. There was nothing on less important people who would only be basic sources of information. Girondou was clearly not interested in local intelligence

- in all probability his sources were better than those of the people in the dossiers. He was more interested in people who could influence the general environment in which he operated. The senior police man and the gendarme were much more useful in controlling policy decisions that would leave him in peace and this was reflected by his investment in them.

There was another whisky waiting for him when he sat in his familiar seat beside Gentry's fire which was, as usual during the winter, blazing merrily. It didn't matter what the temperature was like outside, Gentry was a man of traditional habits. Arthur too had resumed his horizontal afternoon on his particular sofa. Smith handed over the files and settled back to wait. Unlike his friend, Gentry had learned to read very quickly a long time ago and was especially quick reading the sort of files now in front of him. It took him a good deal less time that Smith. He also knew what was important and what wasn't.

'DuPlessis, Lefaivre and Gallion. In that order. The others are nothing to do with this.' He paused with a slightly rueful look on his face.

'Actually, this is really only because they have anti-terrorist connections. For the life of me I can see why, given the story that we have at the moment, why anyone them should want to kill their own men. You don't get to be in charge of these rather specialised ant-terrorist groups by being stupid.'

Smith nodded before replying.

'This means that either we don't know all we should about these men or..'

'We've got the wrong story,' interrupted Gentry.

95

Chapter 9 Bulls and Lunch

Those happy people who hold strong and disapproving opinions about the bullfights that they have never attended or bothered to learn about, also harbour, unsurprisingly, a considerable number of misconceptions about the activity they chose to condemn. One of a multitude of such myths, widely perpetuated on well-meaning but ultimately valueless travel websites, is that the Camargue is stuffed with magnificent fighting bulls that are all destined for the cruellest possible demise in the presence of twenty thousand blood- crazed, demented sub-humans in the great Amphitheatre in Arles. In reality, there are actually very few breeders of fighting bulls in the Camargue. No more than five or six serious ones, each of whom breeds a very small number of animals from Spanish and Portuguese bloodlines not Camargue ones. The vast majority of the more than three thousand cattle of either sex that are bred each year in the great manades of the Camargue meet their end more prosaically in a slaughterhouse en route directly to people's stomachs. Not much sport there one feels. Actually those wonderfully engaged green tourists who poke around in some of the more accessible bits of the Camargue looking for flamingos and a good feeling often fail to realise that the many black bulls they see are at best two hundred kilos in weight – an average that had declined over the years in pursuit of more tender meat – rather than the five to six hundred kilos of nimble cunning rage with a pair of half meter razor-sharp horns that habitually confront a sixty kilo matador armed with the devastatingly aggressive weapon of half a square meter of red cloth and a bent, slim sword that even the least aggressive of them could snap with ease over their knees. The famous Camargue bull is food not death.

Sunday had dawned grey and not too windy. Smith was very much looking forward to his day with the Aubanet family and did not particularly fancy freezing to death or being blown off his horse. Over the last year he had become very familiar with the farm and had always enjoyed the hospitality of a family that had almost become his own. He had become a welcome visitor to the Mas des Saintes as well as to most of its neighbours, and, having valued his solitude for most of his life, he found it a little difficult to adapt to genuine friendship when it was unstintingly shown. He was that most typical of British dilemmas; a loner who craves friendship. An independent who has to rely on others. Like many British he would refuse invitations while being unhappy if he wasn't asked. The rationale had always been that under the cover of a number of rather prosaic business activities of varying success around the world, as well as following a sporadic career in teaching as an art historian, he had worked for Her Majesties Government on a variety of odd but highly secret projects in foreign parts. Long periods away from home – a home in Norfolk that was a county that felt as alien to him as the dark side of the moon – as well as the self-reliance essential to actual survival while he pursued the interests of Queen and Country had combined to make him suspicious of long-term commitments. Being kicked in the balls by two ex-wives only served to reinforce that. The genuine friendship shown by the Aubanet family and, in particular, by Martine, somewhat disconcerted him while being highly valued. The fact that her obvious understanding meant that he did not have to explain himself – never a personal strength – made it more valuable. It may simply be that he saw himself as a fat old man and the idea of a stunningly beautiful, intelligent woman would be attracted to him seemed preposterous.

He turned off the road south out of Arles at Le Sambuc and headed into the depth of the Camargue, relishing the hours ahead. Arthur shifted on the back seat. He was familiar with this trip and made it perfectly plain that he, at least, had no reservations at all about his relationship with the Aubanets. He was spoiled rotten, given the run of the farm and generally thought it was heaven. He knew the routine. As Smith turned into the open gates to the farm, he got up and started looking hungrily around for something to chase. Smith glanced in his mirrors to confirm that the gates shut automatically behind him. Another fortress, he thought a little grimly as he drove into the quadrangle in the middle of the farmhouse.

Martine stood ready to greet him – or rather Arthur who sprang from the back seat of the car at a speed that seemed undiminished from the day when he used to reach up to forty miles an hour within a few paces out of the traps at Harlow race track. Finally he calmed down allowing her to fling both arms around

Smith's neck and make a very public slow of affection at his arrival, much to his embarrassment and the amusement of various staff and retainers who were dotted around the courtyard.

Having returned her greeting with some pleasure he gently disengaged himself and took a large and very badly wrapped soft parcel from the boot of the car. It was his present for his host on his birthday.

There are many things that the French do wonderfully well if one is prepared to think long and hard enough. Winter coats for use in the country are not one of them. For many years the otherwise utterly unremarkable town of Stowmarket in Suffolk in the UK was home to the exotically-named company, Husky of Tostock. This company cornered the market in quilted country clothing, in particular, extremely practical if sartorially dull waistcoats long before the chattering classes discovered the ridiculous word 'gilet'. They were reasonably priced serviceable garments and were a ubiquitous constituent of most country people's wardrobes. The company has long since disappeared as a result of bankruptcy brought on primarily by trying to make a living servicing the notoriously tight-fisted farming community.

However, buried impenetrably deep in their repertoire, was a heavy, shapeless tweed jacket, lined with their usual quilting that was often the difference between life and death for anyone shooting game during the season. They were big, bulky and definitely not for the fashionistas but were superbly made with large pockets that easily contained up to thirty twelve bore shotgun cartridges per pocket, cigarettes and lighter, packets of extra strong mints, hip flasks, handkerchiefs, proper pen knives without little white crosses on them, a medium-sized paperback novel and all the other paraphernalia necessary for a decent day's sport. More than once this remarkable garment had saved Smith from hypothermia and allowed him to shoot grouse on a high Yorkshire moor in howling November sleet with nothing else under it save a shirt. He hated vests. The jackets were expensive but lasted almost forever. Husky had provided a service to repair where necessary, to renew the leather edgings to pockets and sleeves when worn and generally ensure that the jackets outlived their owners.

Husky went bust and the torch was passed to Oliver Brown on Lower Sloan Street. Their jackets are identical in style to the old ones, almost as well-made and now, regrettably available in a wide variety of tweeds, much loved by Americans and the new generation of leisured Norfolk Farmers that would make Toad of Toad Hall look camouflaged. They had also become even more eye-wateringly expensive.

Smith's original old coat had been stolen some years before by a honourable old boy, a fellow guest at a rugby club dinner at the Distinguished Old English Public School where he had tried unsuccessfully to hide as a teacher after retiring from business, marriage and the Service. So much for honour and the Old School tie, he thought. He had spent a not inconsiderable amount of his divorce settlement on a replacement. Emile Aubanet had admired it on a number of occasions and Smith had ordered one of the more conservatively tweeded versions as a birthday present. He was pretty sure it would fit. They always seemed to fit irrespective of the actual dimensions of the wearer.

It was not the sort of thing that you can wrap easily, and Smith hadn't tried very much.

Martine tried to grab the parcel and it took a not inconsiderable combination of brute force and gentlemanly restraint to prevent her doing so. They went inside, and a slightly miffed Martine led him to the study where his host was seated in an armchair reading the morning edition of the local newspaper, La Provence. He rose on the arrival of his guest.

'Peter, it is good to see you again. Thank you for coming.'

'I am delighted to be here, Emile. Happy birthday.' Smith replied holding out the now very distressed parcel somewhat apologetically as he added:

'Sorry about the wrapping.'

The coat virtually undid itself with a little help from gravity. The old man was obviously delighted, as was his daughter who managed to plant a large thank-you kiss on Smith before her father made it across the three metres that separated them.

'Peter, how very kind. It is superb. Do you think it will make me look like a proper Englishman?'

'Sir, if I thought it would do that, I wouldn't have bought it to for you. By the way, I don't think that there is such a thing as a proper Englishman – only improper ones.'

'Oh good.' Martine was not going to be left out of this particular conversation. 'I just thought there was only one.'

The coat was duly tried on.

'What are these?' Emile had discovered a couple of intriguing thin strips of cloth secured to the inside each of the upper slit pockets. The strips each had the male end of small pop stud fasteners sewn into their ends. They actually fitted with their female counterparts that were fixed on the inside flaps that covered the two square pockets below. Smith demonstrated how they fastened.

'They are designed to hold the pocket open so you can get at your cartridges quickly when reloading.'

'Ah,' exclaimed the old man. 'The French would never have thought of something so practical.'

'I suspect,' replied Smith, 'that if the French made jackets like these they would look a good deal more elegant.'

'Perhaps, Peter. But they would also not do their job so well. Keeping warm is something the English understand better than we. However, we must get going. Shall we meet in ten minutes outside?'

Other than changing into a pair of heavy Camargue boots, provided for him some time ago by his hosts and kept for him at the mas thereafter, Smith only had to get his own somewhat shabbier version of the coat from his car. Seeing Jean-Marie he motioned him over and chatted for a few moments. No sooner had they finished, Martine re-joined him. She was dressed in her customary working gear, boots like his, jeans, and a quilted coat. A traditional Camargue guardian's black trilby hat completed the picture. As usual Smith looked at her in wonder. Equally as usual she intercepted his gaze, understood it and blew him a kiss of thanks for the unspoken compliment. Three grey Camargue horses stood, saddled and waiting for them. Martine slid into the saddle with the practiced ease of someone who had been doing it since she was a few months old – which she had, of course. She made it look as difficult as climbing onto a fireside rug. Smith followed with considerably less elegance and more effort but at least by now they had stopped providing someone to stand expectantly near to give him a leg-up had he needed one. The mount was actually not particularly taxing for anyone used to getting onto a full-sized English hunter. The Camargue horse, one of the most ancient breeds on the planet, is not a tall animal, standing at the same height as a large pony, but it is, as they say, as strong as a bull and tough with it.

Monsieur Aubanet was the last of the trio to appear. In addition to being dressed like his daughter in the standard working gear of the *gardian*, the Camargue cowboy, Smith was delighted to see that his present did, indeed, fit very well. Just as well, because the day remained cold and grey and it was getting windier with a spit of rain in the air. Smith pulled a battered cap from his pocket. His last birthday present from Martine had been a gardian hat and, although he treasured it, he had not yet had the courage to wear it. Arles was full of people sporting bits of Provençale costume – black velvet jackets, highly patterned shirts, black trilbies – usually tourists, and Smith had found their adoption of these symbols slightly insulting to the local people. It was a personal thing but one that Martine understood when he had explained.

Father and daughter stationed themselves either side of their guest and the trio rode out to tour the paddocks that contained Emile Aubanet's pride and joy, his herd of bulls. They were joined by the farm manager who rode beside his master within easy conversation distance but a deferential half pace behind. For three hours they toured the farm, stopping regularly to view the animals and the new calves. Aubanet spent much of his time discussing the merits and ultimate destination of the animals in the language known as *provençau*, the Occitan language of the Camargue that had supposedly been rescued from extinction by Frederick Mistral and his literary movement the Félibrige in the nineteenth century. Martine kept up a running commentary that always managed not to sound like a translation. In reality the language had never been lost, but the old Nobel prize winner had a good publicity machine. As always, Smith found it fascinating. In spite of being at the head of a business empire that measured its turnover in tens of millions of Euros, Martine seemed at her happiest in this hard Camargue countryside, as was her father. He was conscious of the fact that farmers from this area had been doing precisely this for probably some two thousand years when the rearing of cattle was started around the Arlelate to supply the large Roman garrison that was stationed in the town in the years following the turn of the first millennium. With the pragmatism that has characterised much of France's history, Arles, originally established as a trading centre by the Greeks in the sixth century BC, was clever enough to side with Caesar in his struggle with Pompey, while their great local rivals, Marseille, chose the wrong side. Caesar's ultimate success was the signal for a huge investment in the town, strategically placed on the first available crossing across the Rhone on Via Aurelia, the road between Italy and Spain. Whether there was a link between the Camargue obsession with raising bulls and the fact that the bull was also the symbol of the Legio VI Ferrata, Caesar's legion raised from Cisalpine Gaul may be debated but the town of Arles was originally developed and expanded to house veterans of that legion. The early wealth that made the development possible, came from the disgraced Marseille and must have represented a source of some satisfaction for the Arlesians over their local rivals. The memory of this particular piece on one-upmanship remains a pleasure to locals even now some two thousand years later.

The quartet made a slow and methodical progress around the flat pastures that made up much of the farm. Arthur, running freely, had exhausted himself within ten minutes and contented himself with trotting along beside them, making the odd unsuccessful lunge into the undergrowth or peering predatorily along each open vista as it presented itself. Most of the fields were only a hectare or two in size and all were bordered by irrigation ditches and hedges made primarily of reeds, stubby bushes and leaning trees. A few brave birds scudding around on the stiff breeze . This was not the Camargue of the tourist. In high summer the place baked and was populated by large numbers of pink flamingos and matchingly hued tourists. The place abounded with wildlife, otters, mink and water rats in the ditches, and a huge variety of birds ranging from circling Camargue eagles to luminous kingfishers darting about the reeds and motionless predator herons standing around managing to combine vigilance with lugubriousness. Today it felt very different. To someone who failed to love this place as much as Smith it could look and feel hard and inhospitable. For Smith it was the best place on earth.

Martine turned to him on one of their many stops. Emile and his manager were in deep and impenetrable conversation.

'You're very quiet, Peter.'

'I was just thinking how much I love this place. There is a sort of greatness about it. It is not a place of great architecture or magnificent rivers or mountains. It has none of the things that usually makes places impressive. It has great skies but having spent twenty unhappy years in Norfolk in England I'm not seduced by the illusory joys of empty skies. In summer it just seems to snooze. But now, especially now, in winter, when you can see the details.'

'Ah, you understand. The Camargue is not a beautiful place to look at. But it makes beauty in your soul. It is a place for the heart not the eye.'

As if to demonstrate her pleasure in knowing that he felt like her about the place, she leaned easily across the narrow gap between their two horses and planted a gentle kiss on his cheek. She also giggled when she saw her father's indulgent smile and the manager's polite downward glance. In high good spirits, she continued:

'One of these days you are going to have to make an honest woman of me, you know. If you don't the entire staff here, to say nothing of most people who live within twenty miles, are going to start thinking there is something wrong with me.'

Her voice darkened slightly. 'After Robert, some of them think that anyway.'

'And why,' he replied, hoping to divert her momentary introspection, 'will they not think that there is something wrong with me instead?'

'After what you did for us all last year, no one will think that. You continue to underestimate the effect of that. However, you are also a man. That means a lot around here.'

Smith felt he was beginning to get into deeper water than that through which they had been riding for much of the morning. He was relieved to have the subject changed by a low drone which took its place along with the sound of the wind in the reeds and they both looked up. A faint, slow moving speck could be seen just below the cloud layer. Martine frowned disapprovingly.

'Those damn micro lights are an increasing pain in the summer and now they even come in winter to disturb our peace and scare our cattle and horses. I hope he gets blown to Algeria. Why they can't at least silence them, I don't know.'

Smith has spotted the thing some time before but didn't feel that that was an appropriate time to discuss the difference between a recreational microlight and a much less benign surveillance drone.

'Martine, in a country that excels in making as much noise as possible at every opportunity, having a silent micro light would not be a great priority. I agree, though, I would shoot everyone who uses them, irrespective of whether they are flying over a nature reserve or not.'

She looked across at him sharply. She understood him much better than he imagined but was still occasionally wrong-footed by a British sense of humour. Knowing whether Smith was being serious or not was often difficult for her.

The tour passed all too quickly and yet again Smith found himself utterly seduced by the farm and the people who worked it. By one o'clock they were back at the mas and, having changed into dry clothes, were seated at the large kitchen table. Smith was touched by the fact that they were not in the rather grand dining room. Being seated around one end of a long plain wooden table with lunch being prepared at the other was an intimate gesture that meant a lot to him. As they sat down, Martine took over the presentation of lunch from the ladies who normally ran the kitchen. Obviously, his hosts felt that their lunch table conversation might not be suitable for the ears of any family retainers, however loyal. As usual Arthur took up his station on the floor just to the side of Emile Aubanet's chair. In general greyhounds are not creatures of great intellect, but it had not taken Arthur long to know the best place to receive offerings from the great man's table – at the great man's feet, obviously.

A glass of red was poured from a bottle bearing no label and the meal started. Characteristically, the old man came quickly to the point.

'Now, Peter, what have you got yourself into this time?'

Not for the first time, Smith felt as if he was in his old headmaster's study. Old intimidations die hard. He saw that the simplest thing was again just to tell his host the whole story. He trusted the Aubanet family completely as he did Girondou's but for very different reasons. After the events of the previous year he was almost family for the Camargue farmer. For Girondou he was a potential threat who turned out to be a trusted friend and ally. As he told the story he could see that Emile Aubanet was wrestling with history. The wartime family split had been irrevocable, to say nothing of his personal part in its solution and he was not of a generation that found it easy, even possible, to forgive and forget. When he had finished, his host looked across the table at him

'I've only one question, Peter. This is a difficult and potentially dangerous business. It is not just some local event. National governments could be involved and while I respect your abilities, heaven knows I have enough reasons to be grateful for them, but is this not, as you British say, biting off more than you can chew? Why are you doing this?'

Smith looked directly at him. The answer was the same as it had been to Girondou.

'Because a friend asked me to.'

The old man stared at him for a long time. Then he nodded slightly, understanding, and started.

'I am afraid on this occasion I can tell you very little. Some of the local people saw what happened but there doesn't seem to have been any local connection. No one seems to know who the person who landed and there is no news about where he went. The three young men who were killed at Beauduc, were gendarmes, members of GIGN, the Groupe d'Intervention de la Gendarmerie Nationale which makes this an army not a civil operation. One was a local boy, Jean Claude Carbot. We know the family well. They were on the beach itself to observe the landing. Another group of some twenty men was supposed to follow the terrorist whichever way he went from the landing and were positioned either side of the Beauduc beach. There was also a third group about one hundred meters inland. I presume they were some sort of protection. '

'So, what happened ? '

'I don't really know. Apparently, all the forces on the beach withdrew a little time before the landing and when our people arrived they just found where three dead policemen had been in the dunes. Their colleagues had not been as conscientious as they imagined in clearing up.'

'Well thank you. I had a feeling that this is not a local thing and you've confirmed that to some extent. '

Emile Aubanet continued:

'I still don't really understand why you want to get involved, Peter. It is very dangerous. To you personally. Both my daughter and I would be very upset if something happened to you. '

Immediately Smith started to feel angry. His choice was his choice, and this was precisely why he avoided the sort of committed relationship that Martine so incongruously but so obviously wanted. After a lifetime of doing for others, at least, he felt that it was now his life to do what he wanted with and he resented this old man telling him what to do. The danger, such as it was, meant nothing, or at least very little. On numerous occasions in the past he had

106

confronted the end of his life. The last time was in Somalia when, with his blood pooling around him on a dirty floor and electrodes attached to his testicles, he had actually said 'fuck it' and decided to give up. His utterly unexpected survival had been orchestrated by Gentry, not for the first time, but the experience had taught him lessons about the value of friendship and life. He would pick his moments, but he would not allow himself nor his friends to be screwed.

'I am afraid it's my choice and that is an end to it.'

He looked across at his host with a very hard look in his eye, a look that surprised the old man. He nodded slowly.

'Ah, as your Edmund Burke said 'The only thing necessary for the triumph of evil is for good men to do nothing' but perhaps he did not consider the matter of inequality. One good man against so many evil ones?'

Smith, able to bandy quotes with anyone, had a reply to that. 'Burke also said 'By gnawing through a dyke, even a rat may drown a nation' but I'm afraid I don't particularly wish to argue the point.'

Still the old man persisted. 'But Peter......'

This time it would end. He was not enjoying this, and he became slightly angry.

'Monsieur, I would not dream of advising you on how you run your life, or what to think. I might have an opinion, but I would not presume to express it. Your life is your business. I would appreciate your extending me the same courtesy.

It was rude and in no small measure unfair for he knew that his host's concern for him and his daughter's feelings was genuine. He had just felt the walls of that Somalian hut closing in around him again. He turned again.

'Emile, that was entirely too rude and I apologise.'

The old man sighed and there was an uneasy silence around

the table. As ever, for she understood, Martine was the first to move things along. She reached out and took Smith's hand and held it very tightly.

'What can we do to help?'

Still not entirely mollified, Smith decided that this was not the moment to be subtle or too conciliatory. The old man had to understand, what his daughter already knew, that there was a very mean streak indeed at the core of this slightly overweight retired Welshman.

'Well you can both ensure that Suzanne knows everything that you do. Her ass is very much on the line at the moment and I doubt that she has many friends in Paris at the moment. She needs help. Your help. Being alone is no easy thing even if you have had a lifetime's practice.'

Emile Aubanet suddenly looked nearer ninety rather than eighty. Personally, Smith had never had time for old enmities – he was entirely too good at creating new ones to keep track. For him there was never any satisfaction in revenge, however cold. Most people simply did not matter enough to him. Whatever had gone on back in nineteen forty-four, and Smith's view was a thoroughly Baxendallian one of viewing the past though a period eye, he was damned if he was going to let that view affect him now.

The silence continued. He sensed that it was a watershed in his relationship with the family. If they accepted what he said, then his place as an unofficial adopted son would be stronger. He could hardly abandon them once they had agreed to do what he wanted. For the first time he might find his roots impossible to pull up. If not, then he could see his connection with the Aubanet family slowly withering, leaving him where he had always sought to be, free and alone. If pushed, Smith was not sure which he preferred.

Characteristically, it was Martine who decided. She was still holding his hand and tightened her grip until it was actually slightly painful.

'OK. What else?'

'Well you can both make sure that you have some full-time protection until we know more. My dear, you must have Jean Marie with you at all times both when you leave the mas and, like today when you travel around the farm. Emile, you too. Martine, you must stay here in the house for the moment, not in your garrigue.'

The old man had still not entirely recovered his humour and so there was an annoyed and slightly exasperated tone to his voice.

'And how long, may I ask, does this babysitting have to go on?'

Smith looked very directly at him. It was the moment when he either took charge or not.

'Until I say it can stop, Monsieur.'

Martine stepped quickly into the conversation.

'Of, course, Peter. But do you think that it is necessary here at home? We're surrounded by people who are loyal and very protective towards us.'

'It's a precaution, Martine, a deterrent, if you like. I don't really think that you either are involved or in danger of becoming so, but whatever is going on, it originates from some part of the officialdom of this country and others may not make the same distinction between Suzanne and her investigation and the rest of her family that you do.'

He fell silent for a moment and thought back to the morning's events. It was a constant wonder to him that Martine understood so much about him. He had always prided himself on being difficult to read but this remarkable woman often saw through him. Her next question therefore was at the same time both a complete surprise and completely unsurprising. It was obviously a complete surprise to her father.

'What did you see this morning, Peter.'

He looked across at her. He knew that she would not be

fobbed off with any old explanation.

'That micro light wasn't a micro light. It was a reconnaissance UAV.'

Anticipating their question, he continued.

'It was an unmanned aerial vehicle – a UAV, a drone if you like. They are very small pilotless aeroplanes designed to fly slowly for long periods of time and can be used, amongst things, to observe ground activities. The one we saw today may be entirely innocent. It could have been under test or some such, and even if it was in a service role, it is much more likely that it was looking for our suspected terrorist or signs of where he has vanished to rather than overflying your farm specifically.'

He went on: 'Have either of you seen one like it here before?' They both shook their heads.

'As I said, it is more likely to be good news rather bad, but it does no harm to understand the possibilities. The point is, of course, that it is a military thing and, at this stage, at least, more likely to be on our side than not. There are still few enough of them in service for it to be quite difficult to use one unofficially no matter how far up the chain of command you are. They require a lot of people to run them and to process and interpret the data they collect. Difficult to use one for nefarious proposes, I would have thought. But it does no harm to take precautions.'

As if realising that it was all getting beyond him, Emil Aubanet finally seemed to capitulate.

'Peter, what do you think happened at Beauduc?'

'I really haven't the slightest idea at this stage. I don't think it was some sort of cock-up. Operations like this are carried out by agencies that are too good at their job for disasters just to happen. No it was all meticulously planned from start to finish. The three men on the beach were killed as part of a planned operation. Effectively they were probably murdered by one of their own.'

As usual Martine understood.

'And that is the reason you want to be involved. You were once one of those men on the beach.'

Smith smiled without humour.

'I was lucky. I could rely on my people. I also had no grandfather to mourn me.'

'Where will you start?'

'Suzanne can do the official investigation of the agencies involved. You can find if there is anything more is known about what actually happened on the beach. There is less than five centimetres of tide at Beauduc at the moment. That beach buggy will have left tracks for a day or two at least. Someone must know where they went. Girondou will see if there is anything, shall we say, unofficial going on in his, ah, general field of expertise.'

'And you?'

'Oh, I will find out about this so-called terrorist who was landed.'

'So-called?'

'Well, time will tell, of course. All I know is that while a night landing on an isolated Provençale beach may be one way of getting into a country as big as France without drawing attention to oneself, it is certainly nowhere near the best. Even if it was the best, killing three observing policemen is not the way to avoid drawing attention to it. Quite the opposite, in fact.'

He turned to his host.

'Emil. I need you to find out where those tracks went. You are the only person who can do this for me.'

The old man looked up from the table from the first time for ages.

'Of course, Peter. One of our friends might know.'

Smith saw a flash of a grateful smile from Martine. Father was reluctantly re-joining the party, possible burying an old devil or two in the process.

Emile Aubanet got up from the table.

'My children, it is now time for an old man to have a nap. Peter, I thank you for my coat and for your company today. I hope you enjoyed the farm. I also thank you for being frank with me. You are right, of course but you must allow me an old man's privilege of never letting you younger people know how right you are. But I will say this to you. Like it or not you are a part of this family however difficult that may be for you to accept.'

All three stood and he departed to his customary siesta bidding good-by to Smith by neither of the customary gestures, a hand shake or kisses on the cheek, but by reaching up and giving a him very gentle cuff on the side of his head. It was an intimate gesture reminiscent of one between father and son. Smith understood a little more. Emile Aubanet had no son.

As soon as he had gone, Smith tuned to Martine.

'I need to talk to Jean Marie. Could you find him and then give us quarter of an hour or so?'

She looked slightly put out.

'Only if you agree to come for a walk before you go.' 'Yes, I can't think of anything nicer.'

Jean Marie presented himself within a minute. Smith was delighted that the young man understood what was required before being asked.

'Well done, this morning, Jean Marie. I am pretty sure that you weren't spotted. Even I found it difficult to be sure. Were you always within range?'

The range mentioned was the 30 metre range; the effective killing range of the Glock 30 that he had taught Jean Marie to use with an accuracy that nearly matched his own.

'About ninety percent of the time. It was sometimes difficult when there was no cover.'

'Yes. You must anticipate. If there's no cover behind you must get in front and wait for people to come to you. However, from now on you will have to be more visible. Who will be with Monsieur Aubanet?

'Roger.'

'Are you happy with that?

'Yes. He is a good man and knows the job.'

'Good. Now I am pretty sure that there is very little danger to the family itself, but you must all take it seriously. Do the men know that you are in charge?'

'Yes, they do.'

Following the events of the previous year, Smith had taken a considerable amount of time training Jean Marie of a number of aspects of security and protection. The mas was an isolated place and the Aubanets were a high-profile family. He was pretty sure that the young man whom Smith had pulled from a bullet-riddled Range Rover on the way back from the Marseille opera one-night last summer was now as competent as anyone.

'Good. Let me know if I can help. In the boot of my car there is parcel with your name on it. It contains a secure satellite phone. My number is on speed dial one. Madame will be on two when I give her hers. Call me even if anything is out of place or if you are not completely comfortable; anything and at any time.'

In answer to Jean Marie's glance, he continued:

'We are dealing with government agencies here, not just your common or garden criminal. The usual telephones may not be as secure as you think.'

Jena Marie nodded. Further explanation was unnecessary.

Their walk was conducted in almost complete silence. After his exertions of the morning, Arthur had opted for the warmth of the kitchen and the generosity of the staff who were clearing up the lunch. The wind had got up to a proper gale and the grey sky was racing. The trees and the reed beds were bending southwards over the groups of bulls huddled under their shelter. The only things in the sky now were a few pigeons careering about on the wind. Martine had her arm tightly through his and she leant her head on his shoulder as they walked. After about twenty minutes they arrived in front of her little garrigue, the small thatched shepherd's house from which his recent instructions had temporarily banned her. It had been a present from her late mother and was her refuge. Other than her father and once by her late unlamented husband, he had been its only visitor in fifteen years. It was an idyllic place and having to stay away from it would be difficult for her. It was, however, much too difficult to protect and she knew it.

They just stood looking at it for a while. In winter its bright white walls and long thatched roof were muted, and it seemed to sink into the marsh rather than stand out from it. She turned up her head and gave him a long gentle kiss on the lips.

'I want you to be careful, Peter. Very careful. I know you to be the most resourceful man I have ever met but this business could get out of hand. I think I understand why you must do this, but you must allow me to care. You may be able to do without people, but I can't. In particular I cannot do without you. However long it takes, I will wait. Do you understand?'

He returned her kiss, unable to say anything and the silence continued for the rest of their walk. At times it was difficult to work out who was holding on to whom. Having collected Arthur and handed over the phone they stood together in the courtyard. Jean Marie hovered under one of the arches leading into the wing that contained the offices. Smith took her hands in his.

'I want you to take very great care, as well, Martine. Jean Marie will be making sure to see you come to no harm. You must promise me that in an emergency you will do what he says.'

She glanced across at the young man. For some time he had just been her driver.

'Don't worry. He's a fast learner. You might be interested to know that he had not been further than thirty metres from you the entire day.'

She looked astonished.

'Even when we were outside the house?'

'Yes'

'Oh.' she giggled and blushed slightly.

'But not, I think, within earshot, however.'

He was unsure whether his attempt at reassurance was successful.

'He has a phone too. Please use it if you want to talk to him and he's not near. He will also organise your father's protection and the security around the farm. By the way, you might like to consider giving him a pay rise at some stage.'

'Does my father have one of these phones?'

'Er no. What do you think? Should he have one? 'He would probably lose it.'

'OK. Just tell him about being careful when he uses the ordinary ones.'

With that he kissed her one final time. 'I'll call you this evening.'

Arthur hopped into the back of his battered Peugeot 307 and

before long they were heading back towards Arles. He sent a text message to Gentry. 'One hour. With you'

One hour later he had got home, parked the car, settled Arthur, walked a circuitous but unobserved route to Gentry's house and was sitting in front of a roaring log fire in his friend's shop-come- study with a whisky in his hand coming straight to the point.

'This morning a UAV was overflying the Aubanet's farm. I need to know what it was doing.'

Gentry met the request with the same calm that would have greeted a request for a cup of sugar but with a sigh.

'You are aware, I trust, that this is a Sunday?'

'Perfectly aware, thank you. That just means that all your famous contacts will be at home with their families. Should make it easier, I would have thought.'

'How long have I got?' 'I'll wait.'

A resigned Gentry sighed artificially loudly, got up from the chair in which he had only recently made himself comfortable and disappeared.

Smith just sat, stared into the fire and spent the time organising his thoughts. After a ridiculously short delay of time, given the task, Gentry returned.

'The drone was a Crecerelle; positively an antique from a technical point of view but owned and operated by the army. It has a five-hour endurance and flies in still conditions at a maximum of 240km. Much less in the wind this morning, I suspect. This does, however, does make it a locally controlled operation. Estimate 60% of that speed and half an hour each for getting there and back and we are talking a control point of less than sixty kilometres away. Very local indeed. Probably the air base at Miramas. As far as I can find out it was on a general pass across the Camargue beaches rather than targeted with any specific location.'

'I'm pleased to hear that, at least. But this morning was very windy. Light levels were low. It was not a good day for an old reconnaissance drone looking for on-the-run Arab terrorists, who, if they had any sense, would hardly be strolling around for all to see. You would be more likely to find them drinking coffee in a Marseille café.'

'Ah, I thought you might pick that up. You might like to know that the drone wasn't fitted with optical cameras.'

He paused for dramatic affect: an attempt at theatricality that failed completely as Smith remained motionless.

'It was equipped with the usual GPS stuff, of course, and but slightly more unusually, radiation sensors.'

'Nothing more? Cameras? Infra-red?'

'No, just the radiation stuff.'

There was a mutual silence. Smith looked at Gentry. In a flash they both knew what was happening and the whole picture changed completely. Gentry was first.

'This isn't about terrorism at all. This is about business; atomic business. It is not about infiltrating a terrorist. It is about the importing a bomb - or at least material to make one.'

'Or exporting it,' Smith muttered. Gentry nodded slowly.

'That would be my guess, too. However, you need proof.'

'Do I?'

'Well, no. Perhaps you don't, but most people would.'

'Bugger most people. I need to know who ordered the flight and who specified the UAV configuration. Hang on.'

Smith picked up his secure phone and called Martine. She answered immediately and slightly grumpily.

'Have you any idea what time it is?'

'Actually, I haven't. I need to know whether any of the locals who saw the RIB coming ashore, stayed around to see it depart.'

'All right. I'll ask around. I'll call you back.'

'I'll wait.'

'I was thinking of tomorrow morning.'

'I'll wait.'

'Tomorrow, Peter. Do you want your information fast or right?' She was right, of course. Smith rang off.

Gentry looked over his half glasses with an amused smile. 'That's rather an interesting gadget, Peter. Bit high tec. for you. You must get to bits of the Arles street markets that I have missed. What's your number?

'No, idea, old chap. Need to know and all that.'

It was no surprise to Gentry. Smith never knew his own telephone number, car number or any other numbers for that matter. He secretly thought that he only remembered his own house number because it was a single digit. What Smith meant, of course, was that he had no need to know this bit of trivia himself. He held out his hand and Smith tossed to phone over to him. Gentry found the number and threw it back and continued:

'This is entirely too sensible an idea for you, Peter. I'd guess Girondou.'

Smith smiled and nodded.

'While I'm compiling a shopping list, David, the story is that the DST requested satellite surveillance, but it was refused. That's obviously bollocks. I need to see that data, if not from the French then from the Americans. These days the Yanks seem to be photographing everything that moves as a matter of routine.'

Gentry looked up sharply.

'I thought the Americans weren't in on this deal, Peter.'

'I have no idea whether they were, or they weren't. Given the French entirely justified xenophobia in matters of national security, I would be surprised. However, there is always a chance.'

'If they weren't involved to begin with, my enquiries might just get them interested. The French might not like that very much.'

'Given the mess that they seem to have made of this whole thing, I hardly think that matters. In any case, where is the least secure place in the whole of France?'

'The Élysée Palace.'

'Precisely. You can always rely on politicians. If the Americans didn't know about all this before, they sure as hell do now.'

'OK, I'll find out. However, Peter, how are you getting on?' 'Well a preliminary view, especially in the light of that drone, is that the terrorist story is a red herring but there is some question as what real story is being obscured. We have a bunch of high-ranking officials in various bits of the police, gendarmerie and what is best described as Special Operations departments all collaborating somewhat reluctantly in varying degrees to escape the wrath of the state in the person Madame Blanchard for screwing up a simple anti-terrorist surveillance operation that in all probability involved no terrorists at all. It looks a bit like someone is going into business for himself. Girondou won't be happy about that. Personally, I can't conjure up much enthusiasm for that particular problem. However, if we are talking about the plutonium trade, then the matter becomes a lot more serious, but again I am less concerned than I might be about that. The state has hundreds of well-paid people to deal with that sort of thing. If they are crap at their job, that is hardly my problem. But three young men have also been murdered because someone didn't keep his mouth shut. Now that is something, I can do something about.'

'Why?'

'Reykjavik ,' was Smith's one-word answer.

Gentry nodded slowly. He knew what his friend thought about betrayal and he began to feel rather sorry for whoever was behind the Beauduc fiasco. They were dead men walking. The two friends sat for a moment remembering in silence. Reykjavik had been one of those routine escort jobs in a neutral country, the last phase of a quiet, low key and, if truth be said, not very important defection from Russia to the UK. Smooth, trouble-free, well away from the public eye. So simple, in fact, that Gentry had been told his presence or his planning input wasn't necessary. Smith was in Iceland ostensibly advising a couple of travel companies about bringing well-heeled but under-educated louts from the financial sector from the City of London to tear noisily around the volcanic waists of the Thorsmork valley in overpowered four- wheel drive vehicles. The actual operation should have been straightforward. Pick up from the hotel. Quick escort trip to the beach for a 2.00 am rendezvous with a landing party from one of Her Majesties submarines, handover, back to the hotel for a scotch and soda and bed. However, one twenty-two-year-old CIA novice drinking too much in a Washington bar and the Russians were waiting on the beach. Four of them. As a last-minute improvisation, Smith decided to get to the beach twenty minutes early. Half an hour later some very surprised submariners collected both Smith, heavier by the weight of three 9mm SP-10 AP slugs and the defector, leaving four dead Russians on the beach. The CIA had had to hide the boy agent from Smith and, for all he knew, still were.

'Don't like beaches.' Smith felt grim at the memory.

Chapter 10 Observations

Martine's call came just as Smith was half way through his morning walk with Arthur. It was working up to being another grey and overcast day from being black and overcast night. At least the wind had dropped but they nevertheless still had most of the town to themselves. They had got down to the eastern end of the old railway bridge across the Rhone that was bombed by the Americans in 1944 and never replaces. They were wandering through the particularly unlovely bus station that stands bleakly alongside the marginally more welcoming train station. A few early rail commuters were arriving for the morning TGV that gets to Paris in not much more than four hours and the local connections to Marseille, Nimes and Avignon in about the same time. In spite of its being at one end of most of the bus services through the town and into the surrounding countryside, busses never seemed to stop for very long. The place looked cursed. Most of it's life is spent deserted, There is no bus company office, no ticket office, certainly no cafés, lit waiting rooms, newspaper shops. Just a few rows of featureless concrete shelters untouched, even by the arguable joys of the graffiti artists. As usual it was deserted and just succeeded in looking like an early sixties Italian science fiction film set. His personal link to outer space jangled in his pocket.

'Good morning, my dear. How are you this morning?' 'I'm fine, Martine, how are you?'

'Fed up with sleeping on my own.'

Smith did not feel up to this sort of banter at six thirty in the morning so didn't make any of a wide range of replies that were possible. She became business-like.

'You were right, of course. A number of people saw what went on at Beauduc. I don't think that they understood much, but they were there. You might like to talk to one man in particular. He is a fruit and vegetable farmer from La Bélugue, just next to Salin de Giraud. He certainly wants to help. He knew Marcel Carbot's grandson. I can tell you how to find him, if you wish.'

'No, thanks, Martine. For his security, I don't think it is a good idea for me to visit him. Does he ever come to Arles?'

'Yes, he supplies a number of our restaurants. I can arrange a delivery whenever you wish.'

'Good. I'll meet him this afternoon in the little park on the Rue André Campra off the Avenue Docteur Robert Morel.'

'Tranquetaille?'

The part of the town on the north bank of the bend in Rhone would never have admitted to being part of Arles proper. Being less susceptible to flooding, it had been settled by the Romans well before they had expanded so magnificently over to the south bank. It remained an independently-minded place in spite of Baedeker's famous blue guide once saying it wasn't worth visiting.

'Only one bridge across the river.'

'Ah I see. How will you recognise him?'

'Let him recognise me.'

'Ah and how will he do that? Will you wear a green carnation and carry a rolled copy of the Times?'

Smith sighed theatrically.

'As usual you have been watching too much bad television, Martine. I suggest that the presence of a large greyhound on a lead might be a hint. Not too many of those in Tranquetaille I believe.'

'Yes, you are probably right, my dear. What time?'

'How about three? Could you ask him to leave his car and walk across the bridge? I might call in to see Madame Durand when we are finished.'

Martine's voice brightened noticeably.

'Oh Peter, that is a nice thought. I know she would love that.

Shall I call her to tell her that you will be coming?'

Smith's reluctance to give advance warning of any part of his life was tempered by the fact that the old lady was well into her nineties.

'Yes, thank you. That would be kind. I shall be there about four. Now can you tell me a little about your farmer. What on earth was he doing wandering around Beauduc in the middle of the night?'

There was a slight hesitation while Martine collected her thoughts.

'I'll paraphrase the history. For many years, much longer than I can remember, we have had a sort of network on the Camargue. Nothing terribly organised, as you might imagine, knowing the people here but nevertheless there is a feeling that we have to look after each other. It may have been going on for centuries, for all I know but it seems to have become serious during the Second World War when the resistance had to keep a look out for Nazis. As you know Arles was occupied and, shall we say, there was a mixed reaction to that occupation. That is why many Camargue people like my father still remain suspicious of people who come from the town itself. Down here there was no question. Many people escaping from Germany and Vichy France, even from Republican Spain, came through here. The beaches, as you are beginning to realise, are good places for small boats to take people away to North Africa or around the coast to Portugal. We needed to know where the Germans were and what they were doing. So a tradition developed that some people would be out and about most of the time just keeping an eye on what was going on.'

'Even at night?'

'Especially at night. The habit remains. These days it is more to do with drugs or other things we don't want to see here but we still keep watch. What happened at Beauduc would have been observed had it happened anywhere between Le Grau du Roi and Port St Louis.'

123

'Who sets the rules?'

'My father.'

'And after him?'

'Thanks to you, when he dies I will be around to carry on.'

'One day you must tell me what I have to do with all this.'

'One day I will, Peter.'

'OK, Martine. That's it. I look forward to meeting your farmer later today.'

'Thank you for wanting to see Madame Durand. She is very special to me. '

Smith smiled at the thought of the old lady.

'She has had enough sorrow in her long life. Anyhow, she pours a good whisky and Arthur likes her. You and she are very similar.'

'Yes, we are. We both love many of the same things, including my father, I think. Although I am not as brown and wrinkly as she is though.'

There was a pause over the satellite link before she continued.

'Don't you want to know the farmer's name?'

'No, better if I don't. A bientôt, ma chère.'

'A presto, il mio più caro.'

The phone call ended with the usual feeling of pleasure whenever he had contact with Marine and an unusual hopeful tug on the lead from Arthur who clearly thought that his master had died. Good as he was at standing still like most greyhounds, the cold was beginning to get to him. Back at home by eight thirty, he called

Girondou.

'Firstly, thank you for your information, Alexei. Very revealing and, as a consequence, very useful indeed. By the way, how many of these dossiers do you have?'

'Enough.' He didn't elaborate. 'There is one I would like to add to my collection but have so far failed to do so.'

'Oh, who is that?'

'You. Do you know you don't exist?'

'Oh Alexei, us girls have to have some secrets, you know. All you have to do is ask, you know.'

'I have a feeling that it would be a waste of time. Why the hell don't you come and work with me and become a very rich man?'

'And ruin a good friendship? I have never been friends with any of my bosses and I certainly don't intend to start now. Possibly also because I don't particularly want to become a rich man. Nothing personal, of course.'

'All right. How are you getting on?'

'I have a feeling that this business is nothing to do with terrorism, Alexei.'

He knew immediately that he had his friend's complete attention. If it wasn't good old-fashioned terrorism, then for Girondou it could be much, much closer to home. That made it important to him. He waited for Smith to continue.

'What do you know about the trade in nuclear material?'

'Not much. Not our field at all. To be honest, I have not heard of it around here at all. Of course, that may because we haven't been looking for it and are obviously not involved.'

'Nothing sure yet, but if I had to guess I would say that there might be a possibility that Beauduc was to do with getting something out rather than someone in.'

There was a silence that extended into the slowly lightening dawn around the Place de la Major. For a second Smith wondered who was picking up the bill for the expensive toy that he held in his hand before common sense prevailed.

'Peter, I feel more than a little uncomfortable about this. The secret of both success and survival in my business is to know what we are good at and what we are not. If you are right, this is way beyond our field of expertise.'

'Why? There is a very great deal of money to be made in the nuclear business. Silly money in fact. What makes it different from anything else?'

'I can't really answer the question, Peter. But all I know is that I feel there is. I don't runs guns to terrorists but I do buy drugs from them. I wouldn't trade nuclear materials. There is a distinction to me but I can't explain it. I don't expect you to understand.'

'Alexei, you are talking to one of the very few people who might.'

'Yes, I know. That's why we're friends. What do you suggest? Is there anything I can do.'

'Until I know a bit more there probably isn't. But thank you anyway.'

Sensing the conversation was over, the gangster felt unusually useless.

'Let me know, Peter, and take care. I don't like this at all.'

'Nor do I, my friend, but my interest is very local. I fully intend to leave the great and the bad to sort their own lives out.'

'Keep that in mind, Peter. The waters shelve very quickly

around here, you know.'

'Yes, my friend. I know.'

He was faintly relieved when the call ended. Not that he felt uneasy about Girondou. A successful major criminal is probably one of the most honest people around. A great one as he was, even more so. But he was beginning to feel uneasy about the number of people who were starting to be involved in this affair. Coordination was not his forte. It was Gentry's. But these were all part of his world not Gentry's and he couldn't simply pass them over like a bunch of files to be actioned by others. If he had any concerns it was about this, not about the nature of the opposition. It was a world he knew better that Girondou or, for that matter, Suzanne Blanchard although she didn't know it. Some of the few people he valued were involved because of him, and that was beginning to weigh on his mind.

Smith waited until the man had come towards him, crossed the Tranquetaille bridge, passed him and set off towards the little park sandwiched between two of the town's more unlovely tenement blocks. From his vantage point in a side street just beyond the north end of the bridge Smith had very little difficulty in spotting him. Apart from the fact that there were very few people indeed braving the wind over the Rhone on foot, he just looked like a very nervous farmer, unable to resist looking over his shoulder every few moments. There was only one other person on the two hundred metre bridge, an old lady, hunched against the wind was making very slow progress indeed in the opposite direction. The farmer was not being followed.

The park was one of those recent institutional creations, formally laid out with immature trees surrounded by their support posts and newly laid out flower beds. Numerous benches were spaced regularly along the tarmac pathways. In time it would probably be quite nice but for the moment it was all a bit stark and open which was precisely why Smith had chosen it. It would be very difficult to be overheard.

The farmer was standing by one of the benches looking confused as Smith walked straight up to him. Another of the random variations to arrangements that had served Smith so well over the years was the decision to leave Arthur at home. The man was obviously expecting the dog. He held out his hand.

'You were expecting a dog.'

It wasn't an apology or even an explanation. It served as an introduction. Smith started.

'Shall we walk? I would like you to tell me exactly what you saw at Beauduc the other night. Were you alone?'

They turned and walked slowly around the new gravel space that in another world could have easily been a prison exercise yard. The wind was very sharp.

'No monsieur, there were four of us spread along the coast.'

Most of the story came as no surprise. A man had been landed from the sea and was taken in an electric beach buggy down the coast for about a kilometre. At this point the farmer confirmed what Smith had suspected. The RIB departed but had come back down the coast, picked up the man and disappeared.

'Did they pick up anything as well as the man?' 'Yes, Monsieur. A package.'

'And the buggy?'

'It was driven into a truck on the road a little further down the coast and they left.

'Did you get the registration number of the truck?'

It was a very long shot. Even if they had it was almost certainly useless.

'Alas no.'

'How long was it between most of the police leaving and the three who remained getting shot?'

'Not much more than five minutes.'

'And the men who shot them, did you see them?'

'Only briefly, Monsieur. They seemed to appear and disappear.

There was no sound.'

'So, you saw the three policemen shot?'

The man's face darkened

'Yes Monsieur. It was not a good way to die.' 'Did you recognise any of the men at all?'

'No. monsieur. They were dressed in black military combat uniform. They all looked the same.'

He had obviously got all he was going to from the man.

'Tell me, was there any particular reason you were on the beach that night?'

'Er no. We have people around and about most nights.'

Smith just avoided falling automatically into interrogation mode. The man was obviously uncomfortable with the question and it wouldn't have taken long to get to know why. However, Smith got the feeling that this was not the time. In any case why they were watching wasn't particularly important. It would keep.

Smith turned to leave but turned back when he heard that his companion has not entirely finished.

'One strange thing, Monsieur. When I went to the places where the young men had been shot, I noticed that their boot prints in the sand made were the same as the prints left made by the people who killed them.'

129

'I am most disappointed, young man.'

Smith was no proverbial spring chicken and very few people would address him in such an endearing, if inaccurate, manner but Madame Durand was an exception; an exception to most things in fact. At ninety-three she had the right to address Smith in whatever way she wished. She had an appearance of a Cellarini handbag, deep brown, lined and hugely valuable. Bright as a button, sharp as a knife; there were numerous platitudes that would describe her, all accurate and each inadequate. She had been Martine's nurse, then an Aubanet family retainer and had retired to Tranquetalle into a rather distinguished eighteenth century town house. The place had luckily escaped the allied bombing of the summer of 1944 that had reduced much of the rest of Tranquetaille to a building site. She now lived out her days surrounded by the comfort she never had during her working life. Her daughter and granddaughter were both dead. Smith had met her the previous year and a friendship had flourished, helped not least by Arthur with whom Madame had struck up an immediate friendship. Smith also adored her. She was also the one person in the whole world he was slightly afraid of and he had no idea why.

The problem was, of course, that he had not brought the dog and no well-prepared excuse about gippy tummies and the consequent danger to people's carpets would assuage her doubts.

'You'd better come in.'

Smith took his usual spot in her surprisingly elegant sitting room while Madame busied herself with the drinks in the kitchen. Neither spoke until she had returned, given him his whisky and sat down at the end of the sofa where Arthur habitually jumped up and laid a sleeping head in her lap. Smith instantly regretted leaving the dog at home.

'You look well, Madame.' She was direct, as usual.

'Thank you, young man, I am well. Now what is this business you have got yourself involved in. I didn't know the boy but I know Marcel Carbot. It is good of you to help him.'

The old lady's information, as usual, was accurate and

completely up to date. She spoke daily with Martine. She continued.

'This is a bad business, Peter, you must take care.'

Smith looked at her sharply. It was the first time he could remember her using his Christian name.

'I will, Madame, I will and before you say it, I'll take care of Martine too.'

An extraordinary look came his way. He had never seen such a combination of threat and vulnerability.

'Mind you do, young man. I wish to dance at your wedding before I die.'

Not for the first time talking to this wonderful old woman he was rendered tongue-tied.

'Er..'

She raised an amused hand slightly.

'Don't worry. I don't intend to die quite yet. Anyhow, Martine tells me that you have yet to take her to bed. I suggest you get on with it. Neither of you is getting any younger. You make rather an attractive couple although you could do to lose a little weight.'

This time he could not even raise an 'er'. She just tossed her head back and laughed.

The next couple of hours passed in easy conversation. They talked again about her life, about the Camargue, about the war. He sensed what she was leading up to and was happy when she finally plucked up courage to broach what was obviously a difficult subject for her.

'It is good that you are helping Suzanne. She has had a difficult life and I don't think she has many friends. That unspeakable husband..'

Her voice faded for a moment. That man was the reason her granddaughter had been murdered. After a while she regained her impetus.

'You must forgive Emil. He lives more in the past that I do. Like most men, he is more sentimental than us women. I too lived through the years of occupation in Arles during the war, and it was ugly. But for him it was worse. We are used to death here, Peter. It is part of life and not necessarily the end of it either. The Camargue is a hard, unforgiving place for those who choose to live there. But to have to do what he did took courage of a sort that most of us cannot understand. It scarred him for life. He can forgive neither the brother he killed nor himself for killing him. You, Martine and I are the only people who can understand this for him. We must. He is a greater man than you will ever know.'

He quickly crossed the few feet separating them and sat beside her. In a gesture utterly uncharacteristic of his hitherto respectful attitude towards her, he put his arm around her thin shoulders. She leant up against him and wept. Suddenly it became clear. She may have been older than he but Emile Aubanet was obviously the love of her life. After a while she straightened, pressed a tiny square piece of lace against her eyes and again became business-like.

'Now, Monsieur Smith, you must go. You have much to do.'

With that she got up and led him to the door. He turned and kissed her tenderly on the cheek. Just once. It was much more familiar than the usual three. Her face brightened with the knowledge.

'Take her to bed, Peter. You need each other, and next time bring Arthur.'

These weren't requests.

He stayed around the door that closed gently behind him for a while, long enough to ensure that no-one inappropriate was hanging around her house and then set course back across the now completely deserted Tranquetaille bridge. It was darker, even windier and there was more than a scud of rain in the air. It was a good evening for being invisible; dark and unfriendly.

Once home, he fed Arthur and, decided against eating. Madame Durand's gentle dart had hit home. No food but he needed to think and that meant whisky.

He sat at one end of the sofa and took stock, Schnabel playing Beethoven's Hammerklavier Sonata in the CD player. It didn't take long to realise that there was very little stock to take. A whole bunch of loose ends was more to the point. It was a mess. No direction and no plan, no progress. However, he had a feeling that now was the time for some precautions.

Gentry answered after the first ring. 'Good evening, Peter.'

'David, we need to get a grip of all this. It's too tatty. I need you to plan.'

'I know.'

'OK. First things first. I am uncomfortable for Martine. Jean-Marie has learned a lot but I am pretty sure that he would be out of his depth if anything serious really happens. Do we still have any friends - alive, that is?'

He could almost hear Gentry's smile.

'I'm slightly ahead of you. Deveraux arrives by TGV tonight at eleven. I will brief him, and he will be on station by one tomorrow morning.'

'Thank you, David. Again, I am in your debt.' 'I know that too.'

John Deveraux, sometime antique dealer, had for years been the department's best killer. The same age as Smith and therefore now somewhat superannuated, he had found it even more difficult than Smith had done to find repose in retirement. More than one precarious head of state around the world owed Deveraux for his continued ability to breathe God's clean air. He was, quite simply the best protection man in the business. He was utterly ruthless, infallible and terminally violent. He was also a great and serious pianist. Smith could never work out which he did to relax. No one at the Mas des Saintes would know anything. Relieved, Smith turned back to the problem.

'Gentry, we need to stir things up a bit.' His friend sighed.

'I was afraid you might say that. You do realise that you are suggesting that we light a fire under some of the most serious and therefore best specialist police and army units in France and that therefore means in the world, under some potentially lethal nuclear terrorists who are not exactly known for their donations to UNICEF, to say nothing of running the risk of getting up the nose of the president of France himself?'

'That all?'

'Well since you ask, I'll continue. There are also the local police and gendarmes, your criminal friends in Marseille, that bunch of hooligans in the Camargue to say nothing of a whole host of interested parties that we haven't identified yet.'

'The money, Gentry. The money.' 'What do you mean?'

'Come on old friend. Get on track for Christ's sake. You should be telling me. Money. That is what this is all about. It must be. If this is a plutonium export, then while the buyers may or not be buying for ideology, the sellers are doing it for money and a hell of a lot of it too. Ascend to that minimalist rooftop eyrie of yours and fucking-well find the money. Then work backwards. That is what you are best at. Leave the troublemaking to me.'

'All right, Peter. This sort of broken-field running was always much more your forté than mine. Just let me know when you intend explode the bomb.'

'And give Deveraux a telephone when he arrives. I'll need him.' 'Yes.'

'And loop him into all mobile calls in and out of the Mas.

He'll take care of the landlines himself.'

Smith rang off and settled onto the sofa beside a slumbering Arthur and slipped gently into thought. Which bit to bite first? The key to all this lay somewhere between the members of Suzanne's committee. Whether or not the killers and the victims at Beauduc were, in fact, from the same unit, and there was little reason to doubt the farmer at the moment, organ grinders rather than monkeys were the ones he had to hurt if he wanted anything to change. The hurt could be terminal. He did not really care very much. Actually, it was a pointless discussion. Gentry would tell him before too long. He sat quietly to think it through. His reverie was interrupted by the phone. It crossed his mind not to answer it. In the normal course of events that is precisely what he would have done - or rather not done. However, these were not normal times and the knowledge of the very few that might call him made him pick up. He listened with a sickening heart and growing anger. He waited for Girondou to calm down before asking:

'And the girls?'

'Here. They're OK'

'How long ago did they call? '

'Five minutes, maybe.'

'Do you have a fast car near?'

'Yes.'

'As soon as you can please. Close your place down completely. Do nothing until I get there. And I mean nothing. No-one in or out. Don't make any calls. They probably won't call again for a while. They want you to spend a few hours worrying. If they do call try just to listen, try to remember exactly what they say and say as little as you can.'

'But..'

'Do as I say, Alexei. Trust me, I know what to do. I'm better at this than you are.'

He rang off and immediately called Gentry.

'Someone else has beaten us to it. They've taken Girondou's wife.'

'Shit.'

'Go to work, old friend. I need you.'

'Yes, of course. You sound angry.'

'Yes, I am, . Very.'

'Oh shit. God help someone.'

'Fuck 'em.' and with that Smith cut the connection.

He went into his study and unlocked the floor safe. The Glock was already in its shoulder holster and he swung it on, pocketed the two spare magazines and went downstairs to hear the sound of a car arriving at the front door.

Chapter 11 War

Not everything that moves fast under a flashing blue light is actually a police car or an ambulance. This one wasn't but it certainly looked like one as it cut through the chaff in the outside lane of the road from Arles to Istres and thence on towards L'Estaque at a speed that seldom dropped below two hundred kilometres an hour. The Mercedes S65 AMG that housed only Smith and a driver had a small blue light magnetically attached to the roof and it was enough to brush aside the light traffic that was out and about at that hour effortlessly into the inside lane. It took very little time for Smith to realise that the driver he sat next to was well up to the job. The car seemed neither to accelerate nor break. It just wafted along at very high speed. He had that calm assurance that only a professionally trained man would possess. Smith took to wondering. Diplomatic protection probably. They were usually the best drivers. The front of the car was a better place to be than the back. Sloping windscreens are always better at diverting a bullet than the windows at the sides, bullet-proof or not.

Smith forced himself to relax and to think it all through. His instinct told him that whether or not this was only a preliminary, it could get fierce. Wherever the leak lay, he was its latest victim. That meant it was close to home and that was not a pleasant thought. He picked up his phone.

'Gentry check my car, please. Now if you would, and take Arthur back home with you, please. Tell Deveraux. This is a no rule game now.'

He knew that these last seven words gave Deveraux instructions to do whatever was necessary. Smith had had enough of rule games. He was unhappy - very unhappy - and people would die now if that was what was necessary. He did not wait for a reply. Gentry knew the war was starting and what was needed without explanation.

Next, he called Martine. He gave her no chance for pleasantries either.

'My love,' for that is what he suddenly realised she was, 'Please don't ask me to explain but I want you to stay at the Mas until I contact you again. It is very important. Your father, too. Keep Jean Marie with you at all times. Do you understand.'

'Yes, of course.'

'Could you take Suzanne in for a day or so? I don't want her on her own for the next twenty-four hours. I know what I am asking but..'

She cut him short.

'I'll tell father, don't worry.'

'Thanks.'

To do her credit she asked for no explanations although she could not resist a gentle admonition.

'Take care, Peter. I don't want to lose you.'

'Nor I, you.'

When it finally came, it was surprisingly easy for him.

'I love you.'

After such a momentous admission he was brought back to reality by her matter-of-fact tone.

'Yes, my dear. I know. Where are you going?'

'To help a friend. They've taken Girondou's wife.'

'He is a fortunate man to have your help, Peter.'

'Remember, Martine. Nothing until I call. Please'.

'OK, bossy boots.'

Given that the next few hours were inevitably going to be

very difficult, he smiled contentedly as he rang off.

The driver passed something across to him without taking his eyes off the road. It was one end of a satellite phone charger. The man was good. Smith plugged it in. Jean Marie was next for a briefing that took no time at all. There was not point in telling him about Deveraux. He would never see him anyway. Suzanne next.

'Suzanne. I don't have the time to explain but you must immediately get in your car and go to the Mas des Saintes and stay there. Martine is expecting you.'

'What is going on Peter. Am I in danger?'

'Probably and I am not prepared to take the chance. Trust me. I will explain but I have something to do first.'

'But to the Mas?'

Smith's reply was purposely brutal.

'It is about time you people started to learn to live with the past. If you don't do as I ask some of you will, in all likelihood, be dead within twenty-four hours. If that includes Martine, then you will die an unforgiven corpse by my hand. Do as I ask for fuck's sake and don't argue.'

By the time the calls were completed, they were sweeping into Girondou's gateway at a perilous speed and plunged down the long serpentine drive. This time security was very obvious. Smith glanced behind as confirmed that the steel bollards were raised after they passed. They drew up into the gravel courtyard with as little delay as there was fuss. Smith turned to his driver with a slightly questioning look. It was all that was needed.

'Henk van der Togt.'

'Are you as good with a gun as you are with this car?' 'Yes.'

'Diplomatic protection? KCT'.

'Shit,' thought Smith. Where the hell had he sprung from? Not all Dutchmen were hop-headed sixties revivalists. The guy would obviously do.

'Thank you. Please stay. I will need you later.'

The man nodded and remained motionless in his seat.

Girondou was seated on the small sofa with his pretty daughters, holding onto him on either side, tearful and terrified. He started to rise but subsided when he saw Smith's upraised hand. Smith walked across, crouched down in front of the sofa and took the girls' hands.

'Your mother will be back safe soon. Trust me. Trust me that I can do this. You have my word. My word, do you understand?'

They didn't, of course, but they nodded anyway.

Smith stood up abruptly, still holding their hands very tightly. They rose with him. He held them both very tightly and kissed them each on the top of the head. Visions of his own daughters filled his head.

'Right. I want you to go to bed. Get into your parents' bed together, hold each other close and under no circumstances leave the room or call anyone until your father tells you. This is really important. Now kiss your father and go. We have work to do and we don't need to be worrying about you. But remember I am very good at this stuff. Very good indeed.'

The two nodded gravely and did as he asked and reluctantly left the room. After they had gone he turned to his friend.

'Do you have a guard for them?' 'Yes.'

'Get him in here.'

Girondou walked to the door of the elegant sitting room and motioned in a squat man who was standing just outside. Girondou made to introduce the man but a quick gesture stopped him. Smith went up to the man and stood very close - purposely too close - to the hostility that was written all over the man's face.

'You are to stand outside the bedroom occupied by Monsieur Girondou's daughters. You are not to let them out until I or Monsieur Girondou tell you. With the exception of Monsieur Girondou and me, you will also kill anyone who comes within ten meters of the bedroom door, without warning or hesitation, even if it's your own mother. If you fail to do this, I will personally kill you and the rest of your family. Do I make myself quite clear.'

The man's expression changed from arrogance to terror in a few seconds. He nodded and left. Girondou looked across at his friend.

'Would you?'

'Oh yes.'

'Shit, Peter, I'm glad you're here - I think.'

'OK, next. Get rid of everyone in the house except five armed men that you can trust and know how to handle themselves. Get them in here. And get me a drink please.'

The whisky arrived before the men but not by much. They were a motley looking bunch but Smith knew from long experience that that was no way to judge. Girondou addressed them.

'As you probably know, we have a problem to solve. This is my friend Mr Smith. You will do exactly what he says as if I was asking you. He is a member of my family and he is also my friend. Please listen to him and do what he says.'

Smith could see a grudging respect dawning in their eyes as they turned their attention on him. The respect turned to shock quite quickly.

'As of now this house contains Monsieur Girondou, his two daughters who are in their parents' bedroom. There is one man outside the bedroom with orders to kill without question anyone who

141

comes close. That includes you. Believe me, he will. If he doesn't, I will. Other than Monsieur Girondou, his two daughters, the man guarding them and you five the only other person here is me and I will be leaving soon. Your job is to lock this house down as tight as the virgin of your basest fantasies. You will let me in when I return but absolutely no one else. You are responsible for the security and safety here and you will answer to me. Fail in this and I will personally rip your balls off while you are still breathing. If you understand, I suggest you get to work. If you don't, please stay and I will explain further.'

Unsurprisingly the all men left the room looking slightly shocked. He replied before his friend asked.

'Oh yes. I would.'

They sat together.

'OK. tell me what happened. Whats not whys or whos. I want bullet points only. Whys and whos come later when Angèle is back safe.'

It was depressingly simple and depressingly casual. Angèle had gone by car into La Couronne to collect some dry cleaning before the shop shut at eight. She drove herself. It was, after all, only four kilometres away. She hadn't returned. That was four hours ago. There had been no contact since. Girondou looked destroyed. The pretence of strength while the girls were with him had completely disappeared. Smith felt completely gutted. This was his fault.

'How were you informed? '

'A call just said they had taken her' 'Nothing more? '

'No. '

'Trace? '

'No.'

'Where does the dry cleaner live?' 'Above the shop, I think.'

'What is Angèle's mobile number.'

'That's no good. I tried to call her but just got the answering service.'

'The answering service. Are you sure? Not a number unobtainable or a switched off announcement?'

'No, the answering service. But how can that help'.

'Be quiet, Alexei. I ask, you answer. Please. Did it answer immediately or after a few rings?'

'Er, after a few rings, I think. Does it matter?' 'Believe me, it does. The number?'

Smith was dialling Gentry as Girondou spoke. He relayed the number to him.

'With any luck the phone might still be on, David. I think that this clever woman has just put it on silent. I need a trace and I need it now. I'll hold.'

The space over the satellite went empty. Girondou still hadn't got his thinking boots on.

'Peter, for Christ's sake, tell me. What are you doing? Who are you calling?'

Smith softened for the first time in fifteen minutes. The man was clearly distraught. Perhaps an explanation would be kind, and, in any case, he had a little time to waste before Gentry came back to him.

'Alexei, you are not only blessed with a wife who is one of the most beautiful women I know, you also have one who is clever. You got through to her answering service which means her phone might still be still switched on although she obviously can't answer it. She must have put it onto silent when she was taken because it would have rung when you called her, and her captors would have taken it away and dumped it. That takes guts. It is not switched off

143

because if it was the answering service would probably have cut in immediately when you called. It also means that the people who took her are pretty stupid. They're not professionals and therefore they will make mistakes. But it also makes them slightly unpredictable, so we must be careful. We need to pray that they stay stupid.'

'But why did someone do this?'

'I'll have a better answer for that after, shall we say, I've had a chat with them. This happened only four hours ago. They won't have gone far. They must have been local or at least looked local to get to Sausset without your people spotting them. Wherever they are, Alexei, we will find them and I will bring her back. She is no use to them dead.'

This was not the time to tell his distraught friend that in reality Angèle had a number of uses dead.

'I presume that her mobile is a modern one? One that can be used all over the world?'

'Well yes, I suppose it is.'

'Then it has a GPS chip and we can find it - or rather my friend can.'

'Your friend?'

'Don't ask'.

Gentry came back on cue.

'Forty-one, Chemin de Coutran , La Bouilladisse.'

'Where the hell's that?'

'About thirty kilometres north of Marseille on the A52.'

'Thanks.'

He closed the phone and turned to his friend.

'Alexei. I am going to leave you here and I will go to get Angèle. I need the car and Henk.'

Girondou looked somewhat perplexed for a moment then protested.

'No, I must come with you, and we need men. An escort?'

'That is precisely what we don't need, Alexei. A bunch of over- hyped thugs trampling in Rambo style led by a man who, unless I miss my guess, hasn't been in a proper fire fight in his entire life.'

Girondou nodded sadly. Smith continued:

'Leave it to me. Please, stay here with your daughters. They need you. Angèle doesn't need you now. She needs me. In any case, people will probably die tonight, and I can get out from under that better than you can. The last thing you need is the flic tramping all over your garden in the hope of at last getting at you. If I could manage it, I would have you far away, but I can't not risk your moving from here until we know a little more of what is going on. Stay here and take care of the girls. Trust me. I will have her back within four hours'

'But, er, Henk?'

Girondou continue to look perplexed. Smith drove on.

'He'll do. In future you might like to find out a little more about your employees. The guy might be wasted as a driver.'

The last thing he saw as he turned to leave was Girondou frowning slightly in a confused sort of way. Smith dismissed it as shock but it did raise a small doubt in his mind as he left the house and headed for the parked Mercedes.

Henk was still there in the same position as Smith had left him. The CD player was playing a Schubert piano sonata and the man looked to be dozing. Smith slid back into the front passenger seat, pulled out his Glock and pointed it at the recumbent driver. The

145

eyes opened but Smith saw neither surprise not panic. Good wasn't the word.

'OK, before we start, who the hell are you and where the hell did you come from?'

The reply was and wasn't surprising at the same time.

'Gentry.'

The wonderful bastard, Smith thought, not for the first time, putting his gun away,

'Ah. OK, I have this and two extra magazines. You?'

'I also have a Glock 30. Three mags. However fortunately Monsieur Girondou's car seems to have some unusual non-factory extras. We have two pump twelve bores in the boot. One hundred rounds. Six stun grenades, four gas, four high explosive. All RWM Arges. Twenty more full clips for the Glocks. Four sets of body armour. The car is a full AMG conversion with all the suspension mods. No armouring, however.'

Smith frowned slightly.

'Which means that it goes like a shit off a stick but can't stop an air gun pellet.'

Henk nodded as Smith continued:

'Perhaps, after this is all over, you might like to advise Monsieur Girondou about spending his money more wisely in future.'

This time Henk's nod was accompanied by a slight grin. Smith continued:

'No automatics?'

'No.' replied the driver, 'don't much like them myself. Too noisy.'

Smith looked sharply across at the man to see if he was talking the piss. He wasn't.

'Have we met before, Henk?'

'No, I don't think so. I think we both might have remembered.

Perhaps we should have, though.' 'My name is Smith.'

'Yes, I know.'

'Where the hell were you when they took Madame Girondou.'

'In Arles outside your house. I had only just arrived.'

Clearly Gentry had called for more reinforcements than he'd admitted.

'How come you are driving this car?'

'Er, shall we say that I changed places with the original driver when he arrived at your house.'

'So how do you manage to find your way around this part of the world?'

The thin Dutchman smiled slightly in the darkness.

'Ah. The joys of factory-fitted GPS systems. Not very secure, though, having your bosses home address programmed into it I think.'

'What the hell happened to the original driver?'

Smith feared the worse. The driver's smile widened a little more.

'Oh. he's in the boot too. Slightly indignant, I would imagine.'

'Dump him out and let's go.'

A few moments later they drove out and turned towards the motorway that would take them around the north of Marseille and towards the A 52.

Smith looked across at his companion. Late forties, fit, tanned.

'We are going to war. Columbia orders.'

Henk nodded slowly. Smith had guessed right. Hostage rescue was a growth industry in South America.

'We need the target safe and one senior man incapacitated. We kill the rest. Have you any idea how many that might be?'

'No.'

'It might be a few, my friend. Are you all right with that?'

Smith sensed rather than heard a slight hesitation before hearing the quiet reply.

'Yes.'

They drove quickly through the night in silence. The télépéage smart card meant that they were not delayed to any great extent at the AutoRoute toll booth and it was less than half an hour before they slowed at AutoRoute exit to La Bouilladisse. The GPS took them around the south of the small town, slightly into the hills and onto a single-track road with houses dotted around irregularly on either side. Smith thought, it seemed a grim little place but perhaps that was his mood. They parked beside road and looked quietly. The house was dimly lit by a few arbitrarily-placed lights at the end of the street which made life easier and had a small garden in the front and a slightly larger one at the back. Smith looked at his watch and was surprised to see it was still only a little past midnight.

'OK, let's have a look. You take the rear. Back here in ten minutes. Turn the car around. Don't bother about concealment too much. We will be long gone before any of the neighbours notice or can figure out what is going on.'

They walked silently but not particularly furtively towards the house. It was a typical small two-story Provençale house. No outbuildings. Fortunately for Smith, all the shutters were open. He hoped that his companion would have equal luck. He didn't want to go in completely blind. Ten minutes later they were back in the car.

'Well?'

'Two plus the target.' replied the driver, clearly familiar with this sort of briefing. 'They are in the bedroom, first floor rear'

Smith added his news.

'I got three in the front ground floor watching football on television. The chances are that the boss isn't on guard duty. So, he will be one of those watching TV and he's the one I want. No alarms. Standard cylinder lock on the front door.'

'Christ, we are dealing with fucking amateurs.' Smith nodded.

'Yes, interesting isn't it?' Henk ventured a suggestion.

'We could get the target and one other out without disturbing the others.'

Smith frowned in the darkness. This was not what he had in mind.

'No. Whoever set this up needs to be sent a message. You sort the three football fans. Just hold them and I will go up. I'll meet you downstairs with the target and the others.

Henk looked sharply at his companion and said nothing. Smith continued.

'Glocks only, I think. Put a set of that body armour on the back seat. I want the target protected on the way home. This doesn't

149

smell like a set-up, but you never know.'

Smith's memory of an entirely too eventful trip back from the Marseille opera only eight months ago was still vivid.

They left the car, doors unlocked and headed back to the house.

The front door opened with a small shiv of flexible steel that lived in Smith's belt and Henk waited just inside the door to the front room while Smith climbed the stairs using the wall side edge only. The stair turned on a small landing and Smith stopped at the point where he would go out of sight of his companion. A five second countdown was started by the raising of a spread hand and he disappeared round the corner. On zero they both simply opened the doors and stepped calmly into their respective rooms.

One of the two guards actually was asleep and took a second or two registering what was going on, slightly ruining the drama of the moment. Smith pointed the Glock at them and said very simply but in quiet immaculate French:

'If either of you moves or says anything at all, you will die.' Simple enough for even them to understand. Madame

Girondou was well awake, lying on the bed bound hand and foot but looking surprisingly spunky for her ordeal. Smith took the little foldable hunting knife that had been a constant companion for years since he had bought it in South Africa into his left hand and cut the bonds. The two men were too busy figuring out what was going on to be much of a threat. They also noticed that whatever movements Smith made the Glock remained completely motionless. Smith kissed the woman on the cheek and whispered into her ear.

'Angèle. I want you to go downstairs quietly and wait by the front door. I'll come down with these two after you and take them into the front room. At that point a friend of mine will come out of the front room and will take you to a car. Go with him please. I'll join you in a few moments. OK?'

She nodded.

150

She had done as he said; standing by the front door looking infinitely more beautiful than any recent kidnap victim has a right to look. Smith took the two guards downstairs after her and into the front room. The three were lined up on their knees with hands on their heads. The two from above joined them in the row. Henk had at least pointed them at the television. He gave Smith a glance as he slipped out of the room and Smith heard the front door opening and closing very softly.

Sensibly Henk had closed the window shutters. Smith stood in front of the football and surveyed the line of kneeling figures. It was time to bite back. They would learn not to mess with his friends. He put on his most kindly face.

'Now then. Who's the boss?'

All five remained sullen and silent.

'I'll ask you once again. Only once. Which of you is in charge? This time I would appreciate the courtesy of an answer. If I don't get one, I might have to ask in a slightly different way.'

Again, there was no reply. Smith could see that the two oldest were beginning to weigh up the possibility of retaliation. There were, after all, five of them and only one of him. It was then that Smith shot the youngest through the forehead. The shutters behind turned a glistening dark maroon and a slow drip started to sink towards the skirting board. The Glock had made less noise than the football commentary.

'You were saying?' he enquired equally politely. The oldest was the first to recover.

'I am.'

'Good. You had better come with me.'

Ten minutes later they were driving swiftly back down the road towards the AutoRoute and home. Smith was in the back with Angèle. Their guest was bound hand and foot with electrical cable ties, gagged with duct tape and strapped into the passenger's seat. He was blindfolded, shivering and completely terrified.

Smith touched the driver lightly on the shoulder. 'Thank you, my friend. You did OK.'

The Dutchman asked the question whose answer he feared he already knew.

'The others?'

Smith felt Angèle taking his hand and holding it very tightly.

The silence grew.

'Whoever it was who did this, did it to warn us. Now they know that we are serious too.'

'But..'

'Henk, no one harms my friends. No one. It would be better if you learned that.'

'It's true, what they say about you, then.'

Smith decided it was time to end the conversation.

'Probably.'

Smith put his arm around Angèle's shoulders and held her as close as the Kevlar body armour would allow. She understood even if the Dutchman found it hard. At some point she reached up and drew Smith's head down towards her and kissed him gently on the cheek.

'Thank you, Peter, thank you.' she whispered.

He turned to his phone. First to Girondou. It connected, and he handed the machine to Angèle. After a while, she handed it back to him. Girondou's voice was thick with emotion.

'Peter, I don't know what to say.'

'Everything is fine, my friend. Tell the girls we will be home in about twenty minutes. I will send Angèle in on her own. I have some business with our passenger. You might like to get the girls downstairs. Be careful though. You don't want to get shot by your own guard. Can we use one of your barns?'

'Yes. The one on the right as you come in is secure and private.'

'Good. Tell the gate guards. I don't want them being silly as we come in.'

'I will. Thank you, Peter. Can I do anything?'

'Just send one of your chaps out to the barn with a very large glass of scotch. I'll come in after having a chat with our friend here.'

The next call was to Gentry. Thanks, were as unnecessary as they would have been inappropriate, as would have been any sort of debrief. One question only came over the air.

'How many?'

'Five.'

'Now?'

'One.'

'Ah.'

'For the present. '

'Ah.'

They arrived back home, and Smith sent Angèle back into the house. He then turned to the driver.

'Henk. What did Gentry ask you to do?'

'Watch your back.'

'How very kind. He should know better. You haven't done much killing yet, have you?'

'No.'

Angry now, Smith turned on the driver.

'Then you are fuck all use to me. You either learn to do what you have obviously been very expensively trained for and do it instantly, without hesitation or, for that matter, regret then you leave now. You're a good driver and you know the job but the sort of people who have problems that need your particular talents will want you to come through for them even if you die in the process. You have to learn that in this particular world the only way to survive is to give more shit than you take. They die, or you do. More importantly they die or the people for whom you're responsible do. If you are not reliable in extreme situations, then you are about as much use as a chocolate teapot.'

He continued unrelentingly.

'You have a choice now. You've done a good job tonight and I am grateful to you. I don't need you for this next bit. What I do need you to do is to stay here with these people for a day or two and organise them to ensure that what happened tonight won't happen again. I'll hold you personally responsible for their safety. If anyone dies around here it had better be you. If you don't like the deal then bugger off home . Sit in the car and think about it. I will be back in five minutes. If your still here when I come out then I will take that as you answer. First, put him in that barn for me.'

Smith nodded at a low building some thirty metres to their right. 'Oh, and unload the armoury before you leave. I will be taking this car home and I don't want all that crap rattling about in the back.'

The man in the barn was not happy. Smith cut the cable ties and let the man get some of his circulation back. He then sat him down on an upright chair and started to talk to him. The man was consumed by the memory of what he had seen less an hour before. Smith had been on the receiving as well as the giving end of this

154

situation himself but one look at the man told him that this was not going to be hard. It was also not likely to be very fruitful. The man looked ignorant.

Smith took a sip of the whisky that was sitting on the bonnet of a ride on lawn-mower in the corner of the barn and pulled a second chair very close to the man. He ripped the tape from the man's mouth ignoring the smell from the stain spreading below the man's waist.

'Now, let's start with your name.' 'Alphonse, Monsieur, Alphonse Didet.'

'OK, Alphonse. My name is not important but unless you answer my questions, I am the last person that you will ever see in your life that has currently slightly less than five minutes to run and I am the man who will end it. Make no mistake. Do you understand me.'

The man nodded.

'You were hired to take Madame Girondou.' The man could not answer quickly enough.

'Yes.'

'What were your instructions?'

'We were told to go to Sausset and take her when she went to collect some dry cleaning. We were to take her to the house in La Bouilladisse and wait to be contacted. We were told not to harm her. We thought it was just a routine kidnap. He offered to pay well.'

'Have you any idea who you were taking?' 'Yes, Monsieur, I did.'

'And you still accepted?'

'Sir, they threatened to kill me and my family.'

Smith inwardly grimaced at the recent memory of using the

same threat.

'OK. How did you get your instructions?'

'I was telephoned yesterday morning and told to take two men and wait in Sausset today from lunchtime on. I got a second instruction at about four o' clock confirming that she was coming.'

'Who telephoned you?'

'I don't know. He just said that tomorrow morning, someone would come to collect the woman and bring our money.'

Smith dug a battered mobile phone out of his pocket. He had taken it off the man before they left the house. He snapped the battery back in.

'This man called you on this?' 'Yes, Monsieur.'

Smith saw that no number was registered and dropped the battery out again.

'Can you think of anything else about this business that might interest me, Monsieur Alphonse Didet.'

'No, Monsieur. Nothing, as God is my judge.' Smith's smile got no further than his lips. 'Believe me, He isn't. I am. Think very carefully.'

The man was clearly desperate, Smith saw him casting about for something - anything. What he finally settled on was interesting.

'Two of the men you, er, left at the house in La Bouilladisse were not ours. They were there when we arrived at the house with the woman.

'Ah,' thought Smith, at least his message would get through to the right people.

'You are absolutely sure that your instructions were specific about Madame Girondou's visit to the dry cleaners.'

'Yes Monsieur.'

As he suspected there was nothing more to be got from the man. Smith leaned very close, putting himself almost touching the sweaty face of his companion. He could smell the bile on the man's breath.

'Monsieur, I have decided that you will live.' The man's relief was indescribable. 'Monsieur, by the grace of God...'

Smith cut him short.

'There is nothing graceful or Christian about your future, my friend. You have done something unforgivable and it is right that you are punished. You will live, certainly, but you will curse me every day of your remaining life. You will wish you were dead. You will also be an example to those who might wish to follow you. It is this message that I want you to pass on. You will be a living warning for anyone who might want again to endanger Monsieur Girondou's family.'

With that, Smith got up and replaced the tape tightly over the man's mouth, took out the Glock, shot the man once through each knee and walked out of the barn. He opened the door to the Mercedes and looked at the driver who seemed not to have moved.

'Well?'

'I'll stay.'

'Good. Sit here. I'll be about ten minutes. Don't go in the barn'

With that he went into the house and was instantly enveloped by three sobbing women. At last he managed to disengage himself and after an uncertain few moments, he took the girls hands in his and bent his head to them.

'My children, I want to have a word with your parents. I will say good night to you. I will come and see you again in a day or two. Tomorrow you will find that your driver will be a rather good-looking Dutchman called Henk. He is going to protect you for a bit so please do what he asks. Now please go to bed. I am sure that your parents will be with you in a few minutes.'

They stood uncertainly, obviously wanting to say something but not knowing what. Smith shooed them out of the door.

'And don't make a pass at Henk. I want him concentrating on the job for a day or two.'

Both the girls managed to flash him a smile as they left.

Not wanting to disturb the other two, he crossed to the side table and poured himself another scotch. It was getting late and he was beginning to run out of energy. Angèle went to say something. Smith held up a gentle hand.

'Angèle. I need to ask you a couple of questions. Are you up to it?'

She nodded.

'Did you hear or see anything?'

'No, Peter. It all happened very quickly. I had just come out of the dry cleaners and I was pushed into the back of a car parked by the side of the road. There was one man in the back and two in the front. They all wore balaclavas. Somebody was put over my head and I was tied up. No one spoke at all, not even when I was taken into the house.'

'Your phone was on silent.'

'Yes, I normally have it on silent.'

'What time did you decide to go to collect the laundry?'
'About four.'

'Yes, it was a last minute thing.'

'Why?'

'Well I had been meaning to go to collect it for some time but never got around to it. But then François, Alexei's brother, asked when I was going as he had a couple of jackets to be picked up as well and he asked me if I could get them for him when I was next passing the shop. He said there was no hurry but I thought there was no reason not to go immediately.'

'Did you tell François when you might go?'

'No, I don't think so. Oh, wait, perhaps I might have said that I would go later this afternoon.'

Again, Smith felt that there was little more to be gained by prolonging the conversation. He had heard enough and, although she didn't know it yet, Madame Girondou was going to need some rest very soon.

'Angèle, would you allow me a few moments with Alexei? Then I will go home. I'm pleased that you are OK and home safe. I suspect that you will find the girls back in your bed and waiting for you.'

She nodded, kissed Alexei lightly and got up and crossed to stand in front of him. She drew long breath as if buying a little time trying to work out what to say. Smith looked tenderly down at her and laid a finger lightly on her lips and shook his head slightly. His next words were a whisper.

'You are my family, Angèle - or as good as. There's nothing more to be said. Please, kiss the girls for me.

After she left there was a long silence. Alexei got up, replenished both their glasses and sat down again opposite Smith still without speaking. Smith knew exactly what was going through his head. Smith offered a few words of warning.

'It may just be some dreadful coincidence, Alexei. You do have to find out first before you do anything.'

'You are probably right, Peter, but my own brother. What possessed him?'

'I think that you have first to ask why. If indeed he did set this up, then why? What does he possibly have to gain? Is he after your position? Does he want to run things down here?'

'I have never thought so, but one never knows.'

'Well, that's the first question you have to answer. The second is how does the kidnapping of Angèle help his ambitions? After that there is the small matter of connecting this to our present enquiries, or at least seeing if there is a connection.'

'What do you think, my friend?' Girondou sounded very, very tired. 'You seem to have a better idea of this sort of think that I have.' 'Alexei, I really don't know. If I had to make a guess, I would think that it is a bit of opportunism. Someone, possibly only François, has spotted a chance to get rid of you under the general confusion of this other business. However, we will soon know.'

'How?'

'I left four bodies in La Bouilladisse and a cripple in your barn who is probably unconscious by now, which, by the way, you should sort out after I am gone. We don't want him ending up dead as well. Someone will get the messages. According to the man who is currently expiring messily over your barn floor, two of the men in the house at La Bouilladisse were apparently strangers so presumably they were from whoever set this up. That is the reaction that will tell us most. In the meantime, go gently with François even if you wish to damage him considerably. He may not have thought he was really endangering Angèle. If he is involved and thinks you don't suspect him, he is more likely to give something away. Try to make him part of a briefing tomorrow. Even ask him to enquire locally. If he is one of the ungodly, he is a channel somewhere else and therefore valuable alive. For Christ's sake, don't tell him I was involved. I don't want a bunch of vengeful thugs coming after me until I know who they are and what they look like. Oh, and get a good tail on François immediately.'

Girondou nodded wearily. The night was beginning to get to him. Smith decided that enough was enough for them both.

'Alexei. I am leaving Henk with you as your bodyguard for a bit. He is as good as it gets apart from a slight squeamishness that I hope I have talked him out of. Let him organise close protection for you and the girls. Trust him. He knows what will happen if he fucks up.'

Girondou nodded. Smith looked at his watch. It was past three in the morning. He continued.

'Right, I am going home for a good sleep. I will borrow the Mercedes, if I may. I will be in touch tomorrow.'

He rose and started towards the door only to be intercepted by Girondou who held him lightly by the arm.

'Peter. I don't know what to say. Nothing in this world can repay you for what you did for me and my family this night. Nothing, nothing can ever repay that.'

Smith nodded awkwardly.

'Just sort that man outside before he bleeds to death all over your pretty barn. As I said, I'll be in touch tomorrow.'

Smith performed the introductions between Girondou and Henk before drawing the Dutchman to one side.

'Henk, I am leaving these people in your charge. I hope that by now you know what that means.'

'Yes, I think I do. They are your friends.'

Smith just nodded a little wearily and walked slowly towards the car.

As he was speeding up the road back towards Arles Smith checked over the last few hours for loose ends and found none. This was not the time to analyse it all. He had forgotten how much this sort of thing took it out of him. He had also forgotten for an hour or

161

two that he was no longer a young man. Suddenly he felt very lonely and rather dirty and the old demons all seemed to come at him in a rush . The ghosts of the past were very near now and he felt threatened. Suddenly, he made up his mind about a number of things. He called Martine.

'Hi, sorry to call ...' She interrupted him.

'Are you all right, Peter?'

'Yes I am and the problem is fixed. You OK?'

'Yes, my dear, now I am.'

There was a silence. They both knew that it was him to speak next and when he did it was very quietly.

'Martine, I need to be with you very much. Can I come now?'

'Yes. How long?'

'About twenty minutes. I am in a black Mercedes.'

'Good. That gives me time to tell the men on the gate to expect you and change the linen on my bed.'

The next call was to Gentry to ask him to tell Deveraux to expect him and described the car. Gentry knew better than to ask questions. There would be time enough for that later.

The night was clear and starry as the Mercedes pressed on at high speed. There was no one on the AutoRoute and he passed no-one until a couple of Spanish camions as he crossed the bridge across the Rhone and turned south towards the Camargue. He was hurting badly now. He swept almost blindly through the mas gates and came to a violent halt scattering gravel to both sides. Martine was waiting for him alone in the courtyard of the Mas. She took his hand gently as he crept stiffly from the car. After a long and passionate kiss on the lips she wordlessly led him inside.

Chapter 12   The Morning After

To say the least the atmosphere at breakfast was odd: not particularly difficult but certainly odd. They were all relaxed but in different ways. Emile Aubanet sat, as usual, at the head of the kitchen table surveying an ensemble that had doubled overnight with a calm detachment and not a little pleasure. Breakfast was usually a deux when he would talk through the events of the day to come with his daughter. This morning he found himself joined by his niece who, when he had gone to bed, had been completely persona non grata in his house who sat to his right looking cool, beautiful and elegant in a plain blouse and jeans and surprisingly relaxed. To his left sat his daughter. In fact while that was topographically accurate she had drawn up her chair up to the far corner and next to the new occupant of the second head of the table as makes no difference. She was making a not inconsiderable fist of devouring coffee, baguette, butter and apricot jam at a joyous rate without once seeming to take any of her three hands off some part of the new occupant of the second senior seat. She was pointedly still dressed in an extravagant flowing multi-coloured Chinese silk dressing gown and looked completely radiant. Smith, on the other hand, looked both slightly embarrassed and very happy simultaneously. He also looked completely shattered. He had an excuse. He was probably the only one around the table who have killed four people and crippled a fifth in the previous twelve hours.

As head of the family Emile Aubanet thought that it was probably his responsibility to attempt some sort of general conversation.

'Well,' he started. 'Some of us have had an exciting night, I gather. I seem to have missed something.' He looked straight ahead of him.

'Peter, I wonder if you might tell me, before you two go back go bed? Oh, Martine, how many shall I tell the cook to expect for lunch?'

It was not without a huge effort that Smith told the whole

story - all of it. He had already told Martine the bare bones at some stage during the night. Now he went back through it all, sparing them some of the details but none of the content. He left little out - apart from Gentry, Deveraux and Henk; these were secrets for Martine alone. At the end he just looked back at the old man. Suzanne was just looking astonished. They all sat in silence. After a while it was the old man who broke it.

'Not for the first time we all have reason to be grateful to you, Peter; Monsieur Girondou and his family in particular but us as well. Again you have rendered a service to us here in the South that we could neither expect nor perhaps deserve. Unlike my daughter who looks happier this morning than at any time since her mother was alive, you look simply dreadful and I am not entirely surprised. Perhaps we might consider all this at lunchtime and make some plans, together this time.'

The nuance was not lost on Smith. He nodded gratefully. Aubanet stretched out his hand to the lady to his right and continued: 'I want to spend some time with Suzanne for I have much to catch up on and some great mistakes of the past to try to put right.' He nodded towards the far end of the table.

'You two clearly have some unfinished business. So off you go.

Lunch will be at 12:30.'

With that, Martine got up, tugged Smith to his feet and they disappeared into the house in the direction of Martine's apartment.

She silenced him every time he wanted to talk. It was the most thrilling and loving few hours of his recent life; not particularly restful but for someone who had basically retired to Arles to die gradually it was a miracle. Their lovemaking was simple and tender, as if they had been doing it for years. While most marriages end in disaster or indifference, a few continue in comfort. It felt like that. When finally they called a temporary truce and lay contentedly and quietly again in each other's arms, he told her about the events that the others did not know.

'A man called Deveraux will be looking after you for a bit.'
'Who?'

'You'll probably never meet him, and you will certainly never see him, but he will be there if Jean Marie can't cope. He is rather good at this sort of thing. He is outside now.'

'But how? Surely our people would have seen him?'

'No. They wouldn't. He is the best. Much better than I am. He will remain to protect you and your father. I don't intend to have to get up in the middle of the night and rescue you as well. You are entirely too precious.'

'But who is he. Why is he doing this?'

'He is from the past but he is also a friend. Perhaps one day you will meet him when we are in less difficult times. He is the most violent and the most sophisticated man I know.'

'And the others?

'The Dutchman is protecting Girondou and his family. He is simply an employee. David Gentry is possible my only true friend. We have worked together for many years. He is the only man I completely trust.'

'The only...?'

Smith took the beautiful face in his hands. 'The only man. You are the only woman.'

With that they subsided again into each other's' arms.

'What is happening Peter, really? Why are you getting involved in something that seems to me to be way too big for one man to change anything.'

'Well,' replied Smith, 'The simple answer to the question is because Gentry and Suzanne asked me to.'

'And they are, of course, friends.'

He smiled and kissed her for the umpteenth time.

'You're beginning to get the idea. The point about it being too big to make a difference is actually precisely the opposite. It is because I am alone that I can. Large governments and their agencies can't do the things I can.'

He paused to collect his thoughts before continuing.

'Originally I had no intention of getting involved. Gentry just wanted to find out what happened to his friend's grandson. But when I discovered that Suzanne was heading up the investigation alarm bells began to ring.'

'Why? Surely it's her job?'

'Perhaps but I have the feeling she is being set up or at least being used by someone who certainly doesn't have her best interests at heart. No one normally gets the sort of authority she has in this investigation. She should have seen that. Perhaps she jumped at the chance too quickly when it came her way. I don't think she has protected herself and unless she gets some advice and some help somebody will screw her. I just want to prevent that.'

'Why? Until last night she wasn't even really part of this family.' 'Because I like her and I respect what she did to her husband.'

They both fell silent as they remembered the shared horrors of the previous year. Both Martine's and Suzanne's husbands had been part of a paedophile organisation. Suzanne had killed hers when she found out. Smith had not bothered to find out who murdered Martine's husband Robert DuGresson in the Arles Arena one afternoon in the previous summer primarily because he guessed that it was Martine herself or at least someone working for the Aubanet family. The reverie was broken with her usual fine timing by Martine whose caress became the sort of grip that in a short time would bring tears to Smith's eyes.

'You're not getting sweet on her, are you? Because if you are, I will do something about it.'

He looked at her not daring to guess what she was capable of doing.

'No, my dear, I am not. She's too thin for me. In any case I thought that the dressing gown of yours at breakfast gave a fairly strong signal.'

Lunch had come and gone without alarm and they had settled into a sort of post-prandial domestic lethargy with newspapers next to the fire. After a while Smith got to his feet slowly and addressed no- one in particular.

'I think I'll just stretch my legs for a few minutes.'

Martine lowered her newspaper a fraction and peered over the. She knew that the weather outside was not nice at all and was a little relieved when he saw a slight shake of his head.

Although it was only mid-afternoon, the sky was already darkening. Clouds raced across, and the wind was well up. Not quite a full Mistral yet but well on the way. Certainly, the temperature was in single figures and the tall pine trees, already bent southwards from years of persistent wind were leaning unsteadily in that direction again. The tall reed beds and scrubby bushes that lined the gravel drive half a kilometre or so to the road were equally unsettled. It was not an afternoon for a gentle constitutional.

It was clear that he had been under observation since he left the courtyard and a brief conversation with Jean-Marie. After a couple of hundred yards and a few bends to take him out of sight of the house, he raised his hand and scratched left ear. It came as no surprise at all that the first thing Smith heard was his voice. On a job like this Deveraux was seen or heard only when he chose to be.

'Good afternoon, Sir.'

Habit, more than experience, caused Smith to turn quickly but gently to come face to face with a face that seemed unchanged since the last time they had met some four years earlier. He was far enough away for Smith to take in the warm but unobtrusive winter clothing of the man who stood at least four inches taller than himself. He looked surprisingly neat, tidy and shaved for a man who had been living outdoors for almost a day in the depths of the Provençale winter.

Smith had no time for pleasantries and just looked expectantly. Deveraux's report was concise.

'The house is reasonably secure, the farm not at all. Entries from all directions. Guarding the main gate seems a bit of an irrelevance. All the principals are in the house including Madame Suzanne. The man Jean-Marie seems to be up to the job. No really weak links with the rest of the staff as far as I can see. No phone traffic of interest.'

'Internet?' Smith asked sharply. 'They have quite a network here used to manage the businesses.'

A smile crossed the taller man's face.

'Down at the moment, Sir. You know what these country areas are like.'

Smith smiled back in appreciation.

'And no one has called anyone about that either?' The smile remained in place.

'No. I suspect they think it is something to do with you.'

'Tactical?'

Deveraux grimaced and looked serious. 'Not good. No better than level four.'

Smith sighed. On this occasion it was not good news to have his own rather pessimistic opinion confirmed. The ability of the Mas with its current personnel to remain secure was well below average. The scale only went down to five. However, at this stage, there was nothing he could do about it. The best defence for the Aubanet family remained in keeping the bad guys in ignorance. If the Girondou kidnapping was associated with the main event, it would take the opposition time to make a connection. If not, then the family was safe for the time being. He addressed the man in front of him once more.

'I suggest that your presence here makes that more like a three.' 'Thank you, Sir. But I think a three and a half would be more accurate.'

'Whatever this is, it will be over in a few couple of days, three at most, I suspect.'

Deveraux frowned. 'I am a little worried about Madame Suzanne Aubanet,'

Smith grinned slightly. 'Join the club.'

'No. It is just that I have intercepted one or two calls from her mobile.'

'You mean the satellite phone I gave her?' 'No, her personal mobile.'

'And why is that a problem? You can listen in, I presume, and Gentry can probably get the cell knocked out if you wish?'

Deveraux continued to frown.

'That's just it. I can't. She seems to have some clever encryption gismo that stops me getting anywhere near the transmission. Maybe Gentry can get me some stuff but at the moment I don't know what she is doing.'

'How many calls?'

'Twelve since she arrived here. All short. One or two just a second or two.'

Smith paused. A few dark thoughts were gathering in the back of his mind. With an effort he put them to one side and forced himself back to the present. Another chat with Gentry was in order. He looked across at his companion with an enquiring glance.

'Anything else?' Deveraux shook his head.

There was nothing more to be said. If Deveraux wanted anything, he would get it himself. Gentry would have made sure he had the basics. If he felt anything needed saying, he would have said it by now. Smith, however, couldn't resist.

'Thanks, Deveraux.'

The tall man shrugged and smiled with genuine warmth. 'I owe you, Sir.'

Smith remembered, nodded and turned away. The whole conversation had lasted less than a minute or two. As he stepped back onto the drive that led back up to the mas he resisted the temptation to look back over his shoulder to confirm what he already knew. Deveraux had silently and invisibly returned to the countryside.

Smith returned to the warmth of the mas to find little changed. There was a generally somnambulant atmosphere which he didn't particularly want to join. In spite of the pleasures of the morning which were considerable, he had business to attend to. The place was becoming all too comfortable and he alone knew that the danger was very far from gone. Before long he took his leave and headed back through a dark rainy evening towards Arles and home.

DuPlessis lay back in bed looking down at the pale naked woman who lay beside him. The moonlight that filtered through the slats in the window shutters striped her legs and torso and although her face was turned away from him he could see her beauty clearly.

It was less than a year ago since he had met her, just after the abortive operation in Chad that had resulted in he and his group being captured by Salafist fighters. Rather than execution, the al-Qaida allied group chose education and the group had been freed with at least half of them, if not actually converted, then certainly thoughtful about the so-called terrorist threat they had been trained so hard to resist to resist. Pouneh and he had met in a Marseille hotel when he had been giving close protection to a conference of Middle East Finance Ministers. She worked as a translator for the Iranian delegation and had an apartment overlooking the Vieux Port; an apartment that was very much more luxurious than a translator's salary might support.

Before long, he had met her friends, talked long into the night and little by little he became, again if not fully believing, at least a fellow-traveller. It was an alliance encouraged by the knowledge that his performance in Chad had fallen under close scrutiny by his bosses in Paris. In a small elitist group like his, failure was punished severely, and his career had been limited ever since, even if it hadn't been before. His new friends promised an infinitely greater pension than the French government would have provided, if indeed they had been minded to give him one at all under the recent circumstances. More likely, a training posting somewhere overseas loomed. Sex, money, religion and politics may have been the heady mixture for most of history but the certainty of a sweaty oblivion in somewhere like the Foreign Legion post in French Guiana ultimately convinced him.

The morality of it all didn't bother him much. He was a street kid from Metz made good. The supercilious bastards who debriefed him at such length after Chad and who sent him and his group on indefinite leave while they figured out what to do with them just looked at him as if he was a piece of shit stuck to their shoes. They conveniently forgot that, hungry for success, he had worked like a dog day and night, had graduated first from his class at St Cyr and had continued to be the very best at everything through the long, hard training that had led to his promotion to Colonel of GIGN. He snorted silently as he thought bitterly that giving France's great enemy an atomic bomb would be adequate revenge for their contempt. The twenty million dollars would help too when he read

172

the inevitable newspaper headline when the bloody thing went off. One thing was for certain. He certainly wouldn't be living anywhere near it.

It has started not very long after he had moved in with Pouneh. He enforced leave was continuing with little prospect on ending in the near future. Indeed, his superiors in the Ministry refused to see him at all. They were at dinner in one of the better fish restaurants in Marseille; one that served its fish simple cooked rather than one of the tourist places that tended to make the whole thing look like Christmas decorations. They had been joined by one of her friends from some embassy or other and, to cut a long story short, he had been persuaded that his erstwhile loyalty to France was misplaced and he would be better advised to join their cause and earn a great deal of money and a new life away from the ignominy that was increasingly surrounding him.

The beach exercise had gone perfectly. The first plutonium had gone, the decoy landed and the biggest of red herrings had been laid with the murder of the three policemen and his erstwhile over Suzanne Blanchard had been appointed to the enquiry. He could keep an eye on all that. Unfortunately, his little disgraced GIGN team had not been big enough to do the job and he had been forced to delve into the Marseille underworld to find some additional men. Payback for the loan of the men had been this ridiculous kidnap idea.

The kidnap of Girondou's wife had been easy enough to organise and its execution had been simple thanks to the two GIGN men who he had leant to the Gangster's brother. Then something had gone very wrong indeed. Something for which he had been totally unprepared. Two completely unknown men had appeared at the house in La Bouilladisse, killed his two men and two of theirs, removed Madame Girondou as easily as if it was a baby from a nursery and returned her safe and sound to her husband within hours of the kidnap. Irrelevant to him, of course, other than the loss of two good men but a fifth member of the kidnap team had been taken too and was in all probability singing like the proverbial canary. The man was one of the locals and his capture didn't worry him too much. He was ignorant of the more important picture. His two men had been highly trained, and he would have put them up against almost anyone. These completely unknown men were obviously someone he should worry about. Presumably they were one of Girondou's men. Dangerous perhaps but still ignorant of what he was up to as was their boss. Fortunately, the conclusion of the plan was only a day or two away.

He felt a momentary flash of regret when he realised that Suzanne would have to die. For a long time, she had been his ride to the top. It was a nasty surprise when he learned that his old lover from their university days had been appointed to investigate his own adventure. Another mental shrug. Tant pis. Maybe he'd give her one last one before he killed her. Maybe at the same time. Suddenly the prospect slightly amused him. If they treated him like a shit, he'd act like it.

He turned, laid a gentle arm across the back of his naked mistress and slipped into an untroubled sleep.

Chapter 13 The Rove Tunnel

Late Morning   The small group was alone in the cold darkness, lit only by a single battery lamp. DuPlessis shuddered in spite of his army training and a heavy overcoat.

'Christ. This is a grim place to plot your campaign to take over in the south of France, especially as it seems to have started with a God almighty fuck up. Where are we?'

Being familiar with the place since childhood, Francois Girondou was more at home with the cold and dank tunnel than his guest. He was, however, extremely nervous. The man in front of him was a professional soldier who showed no fear at all of being alone with a group of heavily armed five strangers, buried deep in a tunnel some thirty metres under the ground with a black, unlit canal lapping indolently against the bank not a metre from his foot. A large, semi-circular brick arched roof vaulted over their heads and disappeared quickly into the blackness in either direction.

'We are in the Rove Tunnel, monsieur. It was built to take barges through a short cut between the Etang de Berre and the Mediterranean. It has been shut since 1963 and we find it a good place to meet and to store things. It is secure from surveillance and easily guarded.'

The GIGN man was not impressed. 'Next time pick somewhere more civilised; a simple bar somewhere would do. Are there any other entrances apart from either end?'

Francois was defensive. 'A rock fall blocks the south exit. There are a few air shafts to the surface, but they have all been sealed. We thought it was somewhere safe to talk.'

'It's a fucking death trap. The sooner I get out the better.' The man's tone turned brisk.

'Now what the hell happened. I lend you two men to help you and they end up dead. One .45 sized hole precisely in the middle of the forehead each. Hollow points.'

Girondou became defensive and shrugged with mock bravado. 'There are plenty of .45 calibre guns around.'

'True Monsieur, but my men were two amongst four, and it takes a very special person to shoot the fourth with the same accuracy as he does the first. The prospective targets tend to get a little restless once they see what's coming. Also this man policed his brass. He was a pro. So who was he? How did they find the house in La Bouilladisse so quickly and how the fuck did they manage to kill four armed men, two of whom were highly trained commandos, take the hostage and vanish without anyone noticing? By the way what the hell happened to the fifth man? We only found four in the house.'

Francois Girondou went pale in the darkness and replied in a low voice.

'He was found on the beach at Port du Bouc, alive but with both knees shattered. His will be in a wheelchair for the rest of his life.'

The GIGN man was a professional soldier but still shuddered at the thought. He got the message even if the idiot in front of him hadn't. He turned to his colleague, drew very close and addressed him in a level monotone.

'Let me sum up. We had a simple arrangement, we two. You supplied some local support for my operation at Beauduc last week, support for which you were handsomely paid, and I agreed to help you replace your brother as the local capo dei capi or whatever you call it here in this part of France.'

The man nodded slowly as DuPlessis continued.

'So now we have a situation where, although everything seems to have gone well at Beauduc, your attempted coup was a disaster. Two of your people are dead as are two of mine. A fifth is a permanent reminder to everyone in the neighbourhood not to mess with your brother insofar as they didn't know it before. The hostage was restored to her loving family almost before she was lifted by person or persons unknown, as they say, and we seem to have collected along the way a highly skilled and completely anonymous killer who seems more likely to get us than we are to get him. You are further away from your cherished seizure of power than you ever were and in all probability you have been rumbled by your bother who is now letting you run around free - or is alive a better word? - in the hope that you would lead him to someone or somewhere interesting - as indeed you have by asking for this meeting. You had better hope that this person is less well informed about my business than he seems to be about yours.'

He looked coldly as his companion. 'Have I left anything out?' Girondou said nothing.

DuPlessis nodded allowing his voice to become friendlier in an attempt to keep Girondou calm.

'In that case, Francois, I suggest that we both lie low for a time while I try to find out who our mystery man is. I don't feel very comfortable about him at all. We have another shipment due to go out soon and I can't afford any mistakes.'

Girondou relaxed.

'Yes, of course. I'll do what I can.' He was obviously relieved that he still seemed to figure in future plans. The four silent men with him also relaxed. Two even finally took their hands from their pockets. The smile that DuPlessis felt inside him did not get anywhere near his face.

'OK. That's it for now. Next time I will organise the meeting.'

The two men exchanged handshakes and the Colonel in charge of the Groupe d'Intervention de la Gendarmerie Nationale walked briskly away through the gloom and back up the tow path beside the black water towards the very dimly lit entrance some four hundred metres away. It would have taken sharp eyes indeed to see the slight nod he gave to two figures standing back invisibly against the tunnel wall, each dressed in full black combat gear carrying

177

silenced Heckler and Koch MP7 A1s and full night vision equipment.

As he passed, they turned noiselessly back down the tunnel towards the group of Frenchmen.

An hour later, sitting in the neat, uncomfortable modern apartment, the home of his next appointment in Greoux-les-Bains, it was DuPlessis who this time felt much less at ease than his host although he didn't show it. He sat in a modest, stiff little arm chair facing a similarly seated, equally anonymous little man in his mid-forties. To one side was a table covered in one of those garish yellow and blue tablecloths covered with images of sunflowers and olives so beloved of Provençale tourist nick-nack sellers. Two small cases lay on the table. One was new, shiny and metal. The other was less stylish, a canvas shoulder bag. DuPlessis had brought the metal case with him and therefore knew what it contained. He also knew what it was supposed to contain. Theoretically, it held half a million Euros; the little man's fee for services rendered. Had the technician dared to count it, he would probably not have seen that all, but a few notes were forged. Neither would he have seen that the case was double skinned and was significantly smaller on the inside than the outside dimensions might have suggested.

No, it was his host's shoulder bag that made him uncomfortable. He had done all the research. He probably knew as much amateur physics about it as any man alive. He knew that the radiation hazard from the alpha particles was virtually nil, the toxicity in a metallic state was lower than many standard poisons. Inhalation was dangerous, but metal gave off very little gas. He knew the bag contained just a small rectangular block of metal, about the size of two king- size cigarette packets stuck together, weighing about 5 kilos. The most danger it posed to him was if he dropped it on his toe and broke something. Nevertheless, it was a malevolent presence in that anodyne room and it made him uncomfortable.

'Right,' he said briskly, looking across at the man. 'That's it. Your payment is in the case. I don't think we have much more to say to each other.'

The other man nodded. DuPlessis had no idea why this middle ranking technician at the nearby Cadaraches nuclear research centre should risk his freedom for a relatively small amount of money - small to his new Iranian friends , that is. Nor did he really know why France had decided some time ago to smuggle shipments of weapons-grade Plutonium 239 from the newly liberated Soviet Union to augment its own, home-produced stock of the stuff and to store them in surprisingly light security at Cadarches rather than at one of their better-known nuclear weapons establishments.

All he knew was that his girlfriend and her friends had known about it and they had convinced him that for Israel to have a nuclear capability while they did not was something that needed to be put right and his new Islamic fundamentalist inclinations required him to do it. The small, shiny metal block a couple of metres away from him was the second of two pieces that, reshaped by machine in a suitable lab and then put together would weigh more than the magical ten kilos which could be made into a critical mass. The first block had gone out from Beauduc a week or so before. This one would follow within a couple of days.

The two men got up together and without further comment or a handshake, DuPlessis lifted the bag off the table and left the room. Rather than putting it on the back seat of his Peugeot, he locked it in the boot, as if, he though grimly, that would make any difference. As he drove back towards Aix-en-Provence past the front gates of Cadaraches itself, he ran through the planning to date. No problem ends that he could think of. The gas main outside the house had been very publicly dug up a couple of weeks before. The announcement of a large explosion in tomorrow's newspapers with a single fatality would be greeted with a resigned Provençale shrug by the readers.

It was a second loose end tied off within a few hours. A good morning's work.

Chapter 14 Briefing with Gentry

The logs crackled in the grate. Outside it was almost dark in spite of only being late afternoon. Both men were stretched out in old leather armchairs, glasses resting on wide stained buttoned arms, both staring moodily into the flames, completely unaware of the similarity of their poses.

Gentry was at his most business-like which clearly meant he had something to say.

'Well, before going on to my stuff, firstly we need to chat about your recent adventure. Any ideas?'

Smith thought for a moment.

'Hum. On the one level, it seems like a simple family squabble if you can describe the internecine strife in the major criminal family in the south of France in those terms. Brother Francois presumably wanted to make a play for power and thought that kidnapping his brother's wife was the way to do it. Pretty bloody stupid, I would have thought, but one can never tell.'

'I agree,' said Gentry taking a pull at his Islay Mist, 'but he would not have reckoned with your intervention, I feel.'

'I'm not sure if that would have made any difference at all. I don't get the impression we are dealing with a criminal mastermind here. However, the actual abduction was reasonably well executed. What interests me is the fact that two of the men at La Bouillardisse weren't locals. Rather more hired guns, I would guess.'

'How do you know?

'Well although it was confirmed by the man I brought back, I knew it back in that room. Two of the men were much too calm. They also both looked at my eyes the whole time, the local peasantry looked at the gun.'

Gentry nodded. It was old field craft. 'So presumably you killed them first?'

'Yes. I did wonder about bringing one of them back but it would have been dangerous on the return journey and I didn't want to waste a lot of time searching them. In any case if they had been properly trained, we wouldn't have got much from them whatever we tried. If they were soldiers, then nothing much would have surprised them. The man we brought back was much more useful, certainly as a messenger.'

'Yes, old friend, I think you got the message through. But if they were hired where did they come from?'

'I've a nasty feeling that they are connected with the Beauduc thing. It always smelt military to me. No real evidence, of course, but if they aren't then we have a very long coincidence on our hands.'

Gentry grunted. He knew what Smith thought about coincidences. Hens' teeth. However, practical as always, he remarked:

'If they were connected then someone's going to be really pissed off.'

'Good, Pissed-off people make mistakes and we need one or two of those at the minute.'

'All very well, Peter. Pushing a stick into a hornet's nest will always get results of some sort, but you don't know how big this particular hornets' nest is.'

'I don't really care, David. If the kidnapping was a purely domestic squabble, then it is really done of our business. Girondou is perfectly capable of sorting the problem out from here. If it was part of a bigger thing, then we will know very soon and be wiser for the knowledge.'

Gentry looked over the rim of his glass and nodded.

'Yes, if Francois is still alive in twenty-four hours then his brother will be allowing him to live. If not, then he will have been disposed of by the others as an obvious security risk.'

'The whole thing was completely stupid and very amateurish so there was probably a very good reason why these two professional soldiers were involved with this bunch of local thugs. However, I can't think of one at the minute.'

'Maybe it was just a matter of manpower. We may be dealing with a very small group of real baddies and perhaps they needed a few more hands at some stage. A sort of quid pro quo. If the baddies aren't locals, they may have needed some local knowledge. Who knows?

Smith felt it was time to move on.

'Thanks for Henk, by the way. Where did you find him?' Gentry waved a vague hand in the air.

'Oh, round and about. You know....'

It was Gentry's way of telling Smith that it was none of his business.

Smith let his anger show slightly.

'Well old friend, next time you find someone 'round and about' as you so quaintly put it, kindly make sure that your discovery isn't gun-shy.'

'What?' Gentry was shocked.

'As you might know if you had actually had to do it more often, Gentry, there is a great deal more to killing someone that being able to shoot. If someone wants to learn the skill, I would suggest he doesn't do it when it is my arse on the line.'

Gentry was stunned.

'Er, he came well recommended. I really don't know what to

say, Peter. I'm truly sorry.'

Smith was not pacified.

'Young Henk may have an immaculate CV and he may indeed end up being good at what he does. But he can get his work experience with someone else, I think. He's not reliable enough for this sort of work at the moment. I rather think that being in the shit with the rest of us is not exactly his metier.'

'Where is he now?'

'I left him doing guard duty with Girondou. You might call him and impress on him the importance of his responsibilities. If he fucks it up, I will kill him myself.'

'Do I tell him that too?'

'He knows it already.'

The two sat in silence while Gentry refilled their glasses. Again it was Smith who moved the conversation along.

'Now tell me what you've got.'

Smith was completely astonished as a section of bookcase in the corner of the room slid silently to one side to reveal a huge plasma screen. In all the years they had been living in Arles, he had never seen Gentry watch a television of any sort let alone something that size. Although there were parts of the great house that Smith had never been in, he was pretty certain that Gentry didn't watch TV. What this monster was used for he couldn't guess. However, his host pressed a remote control and the screen flickered into life. It was by no means perfect. The pictures were slightly indistinct and the motion jerky as the frame rate occasionally slowed but the picture taken from more than three hundred miles up was extraordinarily clear considering it was taken in the middle of an admittedly moonlit night. The drama played out before them. The RIB beached, the buggy arrived. A figure emerged and went ashore. A package was exchanged. At the same time further back three ghostly figures moved up behind three prone figures on the sand some hundred metres back from the shore. The figures jerked once and their assassins turned away. Smith leaned forward slightly towards the screen.

'Wider coverage?'

Gentry shook his head.

'No.'

Smith look across sharply 'Not available or not existing?' Gentry shrugged slightly.

'I am assured that no more exists. Which means..?' Gentry went on as Smith opened his mouth to make the obvious comment. '.. that this was a targeted rather than a random observation.'

They both fell silent digesting the thought that, in spite of French efforts, the Americans had known something about it . Smith looked across.

'This came from...?'

'The CIA.'

'A favour?'

'Not really,' Gentry replied, 'amongst many debts to me, they owe you as well.'

'Me?'

'Yes. Reykjavik you remember .' Smith snorted.

'You can tell your Langley chum that this doesn't even begin to balance that particular account.'

'I already have,' replied Gentry glumly.

'So,' added Smith, 'Apart from confirming what we already knew, or perhaps suspected, all this high-tech stuff adds little more to our picture.'

They sat in silence remembering what they had just seen as well as some previous occasions where there but for the grace of God, or in their case usually Gentry, they would have gone as well. It was he who decided to move the conversation along.

'There is a rumour, a very local one, of course, and a good deal less than reliable, to the effect that the man who was killed in a gas explosion in his house yesterday in Greoux les Bains was up to something at Cadarache.' Smith knew of old that Gentry's reported rumours were invariable true otherwise he would not have bothered mentioning them. Smith had noted a short paragraph at the foot of one of the inside pages of the morning's La Provence, sandwiched between the latest exploits of the Aix-en-Provence High School junior volleyball team and a completely anodyne account of some latest international economic conference that clearly interested the journalist even less than it interested Smith.

'I thought it was a domestic accident. Hadn't they been digging up the gas main in the road? In any case, what do you mean by 'up to something?' Smith's reply was all innocence. Gentry looked sharply over his gold-rimmed glasses at Smith and sighed theatrically.

'The trouble with you, old friend, is that you are getting unimaginative in your retirement. I'm told that this happens sometimes when a lady comes on the scene – or about three in your particular case.'

Smith was first to stop their little game.

'It takes a lot of clout to arrange a team to dig up the road a week before you want to kill someone.'

'Or money,' Gentry nodded, pleased that his companion had not lost the knack of jumping many stages of the analysis at once.

'Tell me about Cadarache.'

Gentry was well prepared for this one and in a few minutes gave a comprehensive account.

'The major installation of the French Nuclear Authority located just outside Aix en Provence. Employs about four thousand people in various departments. Houses a number of the most important nuclear research facilities in Europe including fission and fusion experiments as well as research into handling nuclear materials and general nuclear engineering. It is also, ironically, a major research centre for dealing with nuclear accidents as well as some other departments like microbiology and vegetal research as window dressing for the more sensitive parts of the French chattering classes. All well-publicised and above board - as well as any such facility. What is less public is that it is a major centre for the reception and handling of shipments of plutonium from, shall we say, some of the less respectable parts of the world. For some reason France is buying up a lot of stuff on the black market and most of it comes through Cadarache. Security, I'm told, is not all that it should be as they are trying to draw as little attention to the whole thing as possible. I suspect that this is where our problem originates.'

'What's missing?'

Gentry nodded. Again his friend had jumped to the right conclusion.

'As usual nobody seems to know - or, at least, they're not telling. There are so many things going on at once in the damn place, including some that are secret from most of the people who run it, that their inventory is little more than a hopeful rough guide. The man atomised by his supposedly malfunctioning gas cooker worked officially as a middle grade technician in the new ITER fusion experiment that has recently been located at Cadarache. He had little or no access to anything important.'

Smith's 'but?' didn't need saying.

'He probably was a lab technician but in one of the more embarrassing secret departments.'

Smith remained silent and sure enough a slightly miffed Gentry answered the unspoken question.

'It means that he probably had access to metallic plutonium.'

186

'Shit.'

Instantly Smith felt a frisson crawl up the back of his neck. Like many people he knew enough about plutonium to realise how little, in fact, he really knew. Like most people he was afraid of it and what he imagined it could do. He also knew a little about the world-wide traffic in it that had developed since the new face of the old Soviet Republic had lost control of the second largest nuclear arsenal in the world and started trading it away secretly to maintain its influence. The connections were instant and suddenly the last few days became completely clear in his mind. He understood what was going on. Only the connection between the dead thief and dramatis personae around Suzanne's briefing table remained a bit fuzzy. As usual Gentry supplied the answer, or an important part of it.

'The dead technician worked for a year as a technical advisor to the Special Protection Task Force set up in 1987 within the gendarmerie to escort high risk nuclear shipments around France.'

Smith looked sharply across at his companion. 'And the Task Force Commander was...?'

Gentry nodded grimly.

'Actually, someone completely unremarkable but the second - in - command at the time was your friend Roland DuPlessis'.

Smith sat back in his chair and thought. It now was obvious why the young man had died on the cold beach at Beauduc, why Suzanne's investigation was doomed to get nowhere, why Angèle Girondou had been kidnapped as part of an incidental sub-plot. A few details were imprecise, but the picture was complete. He looked again across at Gentry.

'This isn't finished, is it?'

Gentry shook his head. 'No, otherwise the gas cooker would have exploded a few days ago before that night at Beauduc. There is another shipment to leave. Soon.

Smith replied. 'I need everything on the gendarme Messailles

187

and on DuPlessis. Very fast indeed, David, and I mean everything. I need some documents because the only way to protect Suzanne is to find her an ally and I have a feeling that Messailles might be the man. However, he is an old fashioned, if rather pompous, cop and he will need evidence or at least persuasion. If there is another operation, then obviously this time DuPlessis probably won't rely on anyone local again. He'll have learned his lesson. So, I need to know how many of his elite group are in this with him and who they are. Above all I need to know when and where this all happening.'

'Aren't we drifting a little off our original target, old friend?', Gentry enquired.

'No, I want DuPlessis. This is wrong and that's all I know.'

'You mean you think it's wrong.'

Smith's voice was like granite.

'Yes, and if you don't like it....'

Gentry held up his hand.

'Steady old friend.'

He knew that Smith was more on edge than he appeared. An immediately remorseful Smith grinned an embarrassed apology. No one on earth had held his best interest more closely than Gentry and his comment was plainly ungenerous. He knew it and so did his friend.

There was a silence and they both became thoughtful. Only Gentry, whose relationship with Smith had travelled to and survived many odd places would have the courage to say it.

'You realise, of course, Peter, that killing policemen, however bent, can be a dangerous thing to do, especially if, like DuPlessis, they have friends in high places. He and his little group may not actually be alone. This whole thing seems far too well organised. Someone is backing this from way above the simple operational level. DuPlessis may have to be dealt with but I am not sure if you should probe further up. You might find yourself against someone who you can't just remove from the picture. Even you might need some help from bigger battalions than yours.'

Smith just nodded.

'Voltaire. Very apt under the circumstances. '

Gentry sighed. He knew that one way or another DuPlessis was a dead man. Smith would do it. Smith had always been rather particular about this sort of thing and never delegated.

'Just find out about these two to start with, please, David.

Then I'll see what to do.'

There was an issue that neither had mentioned although for entirely different reasons and it surfaced now. For Gentry it was a matter of analysis. He was the logical one. His pictures were all carefully constructed, piece by interlinking piece. Nothing was added until and unless it derived from something understood and confirmed. The whole structure was had to be accurate, tight, unassailable. Smith's pictures were guesses, illogical jumps, feelings but often annoyingly accurate. He looked at Gentry.

'Suzanne.'

The look of regret in Gentry's eyes was genuine as he nodded slowly. He knew that Suzanne Blanchard was a reluctant favourite of Smith's . Smith felt a dark sadness descend over him.

Gentry continued:

'If you wish it put plainly..' - he ignored Smith's slight shake of the head - 'either she is an innocent patsy put in to do a job, to investigate without success and take the consequent fall or she is up to her slender neck in the whole thing in which case you will have to join the lengthening list of people lining up to kill her. And' - he continued as he saw Smith opening his mouth to reply - 'you will have to tell the Aubanet family either way; once you know, of course. In other words, she is a problem to be added to your list.'

Smith nodded sadly. He had a dreadful feeling that he knew the answer already. There was a long silence before Smith said anything.

'Shit.'

Gentry was uncompromising: 'Yes, I think that just about describes it.'

The silence continued as Gentry listened to Smith sorting it all out in his head. He knew better than to interrupt. Smith was travelling fast now, caught between a problem to resolve and a revenge to plan. This was the moment he stayed silent and waited for instructions. Smith was planning, and people would get hurt. They usually did. Only once in thirty years of working together since the days they were in university together had he ever known Smith to give up. That had been about eight years ago when he had sent Deveraux into Somalia alone to bring Smith home. His friend was brought back to the UK on the broad back of the man who killed so many of them that they had refused to believe that a whole squad had not been sent. One man's bloodbath. It had taken more than a year to put Smith back together, but he had done it, more or less. It had been he who had sent Smith to Somalia in the first place

'The question is: whose side is she actually on?'

It was more a statement than a question because they both knew they didn't have an answer. A thought occurred to Gentry and he looked up sharply to Smith.

'I don't suppose we missed anything the last time, did we?'

Smith nodded slowly. It was a possibility that he had been considering too.

'Maybe. We were possibly too focussed on DuGresson to look much wider. To be fair, at the time, there was very little reason not to be. She could have been involved in the fraud as well but even if she was, it hardly explains any of this.'

'Only to confirm that she's bent as well,' was Gentry's

slightly tired observation.

Smith nodded again.

'It's too much of a coincidence to think that she would have been appointed to investigate the very conspiracy that she was involved in – at least unless the people behind the plot and the investigation are one and the same.

This time it was Gentry nodding. 'Yes. Depressing thought, isn't it?'

Smith rallied.

'No. I can't see it somehow. She would know that she would be under intense scrutiny. She couldn't possibly risk it.' Smith paused and after a moment continued:

'Unless, of course, this all dates from her university days.

Our friend DuPlessis?'

Gentry was pleased. 'Ah now you are getting somewhere, my friend. I don't think that she is in on it, as they say, but she would be an invaluable source of intelligence for DuPlessis if he is actually our man.'

'It also puts her in great danger'.

Finally Smith stirred onto more practical matters. Unsurprisingly it was a shopping list.

'I want to know who appointed Suzanne to this commission of enquiry and why. I know she can call the President but who else? I want to know who she has worked for since she worked for anyone. She is a friend of DuPlessis. I need to know whether he is a friend taking advantage of her or whether they are in this together. If the latter, I want to know what they are doing apart from what we know already. I need to know who she has been calling on that mobile that Deveraux can't crack. I need to know if she is dangerous. I left her at the mas for Christ's sake.'

Gentry said nothing, remembering with some affection the days when he had a staff, a huge library and archive and a Cray T3E at his disposal.

'All right old friend, I'll see what I can dig up.' Smith got up to go.

'I'm having an early supper in town with Martine. Lets talk later.'

Chapter 15 Supper with Martine

In reality, being followed is a state of mind rather than anything much more significant. Although the covert observation of one person by another as they walk or drive along a road has become one of the staple fills for many thriller stories, there is a great deal less to following someone or being followed, melodramatic as it might sound, that meets the eye. There is a rapidly increasing number of ways of following someone or finding out where they are without skulking along behind them looking like a character out of a bad movie. CCTV is everywhere and most of these cameras feed their images into recording devices of some sort with varying degrees of clarity and permanence. Virtually all street lamps in central London, for instance, have integral cameras. Cameras exist now in virtually every public building to which the public has access. Public transport and many roads are covered; many private buildings, too. Add to those tens, probably hundreds of thousands of cameras, GPS chips in telephones, in tablet computers, and in many cars, computer records of credit card use, almost unavoidable in an increasingly cash-free life, toll road date stamps, car park tickets and so on ad infinitum, electronic chips in your dog's neck, even, the fact that almost none of the terabytes of data collected daily end up in remotely secure places makes actually tracking someone increasingly easy. Actually staying a few metres behind them as they walk along the street is unnecessary, fun as it might sound.

The default now is to assume that you are being followed in some way, all the time. Thus, the fact that he was being followed as he set out from his house with Arthur to take a short walk and meet Martine for supper didn't bother Smith too much, primarily because he didn't care. He had realised years before most people that avoiding being followed was impossible. Nor was he particularly interested in why he was being followed. Again, he had stopped asking that particular question years before. Depending of which particular life he was leading at the time the chances of his being followed were either infinitesimal or certain. This time, given that he and Gentry were poking a stick into some very sensitive bits of higher French life, the fact that someone was now following him was no surprise at all. What was a surprise was that the man was good? Very good. Very good indeed. In fact, one of the very best that Smith had ever encountered. There were no oddly frozen members of the public badly reflected in shop windows; no people wearing inappropriate hats. In fact, no-one at all. However, with a lifetime of experience Smith knew. He simply felt it and knew it. He was being followed.

With Arthur ambling along at his side, peering around balefully for cats to kill, he was walking down through the town, down the rue de la Calade, across the place de la République and on down the Rue de la République towards the little cafe in the Roquette. Precisely with this sort of possible diversion in mind he had given himself an extra half an hour. It reminded him of the first time he had shared a meal with her in the same place a year or so back. He had had to shake a tail then, although it had turned out to be her driver rather than one of the bad guys. He hadn't found it difficult then and it wouldn't now in spite of the tail being infinitely more professional. For Smith also knew what many people who had led similar lives had learned. Having a tail was only a problem if you couldn't lose it when you wanted to. That was the secret and he knew he could.

The main point is whether the person who is being followed actually cares or not. Smith would never have tried to avoid being followed, especially by someone so expert. He could however bring the process to an end if he wished. Losing a tail is a matter of knowing where you are better than the person who is tailing you. Whatever his follower may have known, he was almost certainly a stranger to Arles. Professionals like him had little business in the town to make them resident. Smith knew the little streets and alleyways much better than most. He had been walking them since his childhood. He not only knew where they all led and met, crossed and intertwined, he also know which of the street-side doors were open and which were not and where they led. He knew many of the people who lived behind those doors. The Roquette, the old quarter to the west of the town, had been the place where Arles river-based maritime life had flourished from before the Roman occupation to the time the trains arrived early in the nineteenth century and destroyed the river-born transportation of goods that had kept Arles alive for so long. The quarter is riddled with tiny streets narrow enough to remain cool even in high summer, alleys, passages, cut-throughs, and tunnels from one house to the next; from one street to the next. As long as the follower didn't maintain always direct line of sight with the person followed, the next corner would always provide Smith an opportunity to vanish. More than that, it was an opportunity to turn the tables.

Having made a couple of changes of route to bring him onto the road than ran parallel to but a block behind his destination, he turned yet another corner he had about ten seconds before the man followed him. Possibly more because the man wouldn't actually want to turn a blind corner in pursuit without caution. It was all too easy to walk into a gun barrel that way. It was more than enough time to open a stout plain door set flush into the wall slip through, Arthur close behind. He turned and shut the surprisingly silently swinging door behind him and pushed a large deadbolt home.

The evening was drawing in as Smith emerged a few moments from the narrow fisherman's house behind his erstwhile follower not, as he expected, to see a confused person looking this way and that trying to pick up the trail but just in time to see him being picked up by an anonymous black Renault and whisked away. What made the car remarkable was that it was both very clean and undamaged, making it a rare vehicle in Arles. Smith's first and only view of his pursuer was also significant. The head that quickly disappeared into the car sported a very military haircut and it was on top of a lean, fit looking body clothed un-ostentatiously but effectively in black chinos, black polo shirt and sweater. 'A professional,' thought Smith. An amateur would have stayed and tried to continue. This man knew immediately that he had been dumped and that he was therefore now in danger himself from the person he had hitherto been following. Time to bale out and for someone else to pick up the whole thing later. That's the way these things worked in the real world. Smith had no idea which of the many agencies that were part of the picture were actually after him, but it didn't really matter. This was his home turf not theirs and he had just demonstrated that by vanishing. Hopefully the message would get through. He was mildly concerned that they had go onto him so soon. Madam Blanchard might be a good person to ask.

Finding him would have been no problem. The only way to hide from followers was to vary routes and routines almost constantly. Given the size of Arles and the fact that he lived in the middle of town there had never seemed any point of trying to disguise anything. At least whoever it was would know now, if they didn't from the body count a yesterday, they weren't dealing with an amateur.

He continued his perambulation and within a few minutes had confirmed that the man had had no back-up nor were there any other undesirables about - at least not ones that were interested in him. To be sure he did a couple of back doubles and managed to arrive in the cafe exactly on time. Martine, as usual, was there before him, sitting in the high-sided booth at the back. It was where they always sat, well away from the street and nearest the kitchen with its back exit and cellar exits below. One even led directly to the river bank.

Arthur, with every indication of complete intimacy with the place, walked slowly but purposefully around the corner into the kitchen in search of his own supper. He knew that he had not been disappointed in the past and he was a creature of habit. Tradition is important to a greyhound.

Many misconception exist concerning the Mediterranean in general and Provence in particular. Two major ones are that van Gogh painted everything bright yellow and that all Mediterranean cooking is based on the tomato. As he looked down with considerable anticipation at the plate that had just been set in front of him, he smiled at the thought. Tomatoes were actually completely unknown in Mediterranean cooking before the first few decades of the nineteenth century. Many wonderful sauces exist far from the overblown virtues of the dreaded red vegetable. Only small amounts of taste are all that are needed for a well-made pasta. Most modern sauces ignore the fact that pasta actually has a taste of its own without any sauce. Factories that make many thousands of tons of pasta daily course ignore that. Pasta-making is a time consuming and skilled art. Made slowly by hand, not with some badly cleaned complicated a little machine - for that is what they all become after a while - rolled out with a wooden roller that is less than an inch wide at most and about 3 feet long, it is a dish in itself. Even butter, olive oil and a little salt and pepper are not strictly necessary for a good pasta. The Tellines were sweet and, were Smith was relieved to see, out of their shells. The tiny little clams that were one of the precious delicacies of the otherwise pretty barren Camargue coast between Montpellier and Arles were in season for much of the year and formed the basis of a completely delicious pasta sauce, made without the arrivist tomato. Butter, olive oil, salt and pepper, a little white wine and cream and a small bay leaf were all that is needed to bring the taste out and make a simple sauce fit for the gods. God forbid the ubiquitous grated cheese. Chefs have rightly killed for less.

Smith had a real dislike of eating with his fingers, fiddling about getting microscopic pieces of shellfish out of their shells or generally making eating more complicated than it needs to be and was delighted to find that someone in the kitchen, presumably accompanied by instructions from Madame and much shaking of heads as a consequence, had been persuaded to extract the tiny morsels of meat for him. The shells were, of course, essential for the taste of the sauce, but Smith was unrepentant and would have declined the dish had he been required to work for his food. Most shellfish is, after all, he thought, taste not texture. In any case he had a particular antipathy to losing bits of sauce up his finger nails.

Looking across the little table he saw that his companion was smiling in that habitual mocking, loving sort of way that he was having to get used to. They were sitting on one of the small restaurants that the Aubanet family owned or ran in Arles and in some surrounding small towns. In them you ate some of the very best food that Provence could provide. Pure, nourishing, simple but immensely skilled cooking with exclusively local, fresh ingredients, cooked to order and never before. You had to wait. No stars, ratings, listings in important guides or publicity. No credit cards either. Occasionally if the family knew you and you lived in the town, no money either. Locals who had difficulty paying their rent or their taxes could often eat for nothing. Payment was mostly in kind. A little help keeping the cafe clean, doing the proverbial washing up, some fetching and carrying, painting and plumbing when necessary. Local eyes keeping the place secure. There are all sorts of ways of paying for a good meal and a gold card is a long way down the list here.

Madame, as usual was looking devastating. Hire piled up on top of her head in the Arlesian fashion. White blouse and back trousers. A tight belt around her waist and the gold Croix des Saintes on her lapel. Not for the first time did Smith think that he was in the company of the most beautiful woman he had ever met. She had the courtesy to blush slightly when he told her so.

'You know, Martine, this reminds me of Madam Rozier and her little restaurant on the rue Porte de Laure.'

'Madam Rozier?'

'Perhaps we should eat our Tellines as it is a little story and I wouldn't want them to go cold.'

They ate in silence. Conversation usually gets in the way of good food and Martine's cousin who was doing the cooking that evening would have been mortified had they just stuffed their faces while talking. He may willingly have given much of his food away but he was none the less a very proud cook indeed. Good food needs concentration like a good book or a Mozart piano concerto. You keep silent. Anything else is disrespectful.

The dish was quite delicious. There was a real taste of the sea and the Tellines were sweet and tender without being tough from over-cooking. Unlike with many so-called pasts dishes, they could still taste the egg and the flour of the pasta. They both finished more or less together, and Martine looked at him expectantly. Smith was pleased because he could at last talk about an Arles before she was born. He took a sip of his crémant and began.

'I believe that Marc Twain was referring to a view when he said that distance lends enchantment or some such. For me it's probably time. For I have a fond and, by now, probably completely erroneous memory of my all-time favourite place to eat in Arles which closed more than forty years ago. It was just a door about half way along the rue Porte de Laure. I don't recall windows although if there were any, they were certainly shuttered closed in the evening. The mean was entirely too important to be disturbed by passing tourists peering through the windows. The door remained completely closed thought the day and opened at eight 'o clock only for enough time for the first twenty of the larger number of people who had formed an orderly queue in the street outside, to enter. No reservations were possible. There was no telephone. After the twentieth had entered the door was then closed and locked irrespective of whether that split mother from father or husband from wife. You were sat at a single long table, usually next to someone whose acquaintance you had made only a few moments before in the queue outside. You were then fed. No menu. No wine card. No choice. The proprietor, cook, waitress, a large bustling woman of indeterminate age speaking in the broadest Rodanenc, served you a succession of substantial dishes that were handed out to her by a disembodied hand through a small sliding hatch in the wall. The table was lined with unlabelled open bottles of wine. At ten thirty you were completely full, half (or completely) drunk and Madam then put a small stained piece of card in a large earthenware bowl in the middle of the table. The card bore the amount of money that each person had to throw into the bowl. When the settling up had been done, and checked, of course, with forensic intensity, the door was re-opened, and you were ushered out, whereupon the door closed until 8:00pm next evening.'

'The restaurant closed when she died but, on the many occasions when, as a completely penniless teenager, I visited visit Arles, picking up odd jobs like attending in a petrol station on the Route d'Avignon or similar, I used to do the washing up after the guests had departed and then she fed me too. Occasionally when it was raining, I slept on the table too.'

Martine Aubanet held his hand and squeezed it.

'A nice story. Sometimes, Peter, I think you're more Arlesian than I am.'

Smith smiled at the thought.

'Perhaps, my dear, but I think that having a family history here of more than a thousand years here gives you a slight head start, I would have thought.'

'Perhaps. Perhaps. But there is a difference that is important, to me at least. I was born here. It is completely true that I love this little bit of the Camargue and could not seriously think of living anywhere else. But I was born into that love. As a member of the family I was born into its history and its responsibilities. In a way I had no choice. My father had no son and so I must take things forward. My place here is not just a choice, unlike yours, my dear. You could have gone anywhere to live and you chose here. That, amongst many other things, is what makes you special to me and my father. You weren't told to love the place. You just do.'

Smith knew this was true without really being able to explain it. He'd been coming to Arles since he was a child. When, a few years before, he was deciding where to hide in his retirement, in reality, he had had no choice either.

The moment was interrupted by the arrival of their main course. The chef had again been forewarned about Smith's slightly difficult culinary preferences for while Martin had two small but complete pigeons on her plate, Smith was offered three complete pigeon breasts, off the bone and split in half and covered with a simple sauce from the cooking. A plate with a few fresh vegetables was placed on the table together with an unlabelled bottle of wine. Both food and wine were completely delicious and, as before, consumed in near silence. Smith watched with amusement as his beautiful companion took her meal literally in hand and tore it apart with thoroughly un-ladylike relish.

The meal was perfect. A very far cry from what passed for haut cuisine in other, more glamourous Arles restaurants. The food had no foam, no extraneous decorative bits and pieces, swirls of this and that, odd fronds of foreign greenery and other Christmas decorations and was infinitely the better for all that. Simple food, fresh local ingredients cooked expertly with the minimum amount of fuss and the maximum amount of knowledge. All served on simple round white plates. Martine's cousin knew he was a great cook and saw no reason to prove it to anyone. The food did that. His pleasure was obvious and Martine saw it. Reaching across the table she took Smith's hand and smiled.

'You should know how much Philip appreciates it when he
200

sees that look on your face.'

'It's very easy to enjoy food that is as close to perfection as this is.

'Yes,' she replied. But ever more than most, you are a particular customer. He said to me some time ago that he liked cooking for you because he felt you understood what he was doing. He called you my Englishman and said that I was lucky to have found someone who understood food and wine and felt no need to talk about it. You should understand that this is very high praise indeed from a man who hardly ever says anything nice about anyone.'

At that point a slightly lethargic Arthur emerged from the general direction of the kitchen as if to check they were still there. Having confirmed that they were indeed still sitting in the restaurant he turned back the way he had come, not before Smith had noticed a dampness around his muzzle. No supper for you this evening, my friend, Smith thought.

Martine became business-like.

'So, how is your investigation going?'

Smith grimaced, reluctant to be brought back to reality.

'Well, until this afternoon, very slowly but Gentry managed to find some satellite video of the incident.'

'I thought you said there wasn't any.'

'No, that's what Suzanne has been told by her various policemen, but she shouldn't have believed them. Even if there is no French film, there was certainly American footage. They tend to film everything all the time. What we saw was a very well planned, military operation on both sides which was more to do with getting something out of the country than someone into it. It is perfectly reasonable to assume that if all you are doing is observing an operation to land a terrorist into France, there is no real reason why anyone should get killed at all, let alone three. Quite the contrary, you would have thought. The very last thing you would have wanted to do would be to draw attention to what you were doing by needlessly killing people. It should have had the authorities even more determined to find the culprits. These were trained men, Martine, not any old Tom, Dick or Francois. They shouldn't have been easy to kill. The stakes were obviously very much higher'

'What stakes, Peter. What was being shipped out?'
'Plutonium, it seems.'

A substantial glass of a pale, straw-coloured Marc had mysteriously appeared at his elbow and he took a sip and thought a bit more as the smooth fiery river slipped down his throat.

He knew exactly what she was going to say, before she said it.

'Peter this is much too big, surely? You can't possibly do anything about it all yourself.'

Smith let a note of exasperation creep into his voice.

'Firstly, my dear,' he answered a little testily, 'it was never my intention to take on the whole French government, police and military and I'm mildly pissed off that you seem to know me so badly that you would ever think it. I believe I've made my thoughts perfectly plain. Whatever this is all about, I have very little interest in what I believe is known these days as the bigger picture. France can clear up its own mess without my personal help. All I'm interested in is helping a rather noble but very confused old man come to terms with the fact that he has lost a second member of his family within his own lifetime in the service of France. It is bad enough to outlive your son but to outlive your grandson is particularly harsh.'

Martine felt such a depth of emotion in his voice that she wondered momentarily whether there was yet another layer of Smith's past that she knew nothing about. Smith continued:

'He is proud and honourable man who does not deserve to be lied to glibly by a bunch of self-serving senior politician's and

202

military. Nor does he deserve to see the illegal murder of his beloved grandson go un-marked, investigated and, above all, un-revenged. The state has a bad track record for delivering justice to its citizens and France's is worse than most. More than many, I have good reason to know this and I would have thought that you with your family history going back through centuries of pain and difficulty would understand that. I can never bring happiness or even peace to this old man. He will live the rest of his life in sorrow. I will not allow him to live that time in ignorance. He's old, not foolish and has a right to our respect'

Martine again remained silent for she knew there was more to come.

'I'm fully aware that I am putting myself at risk but that doesn't concern me. I am alive today because others put themselves at risk for me from time to time. I regard my life as precious but only up to a point. I also know that I am putting others at risk because of what I believe. Gentry is used to this sort of stuff. I make no apologies either for involving you and your family in this too. I suspect that your father would understand what I mean, and I would have hoped that you would too.'

There was a long silence and Smith again felt that combination of indignation and guilt for having said something in the heat of the moment that he almost instantly regretted. Martine need no reminding by an outsider of what were the standards and morality that governed life in the Camargue. It was because they were so close to his own that he felt so comfortable there himself. His embarrassment was cut short as Martine reached across the narrow table, took his hand and raised it to her lips. She was immediately practical.

'What can we do, Peter. How can we help you?'

Smith squeezed her hand and didn't let it go. Out of the corner of his eye he saw Philippe with a slight smile on his face through the open door to the kitchen as he pretended to busy himself over the stove.

'Most of all, you should keep yourself safe at the Mas. I don't think we are up against too many, but they are well trained and therefore dangerous. I can't see them wasting their time going for you and your father even if they know your connection with me. If they are anything like as professional as I think they are, they will keep focussed on what matters. However, I am unsure about Suzanne and where she stands on all this. While she is staying wth you, then at least you can keep an eye on her. You must move from your cottage into the mas of course and Jean Marie should be reminded about general security. Is he driving you tonight?'

Martine nodded.

'Yes, I can talk to him on the way home.'

Smith continued. 'I think that I need to have a chat with Suzanne. She is either up to her pretty neck in all this or is in considerable danger. Possibly both. I need to have another word with Gentry to see if we can dig up some more information on the Paris end of all this.'

He caught her glance.

'No, my dear, not for any reason other than an attempt to know about our situation here a little more closely. Whether or not she is involved as an investigator or a conspirator, she is certainly involved. If she's not on the side of the ungodly I would be unhappy if harm came to her.'

Martine nodded, leaving the alternative unsaid.

It was time to leave. A reluctant Arthur was retrieved from one of the rooms at the back of the cafe where he had started to sleep off his own supper. Smith thanked the cook and, having waited for the dark shape of the one of the Aubanet's black Range Rover to pull up in front, escorted Martine out of the restaurant. He didn't need to check if the coast was clear. Jean Marie would have checked before coming. Equally he didn't need to tell the young driver to take a different route home. His training over the last few months had found a adept and talented student. He opened the door for her and after a rather perfunctory exchange of kisses watched the car driving off towards the Tranquetaille bridge and the depths of the Camargue.

This time he was concerned. He had decided to walk back to the Hauteur, the part of Arles where he lived, along the Rhone river bank. It was a favourite route and would have normally taken him past the Tranquetaille bridge on to the ruins of the so-called Baths of Constantine, one of the last vestiges of the extensive Roman forum that once made up of most of urban Arles two thousand years ago. The path was high on the riverbank and was built up so that the wall would contain the worst excesses of the flooding that periodically had engulfed the town over the centuries and was lit by the dimmest possible set of streetlights. He felt that for the second time that evening he was being followed. One of the virtues of the riverside bank was that it was very open and thus being followed without being obvious was almost impossible. Obviously, no-one was in sight but again he knew. Apart from his own senses, Arthur stopped to look back over his shoulder from time to time. Sound or smell, the dog knew someone was keeping track of their slow evening perambulation.

He slowed a little to give himself time to think. He could just ignore it of course. Had it been someone amateur or obvious, this is what he would have done. Neither Gentry nor Girondou would put a tail on him, even for benign reasons, without telling him. This was different, and it made him uncomfortable. The image of those dark shapes left on the Beauduc beach came to mind. Never a man to be nervous about anything he was getting a little fed up. Basically, he couldn't figure out why he was being followed. The kidnapping had left no traces for the ungodly to get hold of. Nor had his general investigations with Gentry. The only possibility was Suzanne either inadvertently or on purpose. If the source of the interest in him was Suzanne, then the man following would be official. If it was one of DuPlessis's people then they may or may not be official depending of how dirty DuPlessis was. The only common factor was Suzanne. Either way he found himself getting angry.

Somewhat to Arthur's unhappiness who was walking as usual without any protection against the icy wind, Smith sat on the wall that ran around the top of the river embankment and dug his satellite phone out of his pocket. He started to talk the moment the phone was answered.

'Suzanne, have you put a tail on me?' 'No, of course, not.'

In fact it was the wrong answer. If she knew nothing about it would have been a longer reply.

'That's OK then. That means you won't mind.'

Her uncertainty was clear over the telephone line. After a distinct pause, she re-joined the conversation:

'What do you mean, Peter?'

'It means that you won't be sad to hear that the man following me will be dead within the next five minutes.'

This time the silence was longer. Smith continued: 'Perhaps you might like to try the question again, Suzanne.' This time the voice was somewhat more contrite.

'It is only for your own good.' Smith let the steel show through.

'Suzanne, I have two things to say to you. Withdraw this man immediately. If he is not gone within five minutes you can fish him out of the Rhone with a boat hook in half an hour. I won't answer for whether you will need a hospital or a morgue. You will never out a tail on me again. Also, you will never, and I mean never, again tell anyone where Martine or I can be found. If you do I will come for you and your employers, whoever they might be, will be spared the expense of your old age pension. You may be family, Suzanne, but you are not my family.'

He rang off without encouraging further conversation and continued his walk home. He had only walked a few metres further past the Musée Réattu before both he had Arthur sensed that their companion was no longer there. The next call was to Gentry.

'That bloody woman put a tail on me."

'Oh dear,' Gentry sighed, 'Has the unfortunate person survived to tell the tale?'

Smith, he knew, had very little time for people who tried to follow him and tended to take somewhat extreme measures when he encountered the problem.

'Yes, on this occasion, at least.'

'Peter, old chum. Is all this lovey-dovey stuff making you soft?

Chapter 16   Paris Meeting

One of the best views in Paris was ignored as the four men sat in a rough square of four deep leather armchairs. They were in a large apartment on the fifth and top floor of the building that curved partially around the western end of the Ile St Louis. Below them the four little brasseries that crowded the end of the island where the Pont St Louis bridge spring across to the Ile de la Cité were all quite full. Even in mid-winter the cafes did a good business and there was a good number of tourists wandering around. The view, of course, was across the short distance to the ghostly floodlit shape of the eastern end of the great cathedral of Notre Dame. This was rightly the most expensive real estate in Paris and had long been home to many of the great and the good.

Each had a small table to one side bearing a full glass. The room was lit only by the library lights that cast a gentle glow down over the bookcases that lined the walls between the windows. The books were ornate and the gold blocking and deeply coloured leather on their spines gave a rich and varied patina to the sides of the great room. The huge Venetian chandelier above their heads was unlit and glinted from time to time as the pendants twisted in the slight air currents made by the heating. Darkly lustrous oil paintings in deep gilt frames punctuated the bookcases, each again illuminated by a picture light. The six windows that gave a full three quarter circle view over the city were un-curtained and their folding wooden shutters were left unopened in their recesses on either side of the window casements. Thick, dark, valuable Persian and Afghan rugs covered the Parquet de Versailles floor.

Three were old friends and colleagues Although in public they seemed to represent widely different parts of the political spectrum, in reality on the more important issue of money, they were united. They were well-known public figures of great fame and distinction. Two were current cabinet members. The third was an ex-minister of state of a very different political persuasion to the others. They had collaborated many times in the past and had become powerful and rich in equal measure as a result. The fourth man was slightly darker skinned but to all intents and purposes he was from a similar mould. In their time all had been lawyers, bankers. They were all still freemasons - even the Arab. All four were immaculately dressed in dark suits, white shirts and sober ties. Modest cufflinks, highly polished leather shoes and black socks.

The silence between them was profound interrupted only by the occasional clink of ice melting slowly in the cut glasses. At length one of the men broke the silence.

'So, time to take stock, I believe. Where are we exactly?' A second man put his glass down softly.

'Well. The first shipment went out OK. The operation went as planned.'

The first continued in a calm, low tone, almost conversationally.

'Well not exactly, I fear. The beach operation went as we wished. The investigation was started as we planned. Madam DuGresson was put in charge and she seems to have got nowhere as we anticipated. However, something seems to be happening that we didn't anticipate and, I must admit, I am a little concerned.'

The other two Frenchmen shifted uncomfortably in their chairs. If their host was indeed concerned, then neither would make the mistake of underestimating it. In the past men had died doing that. Before either of them could reply, the Arab raised his hand slightly of the buttoned leather arm and interrupted gently.

'I wonder if we might concentrate for the moment on the core issue; the transfer of the merchandise. What may or may not be happening on the ground is not my concern. We have an agreement; gentlemen and it is very simple one. You have agreed to deliver to me twelve kilos of weapons grade metallic plutonium divided, for obvious reasons, into two shipments and, in return, I have agreed to pay you sixty million dollars. You have safely delivered the first half of the shipment and you have received half the payment. I am told that the plutonium is of the correct specification and we are delighted. My sole concern is the second shipment which I gather is scheduled for the day after tomorrow.'

He paused to take a sip of his drink. No-one said anything for their paymaster was clearly not finished. He put down his glass and stared past them towards that great symbol of a very different faith to his glowing dimly in the night sky. He, alone amongst those present, slightly enjoyed the silence. Finally, he dropped his gaze to his host.

'All I need is your assurance that the second delivery will take place as agreed. If you can give me that, I will leave you to your discussions. Any other matters are not germane, to me at least.'

His host nodded.

'I can give you that assurance.'

The Arab nodded briskly and got up from his chair while at the same time restraining the others from rising with a gesture.

'Good.'

He nodded again to the three, turned and walked towards the door which opened a split second before he reached it. Another silence descended on the remaining group while each marshalled his thoughts for the discussion to come. As usual the host started things off briskly.

'Right. To what extent is this, shall we say, trouble, likely to endanger the second shipment? If the answer is no, then we can look a little at the detail of what seems to be happening.'

'Can we reschedule to transfer until we are a little clearer about what is going on? Take some precautions, for instance.'

'You heard our friend. I didn't get the impression that that is an option.'

'Then we must proceed as planned. Tell DuPlessis that he is to continue and that we expect the right result.'

'OK. Now what is happening down there.' The third man sighed.

'It was always likely to become messy after we heard about the leak from Marseille and DuPlessis decided he wanted to cover his traces on the beach. We agreed, you will remember, because we needed to keep DuPlessis on side and he is, after all, the man on the ground. Although we contained the official enquiry, something more seems to have developed completely outside our control or knowledge. Perhaps we should try to find out and do something about it.'

'Yes, in retrospect that may not have been such a good decision.'

Their host shook his head slightly.

'I rather think not at this stage. However, we are stuck with it and I rather think that we should take a leaf out of our client's book. Concentrate on what is important and leave the whys and wherefores to later - if at all. We have precious little time before the second shipment is handed over and I don't think that we could do much. What is crucial is whether or not this extraneous matter is going to endanger the plan. If it is then we must, of course, act quickly. If not then we can leave it if necessary for later. We keep our eyes focussed on delivering the second shipment. Nothing else matters. If that is screwed up then our Arab friends are going to be unhappy and we know what that means.'

All three did know what it meant, and it was not a happy prospect. He continued after a thoughtful pause.

'We already knew that DuPlessis was a bit of a loose cannon, but he is, unfortunately, the only game in town at the moment. My feeling is that we have no choice but to stick to the original plan. DuPlessis must be told that he is to continue as we agreed and get the shipment out. We don't want any more excursions or excitements on the side. We have plugged the Marseille leak so there is no reason why the arrangements should become public again. My vote is to have a stiff word with DuPlessis and carry on. What do you think?'

The other two nodded, finished their drinks and soon left via the elevator that would take them without stopping down to the small cellar garage and their waiting armoured limousines. A passageway converted from a medieval tunnel would take them under the river to an exit above ground behind the Bibliothèque Fourny on the north bank some hundred metres north of the river bank.

Their host refilled his glass and crossed the room to sit in the Eames recliner placed behind the central window that looked west over the city. He sat looking intently and for a long time across the short distance to the great cathedral standing in a ghostly pale grey light and at the dark river that slipped blackly along either side of it. He was not troubled in any great way. He had anticipated this. Not in the sense that he felt that anything was likely to go wrong with the plan. It was just, he felt, a foolish man who would not cover the possibility. He, more than the others, knew that failure was not an option. They would succeed, and he would receive the additional personal bonus that he had negotiated with the Arabs. If he failed, he was a dead man. It was that simple.

He picked his secure satellite phone from the floor beside him and made a phone call

Chapter 17   Interventions from the Ungodly

Fortunately Smith was excused from making an immediate response by the sound of his satellite phone. He switched it onto the loudspeaker. What came over the 2000 km round trip via the low earth orbit satellite network was a somewhat different Deveraux from the one he had been speaking to a few hours earlier.

'We've had a bit of an incident, boss.' Smith said nothing and waited.

'Three men came over land. Equipped, trained, the lot. They were good. Very good. Some of the best I've seen.'

'And?' Smith's heart had stopped.

'Two dead, one disabled and alive. Just. Household safe and unharmed. I made sure of that. They probably don't know yet what happened.'

Smith came back to life. 'Debt cancelled, Deveraux.'

'Never really was one, boss. You are not the only person to value friendship.'

He was silenced for a moment by the reply. Gentry smiled thinly over his glass of scotch. Neither of them wanted to go down that line yet. Maybe later.

'Your boy Jean Marie was good. He got the third as he was getting into the house. I was a bit busy at the time.'

'You?'

'A few grazes and scrapes. Nothing to worry about.' Gentry leaned over and took the phone.

'Don't piss me off , Deveraux. I want a better answer than that.'

'Sorry, Sir. One 9mm slug in the left upper chest, not fatal but losing blood at a decent rate of knots. Large split in head. I may have been out for a few moments. Bit of a knife wound in the leg. Mobile though.'

'The captive?'

'Jean Marie has him in the stables. I just managed to stop him cutting him up to make stew with tomatoes, garlic and rosemary.'

Gentry continued with the debrief. 'How long, start to finish?'

'About six minutes, give or take.'

'Jesus' thought Smith. 'This was a fire fight.'

He repossessed the phone.

'Get yourself into the house and get some treatment fast. Martine knows about you. I will contact Jean Marie and organise a perimeter. A bunch of reinforcements will arrive. They will look a bit basic, I suspect, they will be at least competent. Try not to kill them. I'll be there in twenty minutes.'

'Oh, by the way, boss.' Smith paused expectantly. 'Yes?'

'Just as the bad guys arrived, Suzanne drove out. Black Citroen.

Very fast. I don't know where to. The gates were open, however.' 'In all how long ago?'

'Forty-five minutes, no more. Sorry, boss, not to call you sooner. I was a little preoccupied. But she did get one of those mysterious calls a few minutes before she left in a hurry.'

Smith stiffened as one of a number of thoughts - all bad or worse - occurred to him

'Make my return time forty-five minutes. Now fuck off and get some treatment. Stay in touch. I doubt whether there are any more to come. They would not have expected to find you there so the chances of a backup plan are small. But you never know.'

Smith broke the connection and remained motionless for a few seconds. Gentry too. This was Smith's game. He was the planner now. They were moving too fast for details.

Smith dialled Martine. She answered calmly and a touch quizzical. Smith's heart went out to her.

'Perhaps you might like to tell me what is going on, Peter?'

'Nothing much, my dear, but in a few moments a man called Deveraux will come into the house. You will recognise him because he has a bullet wound in the chest, a knife wound in the leg and a large bump on the head. Please give him some treatment. Be kind to him as he is the reason you and you father are still alive. He will probably make a great mess on your carpet. If you tie him back together nicely, ask him to play the piano for you. You might be surprised. I'll be back in an hour.'

'Peter,' she interrupted, anxious not finish the call, 'you might like to know..'

'Yes, I do. Suzanne has left. Stupid bitch.' This time he cut her off. Jean Marie was next. 'How is he. Your guest, that is?'

'Not very well, monsieur but still alive. I think he knows that I don't like flics.'

Smith grimaced. For even the most highly trained combat commando, a young and very angry Camargue vaccero with a gun in his hand might look like a creature from another planet.

'Jean Marie. You did well, and I thank you. I am grateful as is the family.'

'You are my family too, monsieur, now. The only person around here who doesn't seem to know this is you.'

Smith digested this particular piece of insubordination without quite as much pleasure as it should have give him and decided to let it go.

'You need to keep him alive for a while, Jean Marie'

'How long, monsieur?'

There was a sound that was suspiciously like a well aimed kick to the balls. The following groan confirmed that the man was indeed still breathing - just.

'I need to talk to him, Jean Marie. It could not be more important.'

'I assumed that monsieur. I will leave his tongue untouched. I am, however, very disappointed.'

Smith could not stop himself smiling inwardly. This young man had grown up a lot in the year or so he had known him.

'I will be back in three quarters of an hour.'

'Take your time, monsieur. This piece of shit is going nowhere.' 'OK. Jean Marie. Organize a small perimeter and sit tight. Five

men only as I taught you. Within fifteen minutes lot of very nasty people from Marseille will appear. They will not be in combat gear. Please don't kill them. They're on your side.'

'OK, boss. Who is in charge?' 'You, of course.'

'Excellent. And boss?' 'Yes?'

'This is better than herding bulls.'

'At least your bulls don't kill you.'

'That only goes to show how much you have to learn about bulls, boss.'

The young man had the good sense to ring off first. The next call was to Girondou.

'There has been an attack. It's over now but I need twenty men at the Mas de Saintes now. Jean Marie Chirou is in charge, but they should do what they know. There is a GIGN man tied up in the stables and he is not to be harmed. He is Jean Marie's supper after I have finished with him. No-one gets into the house, Alexei. No-one. I will arrive within the hour in your black Mercedes. Men on the gate should let me in and no-one else.'

Girondou knew better than to ask for an explanation. 'OK.'

The phone went dead. He called Suzanne more in hope than expectation. No reply. In fact, no connection at all. Smith's mood darkened even more. He dialled Martine's number.

'I've called in some reinforcements from Marseille. Please stop your local farmers throwing pitch forks at them as they arrive. They are here to help and are on our side.'

She snorted and then got back to business.

'Your friend Deveraux is OK although he had two bullets in him not one.'

'Had?'

'Yes, had. See you in an hour.' This time, knowing he had things to do other than to speak to her, it was she who broke the connection.

Smith slumped back in his chair and remained completely motionless for a few seconds. Then with a long, slow intake and exhale of breath he got up. Gentry remained seated. Smith turned and looked down at his old friend.

'Don't bother with the Suzanne stuff until I contact you.'

Gentry nodded slowly and raised a hand from the arm of his chair in a gentle gesture of benediction after his departing guest.

Both new what had happened but someone had to confirm it.

Suzanne's house was less than three minutes' walk away towards the middle of town and he struck west along the river bank until he reached the Tranquetaille bridge. Most of his mind was consumed with the anticipation of what he knew he was going to find. There was no real reason why he knew. He just did. The term gut feeling was a misnomer. There is a sense of the irrational about a 'gut feeling', as if the stomach knows better than the mind. Rubbish, obviously. His knowledge was based an understanding of how things happened - shit primarily. Survival was all too often not to do with avoiding shit but ensuring that someone was deeper in it than you.

Her house might be watched, of course, but the night would help. In truth he didn't really care. He still had the key and the rear entrance he used only few days ago was in a narrow alley with high walls. Getting in without being seen, however, was not a priority. In his anger at what he knew was inevitable he would have actually liked a confrontation for although he was no longer suitably young, he was still as good with the little Glock tucked uncomfortably into the back of his trousers as he had ever been. That meant much better than most. Avenging a death that had still possibly not happened was an odd frame of mind but it was one that settled over him like a fog, or maybe he was just feeling betrayed.

As he reached the bridge he put on a black balaclava and wound a scarf around his head and neck. It was no great disguise, but it would suffice as he wasn't known either to the opposition or to any casual passer-by stupid enough to be wandering around on a cold winter evening. Suzanne's house was a little distance off but the maze of little streets to the north of the Rue de la République allowed him to approach the rear of the house pretty certain that he was undetected, at least until the last few metres. Training told him to stand off and observe. Even professional watchers showed themselves eventually and if they were there, these would be watchers, not killers. People trained to kill were seldom wasted on surveillance. None of this mattered to him for there was still, theoretically at least, a tiny chance that what he feared might not have happened. He couldn't afford the luxury of waiting.

218

It had. Someone – some bastard, he thought - had lit a candle, a tea light in a tiny blood-red glass of all things, and its flickering light confirmed what he had known the second that Deveraux had told him that Suzanne had left the Mas. What remained was a slim, elegant nude, one leg crossed beneath the other, whitening as the remains of her blood seeped into the dark crimson lake that was gradually expanding across the bed. Her throat was cut and the strip of drying blood looked like a courtesan's choker. Not for the first time in recent days he felt his anger rising. He lent down and felt gently in between the tops of her thighs in a sexless gesture. It was one of the last places to lose its temperature and he estimated that she had been killed less than thirty minutes before.

A savage rage swept through him. He left the bedroom without a backward glance. What he had seen would stay with him forever, more so than previous corpses, because he felt that he could have – should have – prevented this one. The rage took him out of the front door which he slammed noisily behind him as a stupid but important defiance. The cold air hit him hard, jolting him back into reality. He dialled Gentry on the satellite phone.

'She's dead.'

'Ah.'

Gentry's reply was a whisper.

There was no need now to take risks and he didn't. In any case it was turning into a very long Tuesday evening indeed. He needed to pace himself and be rather more methodical that he with otherwise have wished. He had too much on his mind. So his speed was only moderate as he took the familiar road south towards Le Sambuc and the Mas des Saintes. He needed Martine's wise council, a fresh look at things while he thought and planned. The bits were fairly clear and the jigsaw was virtually together in his mind. All that remained was the endgame - his endgame where justice would be served unencumbered, if necessary, by proof. He had all the evidence he needed. He swung to a halt in front of the closed steel gates at the entrance to the drive that led up to the mas. The car was surrounded by four men all armed with automatic weapons. Behind the still closed gates Smith recognised the man who only a few days before he had sent to guard his bosses' children. Smith got out of the car to allow the four to inspect it. Nods were exchanged, and the gates swung open. He stopped as he drew level with the man whose scowl deepened.

'Anything?' 'No. All quiet.'

'How many of you?'

'Twenty of us and eight of them.'

Smith grinned in as cheerful a way as he could manage. 'Don't worry. They're friendly.'

'No they're not. They're farmers.' His voice was both contemptuous and fearful.

As he drove into the courtyard, Jean Marie stepped up and opened his door. The young man had obviously had a difficult hour or two but he was together enough to offer a report.

'All OK. No further problems. The family is safe and your friend is in the house being treated.'

'And our guest?'

'Still in the stables and still alive. I left two of these city goons to stare at him. It is the sort of job they are good at.' His voice was equally contemptuous.

Again, Smith smiled a little. The enmity between the gangsters of Marseille and the farmers of Arles went back two thousand years to the rivalry under the Roman occupation. Little had changed.

'Soon we must sit together, and you can tell me what happened. But now I have some other things to do. I will see Madame and Monsieur and then join you in the stables in five minutes. Are you happy with the way things are here?'

Jean Marie pulled himself up a notch in stature, please with the assumption that he was still in charge

'Yes I am. I'll check again before I come to the stables. I don't like these goons much, but I understand why they are necessary. Perhaps you like also tell me about your friend. He is a remarkable man in many ways. Without him we would all be dead, I think.'

Smith laid a hand on the young man's shoulder. 'Without you both, I think, Jean Marie.'

He could tell that he was in trouble the second he walked in the door. Not the sort of trouble that he could deal with easily either. The other sort. An embarrassed Deveraux was sitting in one of the large armchairs ranged on either side of a huge roaring fire, looking to all intents and purposes normal in a borrowed set of clothes, shirt, sweater and corduroy trousers. Rather like an estate agent in a menacing sort of way, thought Smith. Emile Aubanet was in the corresponding chair on the other side of the fire making an unsuccessful attempt to look engrossed in the newspaper. Martine was sitting at one end of the sofa that formed the long side of this rectangle with a very black look on her face.

She was the first actually to speak, somewhat waspishly, Smith thought.

'Derek is staying with us in the house for the moment. He is in no fit state to sleep outside like some common tramp at this time of year.'

Actually, Smith had seen Deveraux doing precisely that in much worse states but he felt that this would be an observation that would not be entirely welcome at that particular moment. He also decided that an enquiry as to what particular time of the year would be suitable might equally be a mistake. He contented himself with:

'Derek??'

It occurred to him that in twenty years he had never known the man's Christian name. Deveraux looked suitably embarrassed.

'Yes sir. Sorry sir!'

'Derek Deveraux, for Chrissakes. Are you OK, by the way?

'Yes sir, Thank you sir!'

'Knock it off, Deveraux.'

'Yes sir. Sorry sir!'

Conscious that this conversation was becoming increasingly silly, Smith turned to Martine.

'We need to talk.'

She nodded in a frumpy sort of way. 'I should think so.'

'No, Martine. We really need to talk.'

They all picked up on the change in tone. Smith was losing patience and becoming business-like in equal measure. Deveraux pulled himself painfully to his feet.

'If you don't mind, I'll rest a little.' Martine wasn't quite done.

'I think I might like you to hear this, Derek.'

Deveraux smiled at her. 'You may want me to hear, Madame Aubanet, but I don't want to listen. It's really none of my business.'

He turned to Smith. 'Everything alright out there?'

'Yes, I think so. Go and lie down and I'll brief you later.' 'Wouldn't you like me to deal with our friend in the stables?' 'Are you up to it?'

Deveraux's eyes darkened. 'Oh yes. If I have Jean Marie's help. I rather think I am. What do you want to know?'

'Where and when the next phase is. Who if possible and, most importantly how many are left. We must have made a bit of a dent in the ungodly between the kidnapping and today's events. It is unlikely that he will know but there is always a chance. He is only a soldier, but this was a small group. Information may be shared more than usual.'

Deveraux nodded.

'Will you need him later?'

Smith shook his head. He was about to ask him to search the two others no matter how unlikely there was to be anything useful on the bodies but realised he didn't have to.

With that Deveraux moved towards the door.

Martine still had not given up. She also stood and ignored the warning glance from her father.

'I really think that he should rest.'

Deveraux seemed to sprint out of the door. He knew what was coming. Smith rounded on the beautiful woman, his anger finally boiling over.

'Sit down, Martine and listen. In the last few hours, a three members of the official GIGN police, arguably the best anti-terrorist forces in the world, have invaded your home with the specific intention of killing me, you and your father - possibly. They were stopped by that man who you have so recently become so fond of and your own bodyguard plus a few others. These so-called policemen are part of a group is on the point of smuggling out of France to God knows where enough metallic plutonium to make a bomb that could vaporise all of Paris and much of the surrounding countryside. They have already got half off it out, killing, amongst other the son of a local family of your precious community who had a wife and two baby children - which is where I came in, you might remember. You also might not know that within the last hour another member of their happy little group has also cut your cousin's throat from one pretty ear to the other and left her to bleed out all over her nice white satin sheets.'

Martine gasped and sat completely motionless. Smith continued without mercy.

'At the moment it is debatable whether she was killed because she was part of the conspiracy or they just thought that she was getting in the way. Maybe they thought she was getting too close to the story. It looks as if she was in regular contact with the very man who is the boss of this particular gang and she seems to have known that you were going to be attacked as she left in a hurry and presumably without telling you. On the other hand, she may have been the target and the three men who came here were just designed to flush her out into the open and had nothing to do with you at all. I rather think that this is the case. They should have had nothing to fear from you two.'

Emil Aubanet nodded gently and adopted the appearance of a man who knew all along that there was something wrong with his late niece and had just been proved right.

Smith continued.

'There is every sign that all this will be coming to an end before very long. I am making arrangements for the bigger picture, as it were, to revert to the people who are best capable of dealing with it, while I'll just settle the little bit that is mine, the murder of a young professional soldier with a young family from the Camargue who was doing his duty and who was betrayed by the people he worked for. Whatever you might think of all this, it matters to me. A lot. So rather than get on your self-conscious high horse and sit on it all disapproving and judgmental, you had better decide where you stand.'

It was one of those speeches where the speaker got angrier the more he speaks. He saw in a flash how his once tranquil retirement had been shattered and this Camargue family seemed slowly to be enveloping him. He saw his past coming alive again and how he seemed to be reverting to something he had hoped he no longer was. All that and much more passed across his mind as he spoke. He knew he had to finish the business but when it was over, then he'd see. Now he needed to get out of there and find a little space to plan the endgame.

Without further comment he turned and walked out of the room leaving a stunned silence behind him. He went quickly through the house and out into the courtyard. He walked over the stable block that formed one side of the quadrangle and met Deveraux coming out. It had been less than five minutes since their last conversation.

'Just a boy, really. Not one of your GIGN people which means..'

'I know what that means, Deveraux. What did you get?'

He handed Smith a piece of paper and a mobile phone SIM card. Smith put them both in his pocket. 'The other two?'

'The real thing. We were lucky.'

'Lucky be damned. You were better than they were. What about these three?'

Deveraux grimaced.

'You can tell Monsieur Aubanet that his pigs won't need

feeding for the next day or so.'

In spite of himself, Smith shuddered slightly and turned towards his old Peugeot 307 that stood in the corner under a canopy. The keys were in the ignition. He shut the door, wound the window down looked at Deveraux.

'You can tell him yourself. I'm going home to get some sleep. Call me or Gentry if you need anything. Oh, the goons from Marseille stay until I say so. Get Jean Marie to organise them into shifts, though I doubt that you will have any more trouble. Get some food and hot coffee out to them too. In the meantime, get some rest. I will probably need you for a long shot within the next day or so. I would put yourself in the arms of Madame Aubanet. It looks as if she needs someone to love at the moment.'

Deveraux had a slight twinkle in his eye. 'I thought that was you, boss.'

Smith gave his friend a very hard stare. 'Any more of that and I will kill you myself.'

Deveraux snorted and stepped back balletically to prevent broken toes being added to his list of current difficulties as Smith took off in a heavy-footed shower of gravel. The man at the gate waved him down but Smith controlled his anger as he remembered that the car was probably unfamiliar. Once he was recognised, the gate was opened and Smith went on his way back to Arles and his little house next to the Arena. It seemed a long time since he had been there.

As he drove, he made a couple of calls. First to Gentry. 'My house, twenty minutes?'

'OK.'

Next to Girondou.

'Thanks for the cavalry, Alexei. I don't think it will be that necessary for more than another day.'

'Are you all right and the family?'

'Yes, just fine. I am on my way back home for a sleep. Please can you fix a meeting for me with Messailles tomorrow morning at the Hotel de Paris on Rue de la Cavalerie in Arles at midday.'

'It that wise, Peter?'

'I don't know whether it's wise, my friend, but it is certainly necessary. I need him to take much of this business over from me.'

There was a rich chuckle from the other end of the call.

'He will certainly like that, mon ami.' Then his voice got lower and more serious.

'I have just heard about Suzanne Blanchard. I'm sorry. This is turning into a shitty business. Francois' body was washed up on the beach outside the Rove tunnel today. One 9mm slug to the head, not from us, however.'

'I am not sure if I am sorry or relieved, Alexei, about either of them, but thank you anyway. At least it reduces the dramatis personae a little.'

He put the phone to one side and not for the first time wondered about Girondou's sources of information.

Gentry was in the house when he arrived. A delighted Arthur leaped from the sofa in front of the fire to greet him. Smith felt a degree of normality returning to proceedings. A pair of whisky glasses stood full on the table. Smith handed over Deveraux's piece of paper and phone chip and waited.

Gentry nodded approvingly, took out a small tablet computer switched it one and inserted the SIM card.

Smith sat silently feeling a bit depressed. His words to Martine and her father had been necessary but he still felt a bit

227

guilty. He was jolted out of his reverie by Gentry.

'Deveraux did well. Firstly, his estimate of DuPlessis' manpower is the same as mine. He started off with no more than eight. I have found some records of an interesting little GIGN operation in Chad a year ago just after he got the top job where DuPlessis and his entire squad of eight vanished for nearly a week. Some of the GIGN top bosses were never quite satisfied with the debrief although you don't accuse the commander of such a group of anything without good proof. He is, however, going to be retired before too long to something slightly less influential.'

'Damn right he is going to be retired,' thought Smith grimly to himself, 'and not to the sort of retirement where you get a pension either.'

Gentry continued:

'This entire squad is currently on leave, at the same time, it should be admitted, as are another thirty or so from the force, although it is all perfectly official and above board. They were all due some R and R. However, the important maths starts from DuPlessis and eight. Now we are down to DuPlessis and three.'

'Four,' said Smith, 'Deveraux thought that the one he talked to was a newcomer, certainly not trained to withstand interrogation. It only took him five minutes to get the information you have. I know he's good, but nobody is that good if the opposition is GIGN trained.' 'OK. Four. The other information Deveraux extracted

comes from the phone chip. You're probably right. The guy must have been an amateur or at least a beginner. No professional takes a phone with him and then uses the contacts memory to store information. I have a date, time and a place for the next rendezvous although I should think they are useless by now because DuPlessis will have at least changed the location. He may have thought the loss of the two men in La Bouilladisse was just bad luck but these latest three will make him uncomfortable even if it doesn't actually prove that someone is onto him.'

'Will he cancel?'

'No, I don't think so. By how he is sitting on a large lump of plutonium and he will not be happy about that even though in reality it is little more dangerous that a chunk of marzipan. No. He will want rid of it and he will want his money. He knows that his days at GIGN are over so he will need the money to disappear. So he will stick to the arrangements as much as he can, not to spook his customers if for no other reason. He is more likely to change the location than the date.'

'So, we might know the when but we don't know the where.' Gentry had the smile of a very self-satisfied Cheshire cat. 'Well actually if we don't yet, we will soon.'

'What do you mean?'

'After your comments about Suzanne using a rather sexy little phone that we couldn't get into I thought I would do a little field work. I nipped round immediately after you left the ladies death bed in your customary huff and pinched it.'

'What do you mean pinched it?'

'Exactly what I say, old boy. This field work isn't as difficult as you people pretend.'

Smith gave his companion a very hard stare indeed.

'May I remind you that you don't do that sort of thing, Gentry. You are precious near being strangled. In fact, you might still not escape that particular fate. However, what have you learned that is making you look so ridiculously self-satisfied?'

'Well the phone is a full-blooded military gismo. All the usual satellite bells and whistles but, and here is the interesting thing, completely military. Military satellite network, military encryptions, secure military channels. My guess is that one of those channels has been hijacked by Du Plessis to run his operation. It could also explain the signals that flew around during the first operation. Rather clever, actually.'

Gentry obviously found it difficult to keep a note of

professional admiration out of his voice. Smith shot him a quick glance and continued:

'Can this be kept separate and secret from the other users of the network.'

'Oh yes. These satellites handle thousands of secure channels and you can't simply find one that might or might not be being used for nefarious purposes without full-time eavesdropping which is by no means as simple as it might sound.'

'Whose military?'

'Ah I wondered when you might ask that. The whole shebang is actually American.'

'Christ.'

Gentry cut across him.

'Now don't start getting ideas. It is entirely possible that this is a cuckoo and they don't know about it. All it would need is a sympathiser to be in the right place and a channel or two could easily by split off and no-one would be the wiser as long as they don't use the arrangement for too long.'

'OK. We can talk about what this might mean later. Can you get into it?'

Gentry gave him a very old-fashioned look indeed.

'Of course, I can. As of one hour ago all conversations over the network are being recorded on my computer at home. If they change the arrangements, I will know at the same time they do.'

Smith suddenly felt very tired.

'OK Gentry, brilliant stuff, as usual. I obviously need to know if there is a change of plan as soon as you do. Now, I only have one other thing I need for now and I am afraid I shall need it before 11 o'clock tomorrow.'

Gentry smiled and slid a USB flash memory stick and a small piece of paper across the table. This will save you a good few hours of explanation when you meet Messailles tomorrow. It has all he needs to mop up the big picture but nothing on the endgame, of course. You can feed him what he needs for that later as you feel necessary. The bit of paper is designed to get his attention in case he is reluctant to chat.'

With that he got up, patted Arthur on the head and his friend on the shoulder - It might have been the other way around, but he was too tired to notice - and walked out into the night.

Half an hour later Smith was back, somewhat gratefully, in his own bed; Arthur lying on the floor at the foot. It felt good to be home and bed had been his constant friend for years. He was acutely unhappy about the situation he had left at the mas but he would deal with that later. He was just beginning to doze off when the front doorbell rang. Not Gentry, he thought, Gentry had a key. Also Arthur didn't bark. Odd. He put his old towelling dressing gown on and took his Glock from under his pillow. He checked the monitor that was fed by a tiny camera in high up on the church at the top of the square outside his house. He went quickly downstairs and opened the door.

Martine entered without a word, kissed him lightly on the cheek, took his hand and led him back up to his bedroom.

Chapter 19   Briefing Messailles

Colonel Claude Messailles, irascible at best, was working up rather a fine head of steam. He had been sitting erect at one of the small tables in the uncomfortable and scruffy café that sported the rather grand name of Hotel de Paris, down near the Porte de Laure on the north edge of city for slightly more than half an hour and his temperature had increased as that of the untouched coffee in front of him declined. He was not a man used to being kept waiting and the fact that he was dressed in mufti rather than in his habitual and, to him at least, more comfortable full uniform of Colonel of the Gendarmerie National did little to relax him or lighten his mood. He had come into the café angry. He had enjoyed a business relationship with Alexei Girondou for a number of years, a relationship that had considerably enriched him, but he still took it very badly to be asked - instructed he felt - to attend a meeting with an anonymous stranger in one of Arles's less salubrious establishments. He thus found himself sitting uncomfortably in a cafe that was less than half full of people who looked as if they would cut his throat for a euro, waiting for someone he had never met and who clearly had no sense of punctuality.

For the umpteenth time he glanced at the Omega Seamaster on his wrist. His patience finally gave out. He had done what his paymaster had asked. It was not his fault if the bloody fellow had not turned up. He tossed a couple of euros on the table and put both hands next to them and started to lift himself to his feet, when the barman appeared at his elbow and thumped a small glass of cognac down on the table in front of him. Caught in a none-too elegant position, half standing, half sitting with his bum pointing out backwards, he turned his head to address something impolite about the mistaken waiter when he caught the scowling man's jerk of the head in the direction of the back of the room. When the Colonel of the Gendarmerie National finally made it to the vertical he turned to follow the waiter's indication to see Smith, sitting in the corner, raising a similar glass in a gesture of greeting. Messailles dimly remembered that the figure had been there reading a newspaper when he had arrived.

He finally finished getting up took the glass in his hand and marched over to the corner table. He was a little taken-aback to find that Smith rose politely, smiled in a friendly manner extended a firm handshake. Automatically the gendarme took the hand and shook it before letting some of his anger come through.

'I suppose you think that keeping me waiting here is funny, Monsieur'.

Smith held his most friendly of faces in place.

'No, monsieur, merely informative. Do please sit down.' Messailles sat with his back to the room looking like thunder.

Smith continued.

'Do please also try your cognac. I think you will find it better than you might expect in a place like this.'

With a snorting noise that Smith associated more with angry horses than with people, Messailles took a sip. Smith was delighted to see that the policeman now had the expression of a man who had been kicked by the horse not sounded like one.

Smith spared the man the indignity of asking. '1886 Moyet.'

Messailles looked over his shoulder at the mirrored bar with undisguised astonishment. Smith continued.

'No. The bottle is mine. I just keep it here for emergencies. This, I suspect, is one such. However perhaps we might start our conversation.'

His companion quickly recovered his poise and no small measure of his previous anger.

'And who the hell are you?' he asked with the sort of glare that one would expect from a full and very angry Colonel of the Gendarmerie National.

Smith looked coldly across the table.

'If by that, you wish me to establish my credentials, Colonel, then I would offer this.'

With a very slight movement he slid his folded newspaper sideways across the table to reveal a small blank piece of paper lying underneath. Messailles frowned, picked it up and turned it over. The next few moments were spent with him fumbling inside his jacket pockets until he located his reading glasses and put them on. Choleric red of his face instantly faded to a much paler hue as he saw that the paper carried two long and familiar numbers, one the number of his Swiss bank account and the second its current balance. He slowly took off his glasses and replaced them in his inside pocket quickly followed by the piece of paper. He looked across at Smith.

'What can I do for you monsieur?'

Smith pitched his voice just loud enough to carry across the small circular table between them but no further.

'Firstly Colonel, this is a briefing. It is not a debate nor is it even a conversation. There will be no questions and after this meeting you and I won't meet again. I have absolutely no interest in your nefarious sources of additional income. However, if I ever get the slightest idea that you are taking any interest in me or any of my friends, your boss at Rue St Didier will get a full file of information about your relationship with Alexei Girondou and one or two similar criminals in the southern half of France. Having said that, however, I am informed that you are good policeman, whatever the hell that actually means, and if you act as I think you should on the information that I am about to give you, then not only will you stop a major crime of treason you will also avenge the murders of a group of your fellow policemen as well as virtually guarantee your ultimate promotion to Director-General of Gendarmerie towards which, I gather you are already making some progress.'

Looking across the table Smith saw that the blustering officer had vanished, and he was being observed very closely and calmly, much more calmly that he expected. Perhaps, Smith thought, there was indeed more to this policeman than meets the eye. He continued:

'You are part of an investigation looking into the killing of three young RAID policeman ago on the beach at Beauduc . Or rather, perhaps it would be better to describe it as presently side-lined from this investigation. You report to Suzanne Blanchard who seems to be working directly for the President. There is a very big conspiracy here; one that affects not only the security of France but could endanger most of its neighbours. I am about to give you almost all of the story and with this information you can not only clean up a very rotten little corner of your government and its police forces but possibly prevent a catastrophe.'

'Almost all the story, monsieur?'

'Yes. You get the rest or as much of the rest as I want to give you a little later. The briefing notes will tell you when and how. But there is a small part that I will keep for myself. You don't need to know what or why. You probably wouldn't believe it if you did.'

'Briefing notes?'

Smith moved his newspaper paper a little further to the side and uncovered the small USB memory stick. The gendarme quickly covered it with his gloves.

'Why me, Monsieur?'

'Because in spite or possibly because of the fact that you exchange information for money, you can be trusted. You are ambitious enough to want to use the information I have given you and you are powerful enough to get it done. As I said, I am told that you are a good policeman and that while you are perfectly prepared to turn a blind eye to the activities of some of the less desirably elements in the South of France, you are nevertheless a soldier who has his country's interests at heart. Oddly enough you are talking to one of the few people who can understand what would seem to many others to be incomprehensible. You are lucky, many other would have fed you to your boss and he would have turned you into fishmeal.'

Making sure that he was watching the policeman very carefully indeed, Smith dropped the bombshell.

'Oh, by the way, Suzanne Aubanet was murdered yesterday evening.'

Messailles' astonishment was quite genuine.

'I hadn't heard. My God, who..' His voice tailed off.

'Perhaps that is one of the things that you can find out monsieur. Maybe being pushed sideways from the investigation was not such a bad thing after all, Colonel.'

'But she was working directly for the President.' Smith long drawn out reply came almost in a whisper. 'Ah, yes. So she was.'

Now there really was a silence.

Smith waited for something more from his reluctant guest but nothing came. Messailles was experienced enough not to ask questions.

Smith got up and looked down the very white-faced gendarme.

'Goodbye, Colonel. You must hope that won't meet again.'

Smith failed to offer a parting handshake and walked straight out of the café into the street.

Chapter 20   Coda

Although he hadn't been there before, Smith felt grimly satisfied. The night was an almost exact repeat of the events that had started all this, slightly more than a week before. Cold, windy with clouds scudding over his back as he lay prone in the sand. He knew how to block out the cold, the wind, the damp - all of it. The mind can do remarkable things when it has to. He imagined how the young man had felt as he lay in a very similar spot on the same Beauduc beach slightly further east. The drop point had indeed been changed but only marginally . He was probably thinking of something warm, familiar, domestic; something to take his mind of the discomfort. He had been young and knew no better. Smith knew that it was the discomfort, the pain, that kept you alert, focussed. Had the young policeman learned to use the pain rather than ignore it he might have heard the approach of his killer before it was too late to do anything about it.

Either side, fifty or so metres away lay Deveraux and Henk. All three had L115A3 sniper rifles. Developed originally for the British forces in Afghanistan, the gun was almost certainly the best

.338 calibre sniper rifle in the world. With the 8.59mm heavy bullet it was deadly up to over a 1000 metres almost irrespective of the wind conditions. Magazines of five rounds of FJM hollow point would be more than enough. The range of the weapon enabled them to be much further back from the seashore than DuPlessis would expect or plan for. God knows where Gentry had found the weapons at such short notice, but the RAID colonel and his colleagues were as good as dead already. Each gun was fitted with Schmidt and Bender 25 x 56 night scopes. No silencers. It would be over too quickly to need them and, in any case, the wind would carry the sounds of the execution away.

Smith glanced to his left without moving his head. The old man lay by his side in a slight depression in the sand, black gloved hands holding a pair of night vision binoculars towards the sea. The man and the binoculars were motionless. Smith smiled to himself as he appreciated the training of all those years ago. Some things you just don't forget.

It had been almost on an impulse when earlier that day Smith had knocked on the door of the little house just to the east of the Boulevard Emil Combes, fetched hard against the crumbling wall of old town cemetery. He didn't quite know why he was doing it but it seemed to him that the man had some rights in all this. The old man had opened the door with the sort of confident suspicion that Smith expected. The man was suspicious because he was Arlesian and Provençale and that is the way they are. He was confident because he had been a soldier, and, in his mind, he still was.

'Monsieur Carbot, my name is Peter Smith. I am a friend of David Gentry. May I speak to you for a moment?'

The old man looked at him with a steady eye, assessing, analysing and then with a fluidity that belied his obvious age stood back and to one side and motioned Smith inside the dark house. The front door gave directly into the kitchen. He was motioned into a narrow, hard armchair on one side of open fireplace, he saw the faded photographs on the walls. Pictures of family in the town and in the countryside around. Grey and white memories of young men in uniform, in France and in Algeria, confident, laughing, arms linked, showing off their newly awarded ribbons and medals with pride. A picture of a group on R and R in Algiers. Again laughter. Either side of the fireplace on the wall he also saw photographs of what were obviously the son and grandson. Both bore multi-coloured strips of medal ribbons over the tops of the frames. Other ribbons, plain black this time, decorated diagonally the bottom right corners. Those of the son, pale and dusty with age; the newer ribbons intense and stark. The old man sat still amongst the images of his dead family. Insofar as he had any doubts, Smith looked around him and dismissed them. The old man waited quietly for Smith to start.

'Monsieur. A little time ago my friend David Gentry asked me to help him to find out how and why your grandson was killed. I have done so and, I believe, the Monsieur Gentry has told you what happened.'

The old man nodded sadly.

'Yes. I know.' The voice was low and lifeless. Smith took a deep breath before continuing.

'Monsieur. I am here because I want to offer you the opportunity, if you wish, to see a wrong righted or, if you prefer, to settle scores. Tonight, the man who caused your son to be killed will himself die at my hand. There is nothing official about this. Nothing legal. Possibly nothing moral. Quite the contrary, in fact. That doesn't concern me. But your grandson was betrayed and murdered while serving his country. I too have also been a soldier, of sorts. If you wish to be there tonight, I'll take you.'

The old man leaned back in his seat and relaxed for the first time since Smith had entered his home. He looked at Smith very directly.

'Ah,' he sighed, 'So you are the one.' There was a long pause before the man spoke again.

'I've seen you walking your beautiful dog around the town.'

Smith was somewhat taken aback and obviously looked so. The old man continued:

'You are the Englishman I have heard of. You are the friend of Emil Aubanet and his daughter.' The man stiffened proudly. 'They are also my friends.'

Smith did not know what to say and therefore, sensibly, said nothing. After a while the older man continued:

'If you are sure that I won't get in the way of what you must do tonight then the answer is yes, I would wish to be there.' 'Very well,' replied Smith. I will pick you up at ten o'clock this evening.'

He got up and turned to go. It had been a good few years since someone had really hurt him enough to make him wince but the old man's grip on his forearm was fiery as a vice. The look was equally hard.

'Thank you, Monsieur Smith, for coming. You're doing the

correct thing.'

The ambiguity of the remark was not lost on him. It crossed his mind to warn his new companion that it would be very cold and that he needed to be dressed in black. A quick glance at the walls of that sombre little room with its iconography of lives spent in military service and their inevitable deaths showed him that he should save his breath.

Some hours later as the four were driving through the labyrinth of pot holes of the road from the main road to the beach at Beauduc, Smith gave the briefing. When he had arrived at the house near the cemetery, he found the old man dressed in full matt black GIGN night operations gear including boots and night vision goggles. The old man answered Smith's unspoken question with the palest of smiles and a shrug of the shoulders.

'My grandson and I were the same size.'

Smith nodded. It was only as he turned away that Smith noticed the light reflecting blackly from a discolouration on the breast of the coverall. Mentally, Smith nodded approvingly. The old man was taking his grandson's blood back to war.

The briefing in the car was short. All four knew what was required. They expected no more than six, possibly eight people, probably fewer. Smith would take the central 30 degrees of the field of fire. Henk, being left handed, took the right sector, Deveraux the left. Traversing is easier away from the dominant eye. Not for the first time Smith found himself marvelling at the fact that Gentry had not only known but also found a fully left-handed L115A3 for Henk. If the beach scenario was repeated, the transfer would be from an electric beach buggy. The execution of its driver, DuPlessis, would fall to whoever had the sector where the buggy stopped. The signal for the rest was to be this first kill.

Now each lay in the dark sand and waited, each alone with his thoughts. For Henk it was a job. He was well paid and having only recently left the Dutch close protection group, he would find regular and well-paid employment. The world continued to need expert killers who could keep secrets and protect their owners. He was a professional and his mind was just cycling on alert. This time it was a long shot with an even longer rifle. Nothing up-close like the last time. In spite of Smith's words, that particular aspect of his new profession would take a little getting used to. Unlike the young policeman lying similarly in the damp sand a week or so before , his Glock 32 was already resting on the sand below his left hand in a small indentation that he had hollowed out to provide fast access while his right lay lightly just behind the front biped support of the sniper rifle. The pistol would be ignored at the last moment. Until then his mind's eye was as much to the rear as his actual vision saw the breaking sea shore greenly through the night sight.

Deveraux was more relaxed. This was familiar stuff for him. Habitually a loner, he had spent all his adult life doing this sort of thing. Had he been bothered to prove it, he could have been known as one of the world's great marksmen. He wasn't bothered but he knew. He was lying on his back, eyes closed, listening intently to the solitude. The view and the targets that would in time present themselves through his night scope could be acquired and dispatched within a second or two. Now he was just watching all their backs and he needed no eyes to do that. Like Henk, a silenced hand gun lay loosely to his right palm.

Smith also lay in the dark sand, relaxed but not completely. He had confidence that the old man next to him would not be a liability. He had not moved in half an hour. He just stared out at the empty beach. Smith was also sure that it was right that he was there. It was the only way he knew to close things and settle accounts. Even now, the memory of the young policeman betrayed and killed made him angry. There were more times in the past than he cared to remember that there but for the grace of God - or in his case, Gentry - the same fate would have befallen him.

After a long, black delay, all four simultaneously picked up the low warble of a silenced outboard and the RIB came into the limited area picked up by the night scopes. It was the old man who saw it first. His binoculars had a wider field of vision than the rifle scopes. It nudged silently into the beach and, as before, four men jumped out and deployed on either side. This time there was no fifth man. In an exact rerun of the events of a week before, the electric dune buggy came from the left. One person only drove it. Smith knew that Deveraux would be tracking it. It stopped directly centrally in their arena. Smith lined up the cross hairs on the man's head. Not for the first time he experienced the slowing of time when doing this sort of job. His forefinger tightened gently on the trigger. He paused in mid-shot as a thought struck him. The decision was only partially his. He gently extended his arm slightly towards the old man lying to his left and rotated his hand, thumb extended, up and down just a few degrees either side of the horizontal in the manner of Roman emperors denoting the fate of a gladiator. His companion silently answered the question. The thumb was down. Smoothly he regained the trigger, squeezed it and felt the gun buck slightly as the .338 Lapua Magnum 19 gram hollow point left the barrel, covered the three hundred metres to its target in considerably less than half a second and punched a hole the size of a tennis ball in Colonel Roland DuPlessis' head. Within a quarter of a second Henk and Deveraux had taken the signal and dropped the first two men. The remaining two fell within a further second. Watching through his scope, Smith saw Henk's second target move slightly on the sand and then twitch finally as Deveraux crossed over and made sure. Within less than two seconds accounts were settled and a great crime stopped in its tracks.

The four men continued to lie in position for a precautionary five minutes, but nothing moved on the beach and silently they withdrew leaving the empty RIB about to be washed out to sea and the buggy with its deadly cargo to be discovered by Messailless and his people. Smith glanced up into the night and saw with grim satisfaction the first seagulls were descending onto the beach for an unexpected evening meal.

It was still completely dark, but Martine had been waiting for them in the old man's house when they got back into Arles. Henk and Deveraux had left for a further precautionary observation of the Mas. Smith didn't bother to ask how she had got into the house, but the fire was made up and roaring, the room dark but warm and hot coffee was ready for them. The three sat in silence around the fire. Smith noted that the medal ribbons on the older photograph were no longer dusty.

At length the old man stirred and got quietly to his feet, crossed over to Smith and looked down at him, a hint of tear in his eyes. He put his hand on Smith's shoulder.

'Killing is never good, young man. We have both been involved with it in different ways and I suspect it has left us both no richer. For people like us it is a difficult and savage life but if we can live with our conscience then we will at least find some peace of mind. Justice is not always right nor is revenge always bad. But what we did today was correct. Tonight, at last, I will sleep, and I thank you for that.'

He extended his hand.

Smith rose and took the old man's hand and, inside the handshake, passed across the long brass cartridge case that an hour or so before had held the charge that sent the soul of his grandson's murderer into oblivion. As he withdrew his hand, Smith saw the old man's knuckles were white as he looked up and nodded. It was a soldier's final gift. It was all that Smith could do and they both knew it.

'Come and visit me again, soon, young man,' the old man said in a strong voice, his face cracking into a genuine smile, 'I suspect that you might make a more interesting opponent at drafts than that friend of yours.'

'Yes,' said Smith as he felt Martine gently take his hand to lead him away. 'Thank you, I will.'

Chapter 20 Finale

Little had changed. The night was moonless, and Notre Dame was again its ghostly self as he looked across from his chair. He had been in his apartment most of the day but midnight had brought him both the news he expected and the confirmation he needed. He had been told of the latest events on the beach with some pleasure. It was always satisfactory when someone did his housekeeping for him. Of more interest was the next call which brought him the good news. The alternative arrangements had worked flawlessly, and his Arab customers was in possession of the second half of their purchase. He himself was now twenty million dollars richer and the business relationship that he had so carefully nurtured was set well for the future. He had successfully created a profitable new business channel that would in time enrich himself and his friends. He had also created a back door into the Middle East that only France possessed. He had carried out his instructions to the letter. The Élysée would be content. It was with a deep sigh of satisfaction that he sank even deeper into the black leather of Charles Eames recliner and waited for the last call of the night.

It was not long coming. His friend simply confirmed that he was satisfied with the shipment, complimented the Frenchman on his foresight in arranging the alternate drop and confirmed that he would be in touch again within a few months.

He expressed no interest in the events at Beauduc earlier that night for it really wasn't his business. Nor, in fact, did the Frenchman. He had already decided that he wasn't at risk from whoever it had been. He would only trouble himself with that if it became either necessary or profitable to do so. At the moment it was neither.

It was a scene that had been repeated often over the years. Gentry always de-briefed Smith in his little office buried in the bowls of that great grey Whitehall building that carefully but anonymously housed their department. From an early stage they had discovered a shared passion for chess and the final meeting of any operation, successful or not, took place over a chess board accompanied by glasses of whisky; Islay Mist for Gentry, supermarket blended for Smith. The games themselves also tended to reflect a little of the way the operation had gone.

This game was no exception all those years later. They sat either side of Gentry's exquisite little Sheraton chess table and slogged through what was developing into a more than unsatisfactory draw. It was gentry's turn to open and, as usual he played a traditional king's pawn advance and the game had

244

progressed along fairly predictable lines. Smith could be quite dangerous when playing black and often sprung surprises but on this occasion, he just fell into a fairly routine Berlin Defence. This by no meant that the game had to lead to the usual draw ; a result does tend to rely on White taking a more innovative approach. In any case Smith was always capable of injecting some unorthodox variation of his owm into proceedings to liven things up had he be minded to. But on this occasion the game meandered and it was some fifteen moves and a second refill of their glasses before Gentry said what they were both thinking:

'Too easy.'

After a long pause, Smith nodded slowly. His mind had been far from his next few moves.

'Yes, I rather think it was. The question is why?'

Gentry shrugged.

'Who knows? At least your particular bit of it is done and dusted. You did what you set out to do and Messailles with have organised the rest. There's little point in agonising about it.'

Even as he spoke, he knew that it was useless. Something had got up Smith's nose and he knew that his friend wouldn't be happy unless he cleared it. Smith stared at the board. The Berlin defence was that relies more on longer term strategies than individual moves and was one that Gentry often found more suited to his general approach to the game. Smith usually avoided it as her preferred to be more proactive in playing Black. It was a few fairly ncutral moved before Smith continued almost as if Gentry hadn't spoken.

'The first bit, before we came on the scene, was obviously authentic. A shipment of plutonium is stolen and passed out of the country. But killing the policemen on the beach was as stupid as it was unnecessary. All it served was to bring down a high-level investigation. That is ignoring our somewhat more unofficial interest.'

245

Gentry stayed silent. He knew Smith was only thinking out loud.

'Almost everything from then on is wrong. DuPlessis was too easy to spot and his team too easy to trace, the whole kidnapping episode served no good reason that I can think of, neither did the attack at the mas unless it was to kill Suzanne who was, by that time dead already. That seems to me to have a touch of the left hand not knowing what the right hand is doing. Add to all that the conveniently available information about the second delivery obtained from someone who was a long way short of the correct level of competence for a job like that. Looking back, it all seems a bit like amateur night. However, given Suzanne's level of authority and the fact that what was going on was the theft or more likely sale of an entire atomic bomb's worth of plutonium, it is more likely that this was a very long way indeed from amateur night.'

Gentry finally stirred himself into moving the game on a little.

'And what, Peter, do you think this means when all said and done.'

'A diversion and a none too subtle one at that.'

'I get the feeling that we have been used to do someone else's housekeeping. For whatever reason, DuPlessis and his men are all dead, as is Suzanne. Most of her committee of investigation are none the wiser in any case. All we seem to have achieved is to help Messailless get a promotion that he was probably going to get anyway. All very convenient for whoever planned all this.'

'We've prevented a plutonium shipment getting into the hands of terrorists, Peter. Don't forget that.'

'Have we, old friend, have we? I've a feeling that that too was a diversion; or if not a diversion than a part of a plan that had a backup. We didn't stop the backup. We never got a sniff of it.'

'If there actually was one.'

'Oh yes, there was one all right. No doubt about it. We just never got high enough in all this. We have been grubbing around in Provence while this was all coming down from somewhere close to the Élysée Palace if not actually in it.'

Gentry tried to stave of the inevitable.

'We have satisfied the old man, Peter. That, at least, was the reason for your getting involved in the first place. '

Smith nodded.

'Yes, we've done that all right. But the rest, David; can we really leave it there?'

'Bigger battalions, old chum, bigger battalions. Too big perhaps.'

Smith wiggled a now-empty glass that had held a very large measure of his favourite supermarket whisky at his host. The game was headed nowhere specific so this time the rather tedious and inconclusive struggle ended a few moves short of the inevitable draw by mutual consent and a slight sense of relief.

They moved from the beautiful old board behind the sofa to the two armchairs on either side of the log fire whose blaze had subsided some time ago into a red mass of glowing embers. The sofa between them was occupied by a supine Arthur who had easily demonstrated for the umpteenth time that greyhounds have no great interest in chess. He had been snoring very gently for the last two hours. He did however raise an eyelid briefly as he verified with some relief that he was not going to have to move immediately.

Smith continued as if there had been no interruption.

'If this was a diversion then it was planned by someone clever. DuPlessis was a soldier. He may have been a good one but he operated at a very low level. This has been all something of what I believe it's fashionable these days to call a backstory.'

'And the main event?' Gentry enquired

Smith grimaced into the amber glass that he held in his hand.

'Oddly I think the story is pretty much the same just with a completely different set of characters; or paymasters and planners, at least.'

Gentry feared the worst as he summed up what they were both feeling.

'Decoys and red herrings come to mind, I think.'

Gentry glanced somewhat nervously across at his friend as Smith nodded and frowned. He knew that this was not the sort of treatment Smith usually put up with. He adopted a placatory tone:

'We have at least satisfied the old man, Peter. We found the truth for him and avenged the boy's death. If you take the local view then that is all that was really required. You did what I asked of you and I thank you for that.'

Smith tilted his glass in acknowledgement as Gentry tried to steer Smith away from the thought that was occupying him.

'Others might can possibly get to the bottom of the rest. Unlikely if you are right about this being a higher-level conspiracy. Maybe Messailles will do some good. I doubt it however. In any case, it is hardly our business, is it?'

'Perhaps, Gentry old chap, perhaps. But only perhaps. I must admit to being a little curious.'

'Oh God.'

Gentry sighed and stooped to fill his friends' glass while Arthur continued gently to snore.

Made in the USA
Las Vegas, NV
02 March 2024

86625224R00152